Beau Brocade

A Romance

Baroness Emmuska Orczy Orczy

Alpha Editions

This edition published in 2021

ISBN : 9789354750052

Design and Setting By
Alpha Editions
www.alphaedis.com
Email - info@alphaedis.com

As per information held with us this book is in Public Domain.
This book is a reproduction of an important historical work. Alpha Editions
uses the best technology to reproduce historical work in the same manner
it was first published to preserve its original nature. Any marks or number
seen are left intentionally to preserve its true form.

Contents

PART I THE FORGE	- 1 -
CHAPTER I	- 3 -
BY ACT OF PARLIAMENT	- 3 -
CHAPTER II	- 10 -
THE FORGE OF JOHN STICH	- 10 -
CHAPTER III	- 14 -
THE FUGITIVE	- 14 -
CHAPTER IV	- 20 -
JOCK MIGGS, THE SHEPHERD	- 20 -
CHAPTER V	- 27 -
"THERE'S NONE LIKE HER, NONE!"	- 27 -
CHAPTER VI	- 35 -
A SQUIRE OF HIGH DEGREE	- 35 -
CHAPTER VII	- 39 -
THE HALT AT THE MOORHEN	- 39 -
CHAPTER VIII	- 44 -
THE REJECTED SUITOR	- 44 -
CHAPTER IX	- 46 -
SIR HUMPHREY'S FAMILIAR	- 46 -

CHAPTER X	- 53 -
A STRANGER AT THE FORGE	- 53 -
CHAPTER XI	- 61 -
THE STRANGER'S NAME	- 61 -
CHAPTER XII	- 64 -
THE BEAUTIFUL WHITE ROSE	- 64 -
CHAPTER XIII	- 68 -
A PROPOSAL AND A THREAT	- 68 -
CHAPTER XIV	- 74 -
THE FIGHT IN THE FORGE	- 74 -
PART II THE HEATH	- 81 -
CHAPTER XV	- 83 -
THE OUTLAW	- 83 -
CHAPTER XVI	- 86 -
A RENCONTRE ON THE HEATH	- 86 -
CHAPTER XVII	- 92 -
A FAITHFUL FRIEND	- 92 -
CHAPTER XVIII	- 96 -
MOONLIGHT ON THE HEATH	- 96 -
CHAPTER XIX	- 106 -
HIS OATH	- 106 -

PART III BRASSINGTON	- 111 -
CHAPTER XX	- 113 -
A THRILLING NARRATIVE	- 113 -
CHAPTER XXI	- 118 -
MASTER MITTACHIP'S IDEA	- 118 -
CHAPTER XXII	- 124 -
AN INTERLUDE	- 124 -
CHAPTER XXIII	- 129 -
A DARING PLAN	- 129 -
CHAPTER XXIV	- 134 -
HIS HONOUR, SQUIRE WEST	- 134 -
CHAPTER XXV	- 138 -
SUCCESS AND DISAPPOINTMENT	- 138 -
CHAPTER XXVI	- 143 -
THE MAN HUNT	- 143 -
CHAPTER XXVII	- 147 -
JOCK MIGGS'S ERRAND	- 147 -
CHAPTER XXVIII	- 153 -
THE QUARRY	- 153 -
CHAPTER XXIX	- 158 -
THE DAWN	- 158 -

PART IV H.R.H. THE DUKE OF CUMBERLAND - 165 -

CHAPTER XXX - 167 -

SUSPENSE - 167 -

CHAPTER XXXI - 171 -

"WE'VE GOTTEN BEAU BROCADE!" - 171 -

CHAPTER XXXII - 174 -

A PAINFUL INCIDENT - 174 -

CHAPTER XXXIII - 178 -

THE AWAKENING - 178 -

CHAPTER XXXIV - 184 -

A LIFE FOR A LIFE - 184 -

CHAPTER XXXV - 191 -

QUITS - 191 -

CHAPTER XXXVI - 196 -

THE AGONY OF PARTING - 196 -

CHAPTER XXXVII - 203 -

REPARATION - 203 -

CHAPTER XXXVIII - 207 -

THE JOY OF RE-UNION - 207 -

PART I
THE FORGE

CHAPTER I

BY ACT OF PARLIAMENT

The gaffers stood round and shook their heads.

When the Corporal had finished reading the Royal Proclamation, one or two of them sighed in a desultory fashion, others murmured casually, "Lordy! Lordy! to think on it! Dearie me!"

The young ones neither sighed nor murmured. They looked at one another furtively, then glanced away again, as if afraid to read each other's thoughts, and in a shamefaced manner wiped their moist hands against their rough cord breeches.

There were no women present fortunately: there had been heavy rains on the Moor these last three days, and what roads there were had become well-nigh impassable. Only a few men—some half-dozen perhaps—out of the lonely homesteads from down Brassington way, had tramped in the wake of the little squad of soldiers, in order to hear this Act of Parliament read at the cross-roads, and to see the document duly pinned to the old gallows-tree.

Fortunately the rain had ceased momentarily, only a cool, brisk nor'-wester came blustering across the Heath, making the older men shiver beneath their thin, well-worn smocks.

North and south, east and west, Brassing Moor stretched its mournful lengths to the distant framework of the Peak far away, with mile upon mile of grey-green gorse and golden bracken and long shoots of purple-stemmed bramble, and here and there patches of vivid mauve, where the heather was just bursting into bloom; or anon a clump of dark firs, with ruddy trunks and gaunt arms stretched menacingly over the sparse young life below.

And here, at the cross-roads, the Heath seemed more desolate than ever, despite that one cottage with the blacksmith's shed beyond it. The roads themselves, the one to Aldwark, the other from Wirksworth, the third little more than a morass, a short cut to Stretton, all bore mute testimony to the remoteness, the aloofness of this forgotten corner of eighteenth-century England.

Then there was the old gallows, whereon many a foot-pad or sheep-stealer had paid full penalty for his crimes! True, John Stich, the blacksmith, now used it as a sign-post for his trade: a monster horseshoe hung there where once the bones of Dick Caldwell, the highwayman, had whitened in the bleak air of the Moor: still, at moments like these, when no one spoke, the wind seemed to bring an echo of ghostly sighs and laughter, for Dick had breathed his last with a coarse jest on his lips, and the ears of the timid seemed still to catch the eerie sound of his horse's hoofs ploughing the ruddy, shallow soil of the Heath.

For the moment, however, the cross-roads presented a scene of quite unusual animation: the Corporal and his squad looked resplendent in their scarlet tunics and white buckskins, and Mr Inch, the beadle from Brassington, was also there in his gold-laced coat, bob-tailed wig and three-cornered hat: he had lent the dignity of his presence to this solemn occasion, and in high top-boots, bell in hand, had tramped five miles with the soldiers, so that he might shout a stentorian "Oyez! Oyez!" whenever they passed one of the few cottages along the road.

But no one spoke. The Corporal handed the Royal Proclamation to one of the soldiers; he too seemed nervous and ill at ease. The nor'-wester, with singular want of respect for King and Parliament, commenced a vigorous attack upon the great document, pulling at it in wanton frolic, almost tearing it out of the hands of the young soldier, who did his best to fix it against the shaft of the old gallows.

The white parchment looked uncanny and ghost-like fluttering in the wind; no doubt the nor'-wester would soon tear it to rags.

"Lordy! Lordy! to think on it!"

There it was, fixed up at last. Up, so that any chance traveller who could might read. But those who were now assembled there—shepherds, most of them, on the Moor—viewed the written characters with awe and misgiving. They had had Mr Inch's assurance that it was all writ there, that the King himself had put his name to it; and the young Corporal, who had read it out, had received the document from his own superior officer, who in his turn had had it at the hands of His Grace the Duke of Cumberland himself.

"It having come to the knowledge of His Majesty's Parliament that certain subjects of the King have lately raised the standard of rebellion, setting up the Pretender, Charles Edward Stuart, above the King's most lawful Majesty, it is hereby enacted that these persons are guilty of high treason and by the laws of the kingdom are therefore condemned to death. It is further enacted that it is unlawful for any loyal subject of the King to shelter or harbour, clothe or feed any such persons who are vile traitors and rebels to their King and country: and that any subject of His Majesty who kills such a traitor or rebel doth thereby commit an act of justice and loyalty, for which he may be rewarded by the sum of twenty guineas."

It was this last paragraph that made the gaffers shake their heads and say "Lordy! Lordy! to think on it! to think on it!" For it seemed but yesterday that the old Moor, aye, and the hamlets and villages of Derbyshire, were ringing with the wild shouts of Prince Charlie's Highland Brigade, but yesterday that his handsome face, his green bonnet laced with gold, his Highland plaid and rich accoutrements, had seemed to proclaim victory to the Stuart cause from one end of the county to the other.

To be sure, that glorious, mad, merry time had not lasted very long. All the wiseacres had foretold disaster when the Prince's standard broke, just as it was taken into my Lord Exeter's house in Full Street. The shaft snapped clean in half. What could that portend but humiliation and defeat?

The retreat from Derby was still fresh in everyone's memory, and there were those from Wirksworth who remembered the rear-guard of Prince Charlie's army, the hussars with their half-starved horses and bedraggled finery, who had swept down on the villages and homesteads round about Ashbourne and had pillaged and plundered to their hearts' content.

But then those were the fortunes of war; fighting, rushing, running, plundering, wild huzzas, mad cavalcades, noise, bustle, excitement, joy of victory, and sorrow of defeat, but this!! ... this Proclamation which the Corporal had brought all the way from Derby, and which had been signed by King George himself, this meant silence, hushed footsteps, a hidden figure perhaps, pallid and gaunt, hiding behind the boulders, or amidst the gorse on the Moor, or perishing mayhap at night, lost in the bog-land up Stretton way, whilst Judas-like treads crept stealthily on the track. It meant treachery too, the price of blood, a fellow-creature's life to be sold for twenty guineas.

No wonder the gaffers could think of nothing to say; no wonder the young men looked at one another shamefaced, and in fear.

Who knows? Any Derbyshire lad now might become a human bloodhound, a tracker of his fellow-creatures, a hunter of men. There were twenty guineas to be earned, and out there on the Heath, in the hut of the shepherd or the forge of the smith, many a pale wan face had been seen of late, which...

It was terrible to think on; for even out here, on Brassing Moor, there existed some knowledge of Tyburn Gate, and of Tower Hill.

At last the groups began to break up, the Corporal's work was done. His Majesty's Proclamation would flutter there in the cool September wind for awhile; then presently the crows would peck at it, the rain would dash it down, the last bit of dirty rag would be torn away by an October gale, but in the meanwhile the few inhabitants of Brassington and those of Aldwark would know that they might deny a starving fellow-creature bread and shelter, aye! and shoot him too, like a wild beast in a ditch, and have twenty guineas reward to boot.

"I've seen nought of John Stich, Master Inch," said the Corporal at last. "Be he from home?"

And he turned to where, just in the fork of the road, the thatched cottage, with a glimpse of the shed beyond it, stood solitary and still.

"Nay, I have not observed that fact, Master Corporal," replied Master Inch, clearing his throat for some of those fine words which had gained for him wide-spread admiration for miles around. "I had not observed that John Stich was from home. Though in verity it behoves me to say that I do not hear the sound of Master Stich's hammer upon his anvil."

"Then I'll go across at once," said the Corporal. "Forward, my men! John Stich might have saved me the trouble," he added, groping in his wallet for another copy of His Majesty's Proclamation.

"Nay, Master Corporal, do not give yourself the futile trouble of traversing the muddy road," said Mr Inch, sententiously. "John Stich is a loyal subject of King George, and by my faith! he would not harbourgate a rebel, take my word for it. Although, mind you, Mr Corporal, I have oft suspicioned..."

Mr Inch, the beadle, looked cautiously round; all the pompousness of his manner had vanished in a trice. His broad face beneath the bob-tailed wig and three-cornered hat looked like a rosy receptacle of mysterious information, as he laid his fat hand on the Corporal's sleeve.

The straggling groups of yokels were fast disappearing down the muddy tracks; some were returning to Brassington, others were tramping Aldwark way; one wizened, solitary figure was slowly toiling up the road, little more than a quagmire, that led northwards across the Heath towards Stretton Hall.

The soldiers stood at attention some fifteen yards away, mute and disinterested. From the shed beyond the cottage there suddenly came the sound of the blacksmith's hammer upon his anvil. Mr Inch felt secure from observation.

"I have oft suspicioned John Stich, the smith, of befriending the foot-pads and highwaymen that haunt this God-forsaken Moor," he said, with an air of excited importance, rolling his beady eyes.

"Nay," laughed the Corporal, good-humouredly, as he shook off Master Inch's fat hand. "You'd best not whisper this confidence to John Stich himself. As I live, he would crack your skull for you, Master Beadle, aye, be it ever so full of dictionary words. John Stich is an honest man, I tell you," he added with a pleasant oath, "the most honest this side of the county, and don't you forget it."

But Mr Inch did not approve of the young soldier's tone of familiarity. He drew up his five feet of broad stature to their full height.

"Nay, but I designated no harm," he said, with offended dignity. "John Stich is a worthy fellow, and I spoke of no ordinary foot-pads. My mind," he added, dwelling upon that mysterious possession with conscious pride, "my mind, I may say, was dominating on Beau Brocade."

"Beau Brocade!!!"

And the Corporal laughed with obvious incredulity, which further nettled Mr Inch, the beadle.

"Aye, Beau Brocade," he said hotly, "the malicious, pernicious, damned rascal, who gives us, that representate the majesty of the law, a mighty deal of trouble."

"Indeed?" sneered the Corporal.

"I dare swear that down at Derby," retorted Mr Inch, spitefully, "you have not even heard of that personage."

"Oh! we know well enough that Brassing Moor harbours more miscreants than any corner of the county," laughed the young soldier, "but methought Beau Brocade only existed in the imagination of your half-witted yokels about here."

"There you are in grave error, Master Corporal," remarked the beadle with dignity. "Beau Brocade, permit me to observe, does exist in the flesh. 'Twas only last night Sir Humphrey Challoner's coach was stopped not three miles from Hartington, and his Honour robbed of fifty guineas, by that pernicious highwayman."

"Then you must lay this Beau Brocade by the heels, Master Inch."

"Aye! that's easily said. Lay him by the heels forsooth, and who's going to do that, pray?"

"Nay, that's your affair. You don't expect His Grace the Duke of Cumberland to lend you a portion of his army, do you?"

"His Grace might do worse. Beau Brocade is a dangerous rascal to the quality."

"Only to the quality?"

"Aye, he'll not touch a poor man; 'tis only the rich he is after, and uses but little of his ill-gotten gain on himself."

"How so?" asked the Corporal, eagerly, for in spite of the excitement of camp life round about Derby, the fame of the daring highwayman had ere now tickled the fancy of the young soldiers of the Duke of Cumberland's army.

"Why, I told you Sir Humphrey Challoner was robbed on the Heath last night—robbed of fifty guineas, eh?" said Master Inch, whispering in eager confidence. "Well, this morning, when Squire West arrived at the court-house, he found fifty guineas in the poor box."

"Well?"

"Well, that's not the first time nor yet the second that such a matter has occurred. The dolts round about here, the lads from Brassington or Aldwark, or even from Wirksworth, would never willingly lay a hand on Beau Brocade. The rascal knows it well enough, and carries on his shameful trade with impunity."

"Odd's fish! but meseems the trade is not so shameful after all. What is the fellow like?"

"Nay, no one has ever seen his face, though his figure on the Moor is familiar to many. He is always dressed in the latest fashion, hence the villagers have called him Beau Brocade. Some say he is a royal prince in disguise—he always wears a mask; some say he is the Pretender, Charles Stuart himself; others declare his face is pitted with smallpox; others that he has the face of a pig, and the ears of a mule, that he is covered with hairs like a spaniel, or has a blue skin like an ape. But no one knows, and with half the villages on the Heath to aid and abet him, he is not like to be laid by the heels."

"A fine story, Master Inch," laughed the Corporal. "And is there no reward for the capture of your pig-faced, hairy, blue-skinned royal prince disguised as a common highwayman?"

"Aye, a reward of a hundred guineas," said Mr Inch, in a whisper that was hardly audible above the murmur of the wind. "A hundred guineas for the capture of Beau Brocade."

The Corporal gave a long significant whistle.

"And no one bold enough to attempt the capture?" he said derisively.

Mr Inch shook his head sadly.

"No one could do it single-handed; the rascal is cunning as well as bold, and..."

But at this point even Mr Inch's voluble tongue was suddenly and summarily silenced. The words died in his throat; his bell, the badge of his important public office, fell with a mighty clatter on the ground.

A laugh, a long, loud, joyous, mirthful laugh, rang clear as a silver gong from across the lonely Moor. Such a laugh as would make anyone's heart glad to hear, the laugh of a free man, of a man who is whole-hearted, of a man who has never ceased to be a boy.

And pompous Mr Inch slowly turned on his heel, as did also the young Corporal, and both gazed out upon the Heath; the patient little squad of soldiers too, all fixed their eyes upon one spot, just beyond John Stich's forge and cottage, not fifty yards away.

There, clearly outlined against the cloud-laden sky, was the graceful figure of a horse and rider; the horse, a sleek chestnut thoroughbred, which filled all the soldiers' hearts with envy and covetousness; the rider, a youthful, upright figure, whose every movement betokened strength of limb and elasticity of muscle, the very pose a model of ease and grace, the shoulders broad; the head, with a black mask worn over the face, was carried high and erect.

In truth it was a goodly picture to look upon, with that massive bank of white clouds, and the little patches of vivid blue as a rich, shimmering dome above it, the gold-tipped bracken, the purple heather all around, and far away, as a mist-covered background, the green-clad hills and massive Tors of Derbyshire.

So good a picture was it that the tardy September sun peeped through the clouds and had a look at that fine specimen of eighteenth-century English manhood, then paused awhile, perchance to hear again that mirthful, happy laugh.

Then came a gust of wind, the sun retreated, the soldiers gasped, and lo! before Mr Inch or Mr Corporal had realised that the picture was made of flesh and blood, horse and rider had disappeared, there, far out across the Heath, beyond the gorse and bramble and the budding heather, with not a handful of dust to mark the way they went.

Only once from far, very far, almost from fairy-land, there came, like the echo of a silver bell, the sound of that mad, merry laugh.

"Beau Brocade, as I live!" murmured Mr Inch, under his breath.

CHAPTER II

THE FORGE OF JOHN STICH

John Stich too had heard that laugh; for a moment he paused in his work, straightened his broad back and leant his heavy hammer upon the anvil, whilst a pleasant smile lit up his bronzed and rugged countenance.

"There goes the Captain," he said, "I wonder now what's tickling him. Ah!" he added with a short sigh, "the soldiers, maybe. He doesn't like soldiers much, doesn't the Captain."

He sighed again and looked across to where, on a rough wooden bench, sat a young man with head resting on his hand, his blue eyes staring moodily before him. The dress this young man wore was a counterpart of that in which John himself was arrayed; rough worsted stockings, thick flannel shirt with sleeves well tucked up over fine, muscular arms, and a large, greasy, well-worn leather apron, denoting the blacksmith's trade. But though the hands and face were covered with grime, a more than casual observer would soon have noticed that those same hands were slender and shapely, the fingers long, the nails neatly trimmed, whilst the face, anxious and careworn though it was, had in it a look of habitual command, of pride not yet crushed out of ken.

John Stich gazed at him for awhile, whilst a look of pity and anxiety saddened his honest face. The smith was a man of few words, he said nothing then, and presently the sound of his hammer upon the anvil once more filled the forge with its pleasant echo. But though John's tongue was slow, his ear was quick, and in one moment he had perceived the dull thud made by the Corporal's squad as, having parted from Mr Inch at the cross-roads, the soldiers ploughed their way through the mud round the cottage and towards the forge.

"Hist!" said John, in a rapid whisper, pointing to the fire, "the bellows! quick!"

The young man too had started in obvious alarm. His ear—the ear of a fugitive, trained to every sound that betokened danger—was as alert as that of the smith. With a sudden effort he pulled himself together, and quickly seized the heavy bellows with a will. He forced his eyes to glance carelessly at the door and his lips to whistle a lively country tune.

The Corporal paused a moment at the entrance, taking a quick survey of the interior of the forge, his men at attention behind him.

"In the King's name!" he said loudly, as he unfolded the Proclamation of His Majesty's Parliament.

His orders were to read it in every hamlet and every homestead in the district; John Stich, the blacksmith, was an important personage all around Brassing Moor, and he had not heard it read from beneath the old gallows at the cross-roads just now.

"Well, Corporal," said the worthy smith, quietly, as he put down his hammer out of respect for the King's name. "Well, and what does His Majesty, King George II., desire with John Stich, the blacksmith, eh?"

"Not with you alone, John Stich," replied the Corporal. "This is an Act of Parliament and concerns all loyal subjects of the King. Who be yon lad?" he asked, carelessly nodding towards the young man at the bellows.

"My nephew Jim, out o' Nottingham," replied John Stich, quietly, "my sister Hannah's child. You recollect her, Corporal? She was in service with my Lord Exeter up at Derby."

"Oh, aye! Mistress Hannah Stich, to be sure! I didn't know she had such a fine lad of her own," commented the Corporal, as the young man straightened his tall figure and looked him fearlessly in the face.

"Lads grow up fast enough, don't they, Corporal?" laughed honest Stich, pleasantly; "but come, let's hear His Majesty's Proclamation since you've got to read it. But you see I'm very busy and..."

"Nay, 'tis my duty, John Stich, 'in every homestead in Derbyshire' 'tis to be read, so says this Act of Parliament. You might have saved this trouble had you come down to the cross-roads just now."

"I was busy," remarked John Stich, drily, and the Corporal began to read:—

"'It having come to the knowledge of His Majesty's Parliament that certain subjects of the King have lately raised the standard of rebellion, setting up the Pretender, Charles Edward Stuart, above the King's most lawful Majesty, it is hereby enacted that these persons are guilty of high treason and by the laws of the kingdom are therefore condemned to death. It is further enacted that it is unlawful for any loyal subject of the King to shelter or harbour, clothe or feed any such persons who are vile traitors and rebels to their King and country; and that any subject of His Majesty who kills such a traitor or rebel doth thereby commit an act of justice and loyalty, for which he may be rewarded by the sum of twenty guineas.'"

There was a pause when the Corporal had finished reading. John Stich was leaning upon his hammer, the young man once more busied himself with the bellows. Outside, the clearing shower of September rain began pattering upon the thatched roof of the forge.

"Well," said John Stich at last, as the Corporal put the heavy parchment away in his wallet. "Well, and are you going to tell us who are those persons, Corporal, whom our village lads are told to murder by Act of Parliament? How shall we know a rebel ... and shoot him ... when we see one?"

"There were forty persons down on the list a few weeks ago, persons who were known to be in hiding in Derbyshire," said the young soldier, "but..."

"Well, what's your 'but,' Corporal? There were forty persons whom 'twas lawful to murder a few weeks ago.... What of them?"

"They have been caught and hanged, most of them," replied the soldier, quietly.

"Jim, lad, mind that fire," commented John Stich, turning to his "nephew out o' Nottingham," for the latter was staring with glowing eyes and quivering lips at the Corporal, who, not noticing him, continued carelessly,—

"There was Lord Lovat now, you must have heard of him, John Stich, he was beheaded a few days ago, and so was Lord Kilmarnock ... they were lords, you see, and had a headsman all to themselves on Tower Hill, that's up in London: some lesser folk have been hanged, and now there are only three rebels at large, and there are twenty guineas waiting for anyone who will bring the head of one of them to the nearest magistrate."

The smith grunted. "Well, and who are they?" he asked roughly.

"Sir Andrew Macdonald up from Tweedside, then Squire Fairfield, you'd mind him, John Stich, over Staffordshire way."

"Aye, aye, I mind him well enough. His mother was a Papist and he clung to the Stuart cause ... young man, too, and hiding for his life.... Well, and who else?"

"The young Earl of Stretton."

"What! him from Stretton Hall?" said John Stich in open astonishment. "Jim, lad," he added sternly, "thou art a clumsy fool."

The young man had started involuntarily at sound of the last name mentioned by the Corporal; and the bellows which he had tried to wield fell with a clatter on the floor.

"Be gy! but an Act of Parliament can make thee a lawful assassin, it seems," added honest John, with a laugh, "but let me perish if it can make thee a good smith. What think you, Master Corporal?"

"Odd's life! the lad is too soft-hearted mayhap! Our Derbyshire lads haven't much sense in their heads, have they?"

"Well, you mind the saying, Corporal, 'Derbyshire born and Derbyshire bred...' eh?"

"'Strong i' the arm and weak i' th' head,'" laughed the soldier, concluding the apt quotation. "That's just it. Odd's buds! they want some sense. What's a rebel or a traitor but vermin, eh? and don't we kill vermin all of us, and don't call it murder either—what?"

He laughed pleasantly and carelessly and tapped the side of his wallet where rested His Majesty's Proclamation. He was a young soldier, nothing more, attentive to duty, ready to obey, neither willing nor allowed to reason for himself. He had been taught that rebels and traitors were vermin ... egad! vermin they were, and as such must be got rid of for the sake of the rest of the kingdom and the safety of His Majesty the King.

John Stich made no comment on the Corporal's profession of faith.

"We'll talk about all that some other time, Corporal," he said at last, "but I am busy now, you see..."

"No offence, friend Stich.... Odd's life, duty you know, John, duty, eh? His Majesty's orders! and I had them from the Captain, who had them from the Duke of Cumberland himself. So you mind the Act, friend!"

"Aye! I mind it well enough."

"Everyone knows *you* to be a loyal subject of King George," added the Corporal in conciliatory tones, for John was a power in the district, "and I'm sure your nephew is the same, but duty is duty, and no offence meant."

"That's right enough, Corporal," said John Stich, impatiently.

"So good-morrow to you, John Stich."

"Good-morrow."

The Corporal nodded to the young man, then turned on his heel and presently his voice was heard ringing out the word of command,—

"Attention!—Right turn—Quick march!"

John Stich and the young man watched the half-dozen red-coated figures as they turned to skirt the cottage: the dull thud of their feet quickly dying away, as they wound their way slowly up the muddy path which leads across the Heath to Aldwark village.

CHAPTER III

THE FUGITIVE

Inside the forge all was still, whilst the last of the muffled sounds died away in the distance. John Stich had not resumed work. It was his turn now to stare moodily before him.

The young man had thrown the bellows aside, and was pacing the rough earthen floor of the forge like some caged animal.

"Tracked!" he murmured at last between clenched teeth, "tracked like some wild beast! perhaps shot anon like a dangerous cur behind a hedge!"

He sighed a long and bitter sigh, full of sorrow, anxiety, disappointment. It had come to this then! His name among the others—the traitors, the rebels! and he an innocent man!

"Nay, my lord!" said the smith, quietly, "not while John Stich owns a roof that can shelter you."

The young man paused in his feverish walk; a look of gentleness and gratitude softened the care-worn expression on his face: with a boyish gesture he threw back the fair hair which fell in curly profusion over his forehead, and with a frank and winning grace he sought and grasped the worthy smith's rough brown hand.

"Honest Stich!" he said at last, whilst his voice shook a little as he spoke, "and to think that I cannot even reward your devotion!"

"Nay, my lord," retorted John Stich, drawing up his burly figure to its full height, "don't talk of reward. I would gladly give my life for you and your family."

And this was no idle talk. John Stich meant every word he said. Honest, kind, simple-hearted John! he loved those to whom he owed everything, loved them with all the devotion of his strong, faithful nature.

The late Lord Stretton had brought him up, cared for him, given him a trade, and set him up in the cottage and forge at the cross-roads, and honest Stich felt that as everything that was good in life had come from my lord and his family, so everything he could give should be theirs in return.

"Ah! I fear me," sighed the young man, "that it is your life you risk now by sheltering me."

Yet it was all such a horrible mistake.

Philip James Gascoyne, eleventh Earl of Stretton, was at this time not twenty-one years of age. There is that fine portrait of him at Brassing Hall painted by Hogarth just before this time. The artist has well caught the proud features, the fine blue eyes, the boyish, curly head, which have been the characteristics of the Gascoynes for many generations. He has also succeeded in indicating the sensitiveness of the mouth, that somewhat feminine turn of the lips, that all too-rounded curve of the chin and jaw, which perhaps robs the handsome face of its virile manliness. There certainly is a look of indecision, of weakness of will about the lower part of the face, but it is so frank, so young, so *insouciant*, that it wins all hearts, even if it does not captivate the judgment.

Of course, when he was very young, his sympathies went out to the Stuart cause. Had not the Gascoynes suffered and died for Charles Stuart but a hundred years ago? Why the change? Why this allegiance to an alien dynasty, to a king who spoke the language of his subjects with a foreign accent?

His father, the late Lord Stretton, a contented, unargumentative British nobleman of the eighteenth century, had not thought it worth his while to explain to the growing lad the religious and political questions involved in the upholding of this foreign dynasty. Perhaps he did not understand them altogether himself. The family motto is "Pour le Roi." So the Gascoynes fought for a Stuart when he was King, and against him when he was a Pretender, and old Lord Stretton expected his children to reverence the family motto, and to have no opinions of their own.

And yet to the hearts of many the Stuart cause made a strong appeal. From Scotland came the fame of the "bonnie Prince" who won all hearts where'er he went. Philip was young, his father's discipline was irksome, he had some friends among the Highland lords: and while his father lived there had as yet been no occasion in the English Midlands to do anything very daring for the Stuart Pretender.

When the Earl of Stretton died, Philip, a mere boy then, succeeded to title and estates. In the first flush of new duties and new responsibilities his old enthusiasm remained half forgotten. As a peer of the realm he had registered his allegiance to King George, and with his youthful romantic nature all afire, he clung to that new oath of his, idealised it and loyally resisted the blandishments and lures held out to him from Scotland and from France.

Then came the news that Charles Edward, backed by French money and French influence, would march upon London and would stop at Derby to rally round his standard his friends in the Midlands.

Young Lord Stretton, torn between memories of his boyhood and the duties of his new position, feared to be inveigled into breaking his allegiance to King George. The malevolent fairy who at his birth had given him that weak mouth and softly rounded chin, had stamped his worst characteristic on the young handsome face. Philip's one hope at this juncture was to flee from temptation; he knew that Charles Edward, remembering his past ardour, would demand his help and his adherence, and that he, Philip, might be powerless to refuse.

So he fled from the county: despising himself as a coward, yet boyishly clinging to the idea that he would keep the oath he had sworn to King George. He wished to put miles of country between himself and the possible breaking of that oath, the possible yielding to the "bonnie Prince" whom none could resist. He left his sister, Lady Patience, at Stretton Hall, well cared for by old retainers, and he, a loyal subject to his King, became a fugitive.

Then came the catastrophe: that miserable retreat from Derby; the bedraggled remains of a disappointed army; finally Culloden and complete disaster; King George's soldiers scouring the country for rebels, the bills of attainder, the quick trials and swift executions.

Soon the suspicion grew into certainty that the fugitive Earl of Stretton was one of the Pretender's foremost adherents. On his weary way from Derby Prince Charles Edward had asked and obtained a night's shelter at Stretton Hall. When Philip tried to communicate with his sister, and to return to his home, he found that she was watched, and that he was himself attainted by Act of Parliament.

Yet he felt himself guiltless and loyal. He *was* guiltless and loyal: how his name came to be included in the list of rebels was still a mystery to him: someone must have lodged sworn information against him. But who?— Surely not his old friends—the adherents of Charles Edward—out of revenge for his half-heartedness?

In the meanwhile, he, a mere lad, became an outcast, condemned to death by Act of Parliament. Presently all might be cleared, all would be well, but for the moment he was like a wild beast, hiding in hedges and ditches, with his life at the mercy of any grasping Judas willing to sell his fellow-creature for a few guineas.

It was horrible! horrible! Philip vainly tried all the day to rouse himself from his morbid reverie. At intervals he would grasp the kind smith's hand and mutter anxiously,—

"My letter to my sister, John?—You are sure she had it?"

And patient John would repeat a dozen times the day,—

"I am quite sure, my lord."

But since the Corporal's visit Philip's mood had become more feverish.

"My letter," he repeated, "has Patience had my letter? Why doesn't she come?"

And spite of John's entreaties he would go to the entrance which faced the lonely Heath, and with burning eyes look out across the wilderness of furze and bracken towards that distant horizon where lay his home, where waited his patient, loving sister.

"I beg you, my lord, come away from the door, it isn't safe, not really safe," urged John Stich again and again.

"Then why will you not tell me who took my letter to Stretton Hall?" said the boy with feverish impatience.

"My lord..."

"Some stupid dolt mayhap, who has lost his way ... or ... perchance betrayed me..."

"My lord," pleaded the smith, "have I not sworn that your letter went by hands as faithful, as trusty as my own?"

"But I'll not rest an you do not tell me who took it. I wish to know," he added with that sudden look of command which all the Strettons have worn for many generations past.

The old habitual deference of the retainer for his lord was strong in the heart of John. He yielded.

"Nay, my lord, an you'll not be satisfied," he said with a sigh, "I'll tell you, though Heaven knows that his safety is as dear to me as yours—both dearer than my own."

"Well, who was it?" asked the young man, eagerly.

"I entrusted your letter for Lady Patience to Beau Brocade, the highwayman—"

In a moment Philip was on his feet: danger, amazement, horror, robbed him of speech for a few seconds, but the next he had gripped the smith's arm and like a furious, thoughtless, unreasoning child, he gasped,—

"Beau Brocade!! ... the highwayman!!! ... My life, my honour to a highwayman!!! Are you mad or drunk, John Stich?"

"Neither, my lord," said John with great respect, but looking the young man fearlessly in the face. "You don't know Beau Brocade, and there are no safer hands than his. He knows every inch of the Moor and fears neither man nor devil."

Touched in spite of himself by the smith's earnestness, Philip's wrath abated somewhat; still he seemed dazed, not understanding, vaguely scenting danger, or treachery.

"But a highwayman!" he repeated mechanically.

"Aye! and a gentleman!" retorted John with quiet conviction. "A gentleman if ever there was one! Aye! and not the only one who has ta'en to the road these hard times," he added under his breath.

"But a thief, John! A man who might sell my letter, betray my whereabouts!..."

"A man, my lord, who would die in torture sooner than do that."

The smith's quiet and earnest conviction seemed to chase away the last vestige of Philip's wrath. Still he seemed unconvinced.

"A hero of romance, John, this highwayman of yours," he laughed bitterly.

Honest John scratched the back of his curly black head.

"Noa!" he said, somewhat puzzled. "I know nought about that or what's a ... a hero of romance. But I do know that Beau Brocade is a friend of the poor, and that our village lads won't lay their hands on him, even if they could. No! not though the Government have offered a hundred guineas as the price of his head."

"Five times the value of mine, it seems," said Philip with a sigh. "But," he added, with a sudden return to feverish anxiety, "if he was caught last night, with my letter in his hands..."

"Caught!!! Beau Brocade caught!" laughed John Stich, "nay, all the soldiers of the Duke of Cumberland's army couldn't do that, my lord! Besides, I know he wasn't caught. I saw him on his chestnut horse just before the Corporal came. I heard him laughing, at the red coats, maybe. Nay! my lord, I beg you have no fear, your letter is in her ladyship's hand now, I'll lay my life on that."

"I had to trust someone, my lord," he said after awhile, as Lord Stretton once more relapsed into gloomy silence. "I could do nothing for your lordship single-handed, and you wanted that letter to reach her ladyship. I scarce knew what to do. But I did know I could trust Beau Brocade, and your secret is as safe with him as it is with me."

Philip sighed wearily.

"Ah, well! I'll believe it all, friend John. I'll trust you and your friend, and be grateful to you both: have no fear of that! Who am I but a wretched creature, whom any rascal may shoot by Act of Parliament."

But John Stich had come to the end of his power of argument. Never a man of many words, he had only become voluble when speaking of his friend. Philip tried to look cheerful and convinced, but he was chafing under this enforced inactivity and the dark, close atmosphere of the forge.

He had spent two days under the smith's roof and time seemed to creep with lead-weighted wings: yet every sound, every strange footstep, made his nerves quiver with morbid apprehension, and even now at sound of a tremulous voice from the road, shrank, moody and impatient, into the darkest corner of the hut.

CHAPTER IV

JOCK MIGGS, THE SHEPHERD

"Be you at home, Master Stich?"

A curious, wizened little figure stood in the doorway peering cautiously into the forge.

In a moment John Stich was on the alert.

"Sh!" he whispered quickly, "have no fear, my lord, 'tis only some fool from the village."

"Did ye say ye baint at home, Master Stich?" queried the same tremulous voice again. "I didn't quite hear ye."

"Yes, yes, I'm here all right, Jock Miggs," said the smith, heartily. "Come in!"

Jock Miggs came in, making as little noise, and taking up as little room as possible. Dressed in a well-worn smock and shabby corduroy breeches, he had a curious shrunken, timid air about his whole personality, as he removed his soft felt hat and began scratching his scanty tow-coloured locks: he was a youngish man too, probably not much more than thirty, yet his brown face was a mass of ruts and wrinkles like a furrowed path on Brassing Moor.

"Morning, Mr Stich ... morning," he said with a certain air of vagueness and apology, as with obvious admiration he stopped to watch the broad back of the smith and his strong arms wielding the heavy hammer.

"Morning, Miggs," retorted John, not looking up from his work, "how's the old woman?"

"I dunno, Mr Stich," replied Miggs, with a dubious shake of the head. "Badly, I expec' ... same as yesterday," he added in a more cheerful spirit.

"Why! what's the matter?"

"I dunno, Mr Stich, that there's anything the matter," explained Jock Miggs with slow and sad deliberation, "but she's dead ... same as yesterday."

Involuntarily Philip laughed at the quaint, fatalistic statement.

"Hello!" said Miggs, looking at him with the same apathetic wonder, "who be yon lad?"

"That's my nephew Jim, out o' Nottingham," said John, "come to give me a hand."

"Morning, lad," piped Miggs, in his high treble, as he extended a wrinkled, bony hand to Stretton.

"Lud, John Stich," he exclaimed, "any one'd know he was one o' your family from the muscle he's got."

And gently, meditatively, he rubbed one shrivelled hand against the other, looking with awe at the fine figure of a man before him.

"A banging lad your nephew too," he added with a chuckle; "he'll be turning the heads of all the girls this side o' Brassington, maybe."

"Oh! I'll warrant he's got a sweetheart at home, eh, Jim lad?—or maybe more than one. But what brings ye here this day, friend Miggs?"

The wizened little face assumed a puzzled expression.

"I dunno..." he said vaguely, "maybe I wanted to tell ye about the soldiers I seed at the Royal George over Brassington way."

"What about 'em, Miggs?"

"*I* dunno.... I see a corporal and lots of fellers in red .... some say there's more o' them ... I dunno."

"Ha!" said Stich, carelessly, "What are they after?"

"*I* dunno," commented Miggs, imperturbably. "Some say they're after that chap Beau Brocade. There was a coach stopped on the Heath 'gain last night. Fifty guineas he took out of it, he did...." And Jock Miggs chuckled feebly with apparent but irresponsible delight. "Some folk say it were Sir Humphrey Challoner's coach over from Hartington, and no one's going to break their hearts over that! he! he! he! ... but *I* dunno," he added with sudden frightened vagueness.

"Be they cavalry soldiers over at the Royal George, Miggs?" asked John.

"*I* dunno ... I seed no horses ... looks more like foot soldiers ... but *I* dunno. The Corporal he read out something just now about our getting twenty guineas if we shoot one o' them rebels. I'd be mighty glad to get twenty guineas, Master Stich," he said reflectively, "but I dunno as how I could handle a musket rightly ... and folks say them traitors are mighty desperate fellows ... but I dunno..."

Then with sudden resolution Jock Miggs turned to the doorway.

"Morning, Master Stich," he said decisively. "Morning, lad! ... morning."

"Morning, Miggs."

However, it seemed that Jock Miggs's visit to the forge was not so purposeless as it at first appeared.

"He! he! he!" he chuckled, as if suddenly recollecting his errand. "I'd almost forgot why I came. Farmer Crabtree wanted to know, Master Stich, if you'm got the wether's collar mended yet?"

"Oh, yes, to be sure," replied the smith, pointing to a rough bench on which lay a number of metal articles. "You'll find it on that there bench, Jock. Farmer Crabtree sold his sheep yet?"

Jock toddled up to the bench and picked up the wether's collar.

"Noa!" he muttered, "not yet, worse luck! And his temper is that hot! So don't 'ee charge him too much for the collar, Master Stich, or it's me that'll have to suffer."

And Miggs rubbed his shoulder significantly. Stich laughed. Philip himself, in spite of his anxiety, could not help being amused at the quaint figure of the little shepherd with his wizened face and gentle, vaguely fatalistic manner.

Thus it was that no one in the forge had perceived the patter of small feet on the mud outside, and when Jock Miggs, with more elaborate "Mornings" and final leave-takings, once more reached the doorway, he came in violent collision with a short, be-cloaked and closely-hooded figure that was picking its way on very small, very high-heeled shoes, through the maze of puddles which guarded the entrance to the forge.

The impact sent Jock Miggs, scared and apologetic, stumbling in one direction, whilst the grey hood flew off the head of its wearer and disclosed in the setting of its shell-pink lining a merry, pretty, impudent little face, with brown eyes sparkling and red lips pouting in obvious irritation.

"Lud, man!" said the dainty young damsel, withering the unfortunate shepherd with a scornful glance, "why don't you look where you're going?"

"I dunno," replied Jock Miggs, with his usual humble vagueness. "Morning, miss ... morning, Master Stich ... morning."

And still scared, still in obvious apology for his existence, he pulled at his forelock, re-adjusted his hat over his yellow curls, took his final leave, and presently began to wend his way slowly back towards the Heath.

But within the forge, at first bound of the young girl's voice, Stretton had started in uncontrollable excitement.

"Betty!" he whispered, eagerly clutching John Stich's arm.

"Aye! aye!" replied the cautious smith, "but I beg you, my lord, keep in the background until I find out if all is safe."

Mistress Betty's saucy brown eyes followed Jock Miggs's quaint, retreating figure.

"Well! you're a pretty bit of sheep's wool, ain't ye?" she shouted after him, with a laugh and a shrug of her plump shoulders.

Then she peered into the forge.

"Lud love you, Master Stich!" she said, "how goes it with you?"

In obedience to counsels of prudence, Stretton had retired into the remote corner of the forge. John Stich too was masking the entrance with his burly figure.

"All the better, Mistress Betty," he said, "for a sight of your pretty face."

He had become very red, had honest John, and his rough manner seemed completely to have deserted him. In fact, not to put too fine a point upon it, the worthy smith looked distinctly shy and sheepish.

She looked up at him and laughed a pleased, coquettish little laugh, the laugh of a woman who has oft been told that she is pretty, and has not tired of the hearing. John Stich, moreover, was so big and burly, folks called him hard and rough, and it vastly entertained the young damsel to see him standing there before her, as awkward and uncomfortable as Jock Miggs himself.

"Am I not to step inside, Master Stich?" she asked.

"Yes, yes, Mistress Betty," murmured John, who seemed to have lost himself in admiration of a pair of tiny buckled shoes muddy to the ankles—such ankles!—which showed to great advantage beneath Betty's short green kirtle.

An angry, impatient movement behind him, however, quickly recalled his scattered senses.

"Did her ladyship receive a letter, mistress?" he asked eagerly.

"Oh, yes! a stranger brought it," replied Betty, with a pout, for she preferred John's mute appreciation of her small person to his interest in other matters. However, the demon of mischief no doubt whispered something in her ear for the further undoing of the worthy smith, for she put on a demure, mysterious little air, turned up her brown eyes, sighed with affectation, and murmured ecstatically,—

"Oh! such a stranger! the fine eyes of him, Master Stich! and such an air, and oh!" added little madam with unction, "such clothes!"

But though no doubt all these fine airs and graces wrought deadly havoc in poor John's heart, he concealed it well enough under a show of eager impatience.

"Yes! yes! the stranger," he said, casting a furtive glance behind him, "he gave you a letter for my lady?"

"La! you needn't be in such a hurry, Master Stich!" retorted Mistress Betty, adding with all the artifice of which she was capable, "the stranger wasn't."

But this was too much for John. There had been such a wealth of meaning in Betty's brown eyes.

"Oh! he wasn't? was he?" he asked with a jealous frown, "and pray what had he to say to you? There was no message except the letter."

But the demon of mischief was satisfied and Betty was disposed to be kind, even if slightly mysterious.

"Oh, never mind!" she rejoined archly, "he gave me a letter which I gave to my lady. That was early this morning."

"Well? ... and?"

But matters were progressing too slowly at anyrate for one feverish, anxious heart. Philip had tried to hold himself in check, though he was literally hanging on pretty Mistress Betty's lips. Now he could contain himself no longer. Lady Patience had had his letter. The mysterious highwayman had not failed in his trust, and the news Betty had brought meant life or death to him.

Throwing prudence to the winds, he pushed John Stich aside, and seizing the young girl by the wrist, he asked excitedly,—

"Yes? this morning, Betty? ... then ... then ... what did her ladyship do?"

Betty was frightened, and like a child was ready to drown her fright in tears. She had not recognised my lord in those dirty clothes.

"Don't you know me, Betty?" asked Philip, a little more quietly.

Betty cast a timid glance at the two men before her, and smiled through the coming tears.

"Of course, my lord ... I ..." she murmured shyly.

"'Tis my nephew Jim out o' Nottingham, mistress," said John, sternly, "try and remember that: and now tell us what did her ladyship do?"

"She had the horses put to, not an hour after the stranger had been. Thomas is driving and Timothy is our only other escort. But we've not drawn rein since we left the Hall!"

"Yes! yes!" came from two pairs of eager lips.

"And my lady stopped the coach about two hundred yards from here," continued Betty with great volubility, "and she told me to run on here, to see that the coast was clear. She knew I could find my way, and she wouldn't trust Timothy as she trusts me," added the young girl with a pretty touch of pride.

"But where is she, Betty? where is she?"

Betty pointed to the clump of firs, which stood like ghostly sentinels on the crest of the hill, just where the road turns sharply to the east.

"Just beyond those trees, my lord, and she made Timothy watch until I came round the bend and in sight of the forge. But la! the mud on the roads! 'tis fit to drown you."

But already John Stich was outside, beckoning to Mistress Betty.

"Come, mistress, quick!" he said excitedly, "her ladyship must be nigh crazy with impatience. By your leave, my lord, I'll help Mistress Betty on her way, and I'll keep this place in sight. I'll go no further..."

"Yes, yes," rejoined Philip, feverishly, "go, go, fly if you can! I'll be safe! I'll not show myself. God give you both wings, for I'll not live now till I see my sister."

Eager, boyish, full of wild gaiety, he seemed to have thrown off his morbid anxiety as he would a mantle. He even laughed whole-heartedly as he watched Betty, with many airs and graces, "Luds!" and "I vows!" making great pretence at being unable to walk in the mud, and leaning heavily on honest Stich's arm.

He watched them as they picked their way up the so-called road, a perfect quagmire after the heavy September rains.

The air seemed so different now, the Heath smelt good, there was vigour and life in the keen nor'-wester; how green the bracken looked, and how harmoniously it seemed to blend with the purple shoots of the bramble laden with ripening fruit! how delicate the more tender green of the gorse, and there that vivid patch of mauve, the first glimpse of opening heather! the heavy clouds too were rolling away; the September sun was going to have his own way after all and spread his kingdom of blue and gold over the distant Derbyshire hills.

Hope had come like the divine magician to chase away all that was grey and sad and dreary, and Hope had met Youth and shaken him by the hand: they are such friends, such inseparable companions, these two!

What mattered it that some few yards away the old gallows, like some eerie witch, still spread its gaunt arm over that fluttering bit of parchment: the Proclamation of His Majesty's Parliament? What though it spoke of death, of treachery, of bills of attainder, of Tower Hill?

Did not the good nor'-wester from the Moor flutter round it, and in wanton frolic attack it now with madcap fury and a shrill whistle, and now with a long-drawn-out sigh. The parchment resisted with vigour, it bore the onslaught of the wind twice, thrice, and once again. But the nor'-wester was not to be outdone, and again it renewed the attack, took the parchment by the corner, pulled and twisted at it, until at last with one terrific blast it tore the Royal Proclamation off the old gallows, and sent it whirling in a mad gallop across the Moor, far, very far away on to Derby, to London, to the place where all winds go.

CHAPTER V

"THERE'S NONE LIKE HER, NONE!"

There was something more than ordinary affection between Philip, Earl of Stretton, and his sister, Lady Patience Gascoyne. Those who knew them in the days of their happiness said they seemed more like lovers than brother and sister, so tender, so true was their clinging devotion to one another.

But those who knew them both intimately said that they were more like mother and son together; though Philip was only a year or two younger than Patience, she had all a mother's fondness, a mother's indulgence and sweet pity for him, he all a son's deference, a son's trust in her.

Even now, as he instinctively felt her dear presence nigh, hope took a more firm, more lasting hold upon him. He knew that she would act wisely and prudently for him. For the first time for many days and weeks he felt safe, less morbidly afraid of treachery, more ready to fight adverse fate.

The heavy coach came lumbering along the quaggy road, the old coachman's "Whoa! whoa! there! there!" as he tried to encourage his horses in the heavy task of pulling the cumbersome vehicle through the morass, sounded like sweetest music in Philip's ear.

He did not dare go to meet them, but he watched the coach as it drew nearer and nearer, very slowly, the horses going step by step urged on by the coachman and by Timothy, who rode close at their heads, spurring them with whip and kind words, the wheels creaking as they slowly turned on their mud-laden axles.

Thus Patience had travelled since dawn, ever since the stranger had brought her the letter which told her that her brother had succeeded in reaching this secluded corner of Derbyshire, and was now in hiding with faithful John Stich, waiting for her guidance and help to establish his innocence.

Leaning back against the cushions of the coach, she had sat with eyes closed and hands tightly clutched. Anxious, wearied, at times hopeful, she had borne the terrible fatigue of this lumbering journey from Stretton Hall, along the unmade roads of Brassing Moor, with all the fortitude the Gascoynes had always shown for any cause they had at heart.

At the cross-roads Thomas, the driver, brought his horses to a standstill. Already, as the coach had passed some fifty yards from the forge, Patience had leaned out of the window trying to get a glimpse of the dear face which she knew would be on the lookout for her.

John Stich had escorted Betty as far as the bend in the road, and within sight of Timothy waiting some hundred yards further on, then he had retraced his steps, and was now back at the cross-roads ready to help Lady Patience to alight.

"Let the coach wait here," she said to the driver, "we may sleep at Wirksworth to-night."

"Ah! my good Stich," she added, grasping the smith's hand eagerly, "my brother, how is he?"

"All the better since he knows your ladyship has come," replied Stich.

A few moments later brother and sister were locked in each other's arms.

"My sweet sister! My dear, dear Patience!" was all Philip could say at first.

But she placed one hand on his shoulder and with a gentle motherly gesture brushed with the other the unruly curls from the white, moist forehead. He looked haggard and careworn, although his eyes now gleamed with feverish hope, and hers, in spite of herself, began to fill with tears.

"Dear, dear one," she murmured, trying to look cheerful, to push back the tears. All would be well now that she could get to him, that they could talk things over, that she could *do* something for him and with him, instead of sitting—weary and inactive—alone at Stretton Hall, without news, a prey to devouring anxiety.

"That awful Proclamation," he said at last—"you have heard of it?"

"Aye!" she replied sadly, "even before you did, I think. Sir Humphrey Challoner sent a courier across to tell me of it."

"And my name amongst those attainted by Act of Parliament!"

She nodded, her lips were quivering, and she would not break down, now that he needed all her courage as well as his own.

"But I am innocent, dear," he said, taking both her tiny hands in his own, and looking firmly, steadfastly into her face. "You believe me, don't you?"

"Of course, Philip, I believe you. But it is all so hard, so horrible, and 'tis Heaven alone who knows which was the just cause."

"There is no doubt as to which was the stronger cause, at anyrate in England," said Stretton, with some bitterness. "Charles Edward was very ill-advised to cross the border at all, and in the Midlands no one cares about the

Stuarts now. But that's all ancient history," he added with a weary sigh, "it's no use dwelling over all the wretched mistakes that were committed last year, 'tis only the misery that has abided until now."

"Why did you run away, Philip?" she asked.

"Because I was a fool ... and a coward," he added, while a blush of shame darkened his young Saxon face.

"No, no..."

"I thought if I remained at Stretton Charles Edward would demand my help ... and you know," he said with a quaint boyish smile, "I was never very good at saying 'Nay!' I knew they would persuade me. Lovat and Kilmarnock were such friends, and..."

"So you preferred to run away?"

"It was cowardly, wasn't it?"

"I am afraid it was," she said reluctantly, her tenderness and her conviction fighting an even battle in her heart. "But why wouldn't you tell me, dear?"

"Because I was a fool," he said, cursing himself for that same folly. "You were away in London just then, you remember?"

She nodded.

"And there was no one to advise me, except Challoner."

"Sir Humphrey? Then it was he?..."

Philip looked at her in astonishment. There was such a strange quiver in her voice; a note of deep anxiety, of almost hysterical alarm. But she checked herself quickly, and said more calmly,—

"What did Sir Humphrey Challoner advise you to do?"

"He said that Charles Edward would surely persuade me to join his standard, that he would demand shelter at Stretton Hall, and claim my allegiance."

"Yes, yes?"

"And he thought that it would be wiser for me to put two or three counties between myself and the temptation of becoming a rebel."

"He thought!..."

There was a world of bitter contempt in those two words she uttered. Even Philip, absorbed as he was in his own affairs, could not fail to notice it.

"Challoner has always been my friend," he said almost reproachfully. "I fancy, little sister," he added with his boyish smile, "that it rests with you that he should become my brother."

"Hush, dear, don't speak of that."

"Why not?"

She did not reply, and there was a moment's silence between them. She was evidently hesitating whether to tell him of the fears, the suspicions which the mention of Sir Humphrey Challoner's name had aroused in her heart, or to leave the subject alone. At last she said quite gently,—

"But when I came home, dear, and found you had left the Hall without a message, without a word for me, why did you not tell me then?"

The boy hung his head. He felt the tender reproach, and there was nothing to be said.

"I would have stood by you," she continued softly. "I think I might have helped you. There was no disgrace in refusing to join a doomed cause, and you were a mere child when you made friends with Lovat."

"I know all that now, dear," he said with some impatience. "Heaven knows I am paying dearly enough for my cowardice and my folly. But even now I cannot understand how my name became mixed up with those of the rebels. Somebody must have sworn false information against me. But who? I haven't an enemy in the world, have I, dear?"

"No, no," she said quickly, but even as she spoke the look of involuntary alarm in her face belied the assurance of her lips.

But this was not the moment to add to his anxiety by futile, worrying conjectures. He had sent for her because he wanted her, and she was here to do for him, to help and support him in every way that her strength of will and her energy would dictate.

"You sent for me, Philip," she said with a cheerful, hopeful smile.

Her look seemed to put fresh life into his veins. In a moment he tried to conquer his despondency, and with a quick gesture he tore open the rough, woollen shirt he wore, and from beneath it drew a packet of letters. Not only his hand now, but his whole figure seemed to quiver with excitement as he gazed at this packet with glowing eyes.

"These letters, dear," he said in a whisper, "are my one hope of safety. They have not left my body day or night ever since I first understood my position and realised my danger, and now, with them, I place my life in your hands."

"Yes, Philip?"

"They prove my innocence," he continued, as nervously he pulled at the string that held the letters together. "Here is one from Lovat," he added, handing one of these to Patience, "read it, dear, quickly. You will see he begs me to join the Pretender's standard. Here's another from Kilmarnock—that was after the retreat from Derby—he upbraids me for holding aloof. I was in hiding at Nottingham then, but *they* knew where I was, and would not leave me alone. They would have followed me if they could. And here ... better still ... is one from Charles Edward himself, just before he fled to France, calling me a traitor for my loyalty to King George."

Feverishly he tore open letter after letter, thrusting them into her hand, scanning them with burning, eager eyes. She took them from him one by one, glanced at them, then quietly folded each precious piece of paper, and tied the packet together again. Her hand did not shake, but beneath her cloak she pressed the letters to her heart, the letters that meant the safety of her dear one's life.

"Oh! if I had known all this sooner!" she sighed involuntarily.

But that was the only reproach that escaped her lips for his want of confidence in her.

"I nearly yielded to Lovat's letter," said the boy, hesitatingly.

"I know, I know, dear," she said with an infinity of indulgence in her gentle smile. "We won't speak of the past any more. Now let us arrange the future."

He tried to master his excitement, throwing off with an effort of will his feverishness and his morbid self-condemnation.

He had done a foolish and a cowardly thing; he knew that well enough. Fate had dealt him one of those cruel blows with which she sometimes strikes the venial offender, letting so often the more hardened criminal go scatheless.

For months now Philip had been a fugitive, disguised in rough clothes, hiding in barns and inns of doubtful fame, knowing no one whom he could really trust, to whom he dared disclose his place of temporary refuge, or confide a message for his sister. Treachery was in the air; he suspected everyone. The bill of attainder had condemned so many men to death, and rebel-hunting and swift executions were in that year of grace the order of the day.

"I could do nothing without you, dear," he said more quietly. "I must hide now like a hunted beast, and must be grateful for the sheltering roof of honest Stich. I have been branded as a traitor by Act of Parliament, my life is forfeit, and it is even a crime for any man to give me food and shelter. The lowest footpad who haunts the Moor has the right to shoot me like a mad dog."

"Don't! don't, dear!" she pleaded.

"I only wished you to understand that I was not such an abject coward as I seemed. I could not get to you or reach the Hall."

"I quite understood that, dear. Now, tell me, you wish me to take these letters to London?"

"At once. The sooner they are laid before the King and Council the better. I must get to the fountain head as quickly as possible. Once I am caught they will give me no chance of proving my innocence. I have been tried by Act of Parliament, found guilty and condemned to death. You realise that, dear, don't you?"

"Yes, Philip, I do," she replied very quietly.

"Once in London, who do you think can best help you?"

"Lady Edbrooke, of course. Her husband has just been appointed equerry to the King."

"Ah! that's well! Aunt Charlotte was always fond of me. She'll be kind to you, I know."

"I think you should write to her. I'd take that letter too."

"When can you start?"

"Not for a few hours unfortunately. The horses must be put up. We have been on the road since dawn."

They were both quite calm now, and discussed these few details as if life or death were not the outcome of the journey.

Patience was glad to see that the boy had entirely shaken off the almost hysterical horror he had of his unfortunate position.

They were suddenly interrupted by John Stich's cautious voice at the entrance of the shed.

"Your ladyship's pardon," said John, respectfully, "but there's a coach coming up the road from Hartington way. I thought perhaps it might be more prudent..."

"Hartington!"

Brother and sister had uttered the exclamation simultaneously. He in astonishment, she in obvious alarm.

"Who can it be, John, think you?" she asked with quivering lips.

"Well, it couldn't very well be anyone except Sir Humphrey Challoner, my lady. No one else'd have occasion to come down these God-forsaken roads. But they are some way off yet," he added reassuringly, "I saw them first on the crest of the further hill. Maybe his Honour is on his way to Derby."

Patience was trying to conquer her agitation, but it was her turn now to seem nervous and excited.

"Oh! I didn't want him to find me here!" she said quickly. "I ... I mistrust that man, Philip ... foolishly perhaps, and ... if he sees me ... he might guess ... he might suspect..."

"Nay, my lady, there's not much fear of that, craving your pardon," hazarded John Stich, cheerfully. "If 'tis Sir Humphrey 'twill take his driver some time yet to walk down the incline, and then up again to the cross-roads. 'Tis a mile and a half for sure, and the horses'll have to go foot pace. There's plenty of time for your ladyship to be well on your way before they get here."

She felt reassured evidently, for she said more calmly,—

"I'll have to put up somewhere, John, for a few hours, for the sake of the horses. Where had that best be?"

"Up at Aldwark, I should say, my lady, at the Moorhen."

"Perhaps I could get fresh horses there, and make a start at once."

"Nay, my lady, they have no horses at the Moorhen fit for your ladyship to drive. 'Tis only a country inn. But they'd give your horses and men a feed and rest, and if your ladyship'll pardon the liberty, you'll need both yourself."

"Yes, yes," said Philip, anxiously regarding the beautiful face which looked so pale and weary. "You must rest, dear. The journey to London will be long and tedious ..."

"But Aldwark is not on my way," she said with a slight frown of impatience.

"The inn is but a mile from here, your ladyship," rejoined Stich, "and your horses could never reach Wirksworth without a long rest. 'Tis the best plan, an your ladyship would trust me!"

"Trust you, John!" she said with a sweet smile, as she extended one tiny hand to the faithful smith. "I trust you implicitly, and you shall give me your advice. What is it?"

"To put up at the Moorhen for the night, your ladyship," explained John, whose kindly eyes had dropped a tear over the gracious hand held out to him, "then to start for London to-morrow morning."

"No, no! I must start to-night. I could not bear to wait even until dawn."

"But the footpads on the Heath, your ladyship..." hazarded John.

"Nay, I fear no footpads. They're welcome to what money I have, and they'd not care to rob me of my letters," she said eagerly. "But I'll put up at the Moorhen, John. We all need a rest. I suppose there's no way across the Heath from thence to Wirksworth."

"None, your ladyship. This is the only possible way. Back here to the cross-roads and on to Wirksworth from here."

"Then I'll see you again, dear," she said tenderly, clinging to Stretton, "at sunset mayhap. I'll start as soon as I can. You may be sure of that."

"And guard the letters, little sister," he said as he held her closely, closely to his heart. "Guard them jealously, they are my only hope."

"You'll write the letter to Lady Edbrooke," she added. "Have it ready when I return, and perhaps write out your own petition to the King—I'll use that or not as Lord Edbrooke advises."

Then once more, womanlike, she clung to him, hating to part from him even for a few hours.

"In the meanwhile you will be prudent, Philip," she pleaded tenderly. "Trust *nobody* but John Stich. *Any* man may prove an enemy," she added with earnest emphasis, "and if you were found before I could reach the King..."

She tore herself away from him. Her eyes now were swimming in tears, and she meant to seem brave to the end. Stich was urging her to hurry. After all she would see Philip again before sunset, before she started on the long journey which would mean life and safety to him.

Two minutes later, having parted from her brother, Lady Patience Gascoyne entered her coach at the cross-roads, where Mistress Betty had been waiting for her ladyship with as much patience as she could muster.

By the time Sir Humphrey Challoner's coach had reached the bottom of the decline on the Hartington Road, and begun the weary ascent up to the blacksmith's forge, Lady Patience's carriage was well out of sight beyond the bend that led eastward to Aldwark village.

CHAPTER VI

A SQUIRE OF HIGH DEGREE

The Challoners claimed direct descent from that Sieur de Challonier who escorted Coeur de Lion to the crusade against Saladin.

Be that as it may, there is no doubt that a De Challonier figures in the Domesday Book, as owning considerable property in the neighbourhood of the Peak.

That they had been very influential and wealthy people at one time, there could be no doubt. There was a room at Old Hartington Manor where James I. had slept for seven nights, a gracious guest of Mr Ilbert Challoner, in the year 1612. The baronetcy then conferred upon the family dates from that same year, probably as an act of recognition to his host on the part of the royal guest.

Since that memorable time, however, the Challoners have not made history. They took no part whatever in the great turmoil which, in the middle of the seventeenth century, shook the country to its very foundations, lighting the lurid torch of civil war, setting brother against brother, friend against friend, threatening a constitution and murdering a king.

The Challoners had held aloof throughout all that time, intent on preserving their property and in amassing wealth. The later conflict between a Catholic King and his Protestant people touched them even less. Neither Pretender could boast of a Challoner for an adherent. They remained people of substance, even of importance, in their own county, but nothing more.

Sir Humphrey Challoner was about this time not more than thirty-five years of age. Hale, hearty, boisterous, he might have been described as a typical example of an English squire of those days, but for a certain taint of parsimoniousness, of greed and love of money in his constitution, which had gained for him a not too enviable reputation in the Midlands.

He was thought to be wealthy. No doubt he was, but at the cost of a good deal of harshness towards the tenants on his estates, and he was famed throughout Staffordshire for driving a harder bargain than anyone else this country side.

Any traveller—let alone one of such consequence as the Squire of Hartington—was indeed rare in these out-of-the-way parts, that were on the way to nowhere. Sir Humphrey himself was but little known in the neighbourhood of Aldwark and Wirksworth, and only from time to time passed through the latter village on his way to Derby.

John Stich, the blacksmith, however, knew every one of consequence for a great many miles around, and undoubtedly next to the Earls of Stretton the Challoners were the most important family in the sister counties. Therefore when Sir Humphrey's coach stopped at the cross-roads, and the Squire himself alighted therefrom and walked towards the smith's cottage, the latter came forward with all the deference due to a personage of such consequence, and asked respectfully what he might do for his Honour.

"Only repair this pistol for me, master smith," said Sir Humphrey; "you might also examine the lock of its fellow. One needs them in these parts."

He laughed a not unpleasant boisterous laugh as he handed a pair of silver-mounted pistols to John Stich.

"Will your Honour wait while I get them done?" asked John, with some hesitation. "They won't take long."

"Nay! I'll be down this way again to-morrow," replied his Honour. "I am putting up at Aldwark for the night."

John said nothing. Probably he mistrusted the language which rose to his lips at this announcement of Sir Humphrey's plans. In a moment he remembered Lady Patience's look of terror when the squire's coach first came into view on the crest of the distant hill, and his faithful, honest heart quivered with apprehension at the thought that a man whom she so obviously mistrusted was so close upon her track.

"I suppose there is a decent inn in that God-forsaken hole, eh?" asked the Squire, jovially. "I've arranged to meet my man of business there, that old scarecrow, Mittachip, but I'd wish to spend the night."

"There's only a small wayside inn, your Honour..." murmured John.

"Better than this abode of cut-throats, this Brassing Moor, anyway," laughed his Honour. "Begad! night overtook me some ten miles from Hartington, and I was attacked by a damned rascal who robbed me of fifty guineas. My men were a pair of cowards, and I was helpless inside my coach."

John tried to repress a smile. The story of Sir Humphrey Challoner's midnight adventure had culminated in fifty guineas being found in the poor box at Brassington court-house, and Mr Inch, the beadle, had brought the news of it even as far as the cross-roads.

"I must see Squire West about this business," muttered Sir Humphrey, whilst John stood silent, apparently intent on examining the pistols. "'Tis a scandal to the whole country, this constant highway robbery on Brassing Moor. The impudent rascal who attacked me was dressed like a prince, and rode a horse worth eighty guineas at the least. I suspect him to be the man they call Beau Brocade."

"Did your Honour see him plainly?" asked John, somewhat anxiously.

"See him?" laughed Sir Humphrey. "Does one ever see these rascals? Begad! he had stopped my coach, plundered me and had galloped off ere I could shout 'Damn you' thrice. Just for one moment, though, one of my lanterns flashed upon the impudent thief. He was masked, of course, but I tell thee, honest friend, he had on a coat the Prince of Wales might envy; as for his horse, 'twas a thorough-bred I'd have given eighty guineas to possess."

"And everyone knows your Honour is clever at a bargain," said John, with a suspicion of malice.

"Humph!" grunted the Squire. "By Gad!" he added, with his usual jovial laugh, "the rogue does not belie his name—'Beau Brocade' forsooth! Faith! he dresses like a lord, and cuts your purse with an air of gallantry, an he were doing you a favour."

It was difficult to tell what went on in Sir Humphrey Challoner's mind behind that handsome, somewhat florid face of his. The task was in any case quite beyond the powers of honest John Stich, though he would have given quite a good deal of his worldly wealth to know for certain whether his Honour's journey across Brassing Moor and on to Aldwark had anything to do with that of Lady Patience along the same road.

Nothing the Squire said, however, helped John towards making a guess in that direction. Just as Sir Humphrey, having left the pistols in the smith's hands, turned to go back to his coach, he said quite casually,—

"Whose was the coach that passed here about half an hour before mine?"

"The coach, your Honour?"

"Aye! when we reached the crest of the hill my man told me he could see a coach standing at the cross-roads, whose was it?"

For one moment John hesitated. The situation was just a little too delicate for the worthy smith to handle. But he felt, as Sir Humphrey was going to Aldwark and therefore would surely meet Lady Patience, that lying would be worse than useless, and might even arouse unpleasant suspicions.

"'Twas Lady Patience Gascoyne's coach," he said at last.

"Ah!" said the Squire, with the same obvious indifference. "Whither did she go?"

"I was at work in my forge, your Honour, and her ladyship did not stop. I fancy she drove down Wirksworth way, but I did not see or hear for I was very busy."

"Hm!" commented his Honour, whilst a shrewd and somewhat sarcastic smile played round the corners of his full lips.

"I'll stay the night at Aldwark," he said, nodding to the smith. "Faith! no more travelling after dark for me on this unhallowed Moor; and for sure my horses could not reach Wirksworth now before nightfall. So have the pistols ready for me by seven o'clock to-morrow morning, eh, mine honest friend?"

Then he entered his carriage, and slowly, with many a creak and a groan, the cumbersome vehicle turned down the road to Aldwark, whilst John Stich, with a dubious, anxious sigh, went back into his forge.

CHAPTER VII

THE HALT AT THE MOORHEN

Patience herself would have been quite unable to explain why she mistrusted, almost feared, Sir Humphrey Challoner.

The fact that the Squire of Hartington had openly declared his admiration for her, surely gave her no cause for suspecting him of enmity towards her brother. She knew that Sir Humphrey hoped to win her hand in marriage—this he had intimated to her on more than one occasion, and had spoken of his love for her in no measured terms.

Lady Patience Gascoyne was one of the richest gentlewomen in the Midlands, having inherited vast wealth from her mother, who was sister and co-heiress of the rich Grantham of Grantham Priory. No doubt her rent-roll added considerably to her attractions in the eyes of Sir Humphrey; that she was more than beautiful only helped to enhance the ardour of his suit.

Women as a rule—women of all times and of every nation—keep a kindly feeling in their heart for the suitor whom they reject. A certain regard for his sense of discrimination, an admiration for his constancy—if he be constant—make up a sum of friendship for him tempered with a gentle pity.

But in most women too there is a subtle sense which for want of a more scientific term has been called an instinct: the sense of protection over those whom they love.

In Patience Gascoyne that sense was abnormally developed: Philip was so boyish, so young, she so much older in wisdom and prudence. It made her fear Sir Humphrey, not for herself but for her brother: her baby, as in her tender motherly heart she loved to call him.

She feared and suspected him, she scarce could tell of what. Not open enmity towards Philip, since her reason told her that the Squire of Hartington had nothing to gain by actively endangering her brother's life, let alone by doing him a grievous wrong.

Yet she could not understand Sir Humphrey Challoner's motive in counselling Philip to play so cowardly and foolish a part, as the boy had done in the late rebellion. Vaguely she trembled at the idea that he should know of her journey to London, or worse still, guess its purpose. Philip, she feared, might have confided in him unbeknown to her: Sir Humphrey, for aught she knew, might know of the existence of the letters which would go to prove the boy's innocence.

Well! and what then? Surely the Squire could have no object in wishing those letters to be suppressed: he could but desire that Philip's innocence *should* be proved.

Thus reason and instinct fought their battle in her brain as the heavy coach went lumbering along the muddy road to the little wayside inn, which stood midway between the cross-roads and the village of Aldwark.

Here her man Timothy made arrangements for the resting and feeding of himself, the horses and Thomas, the driver, whilst Lady Patience asked for a private room wherein she and her maid, Betty, could get something to eat and perhaps an hour's sleep before re-starting on their way.

The small bar-parlour at the Moorhen was full to overflowing when her ladyship's coach drove up. Already there had been a general air of excitement there throughout the day, for the Corporal in his red coat, followed by his little squad, had halted at the inn, and there once more read aloud the Proclamation of His Majesty's Parliament.

The soldiers had stayed half an hour or so, consuming large quantities of ale the while, then they had marched up to the village, read the Proclamation out on the green, and finally tramped along the bridle-path back to Brassington.

And now here was the quality putting up at the Moorhen. A most unheard-of, unexpected event. Mistress Pottage, the sad-faced, weary-eyed landlady, had never known such a thing to happen before, although she had been mistress of the Moorhen for nigh on twenty years. Usually the quality from Stretton Hall or from Hartington, or even Lady Rounce from the Pike, preferred to drive a long way round to get to Derby, sooner than trust to the lonely Heath, with its roads almost impassable four days out of five.

Master Mittachip, attorney-at-law, who had ridden over from Wirksworth with his clerk, Master Duffy, recognised her ladyship as she stepped out of her coach.

"Sir Humphrey will be astonished," he whispered to Master Duffy, as he rubbed his ill-shaven chin with his long bony fingers.

"He! he! he!" echoed the clerk, submissively.

Master Mittachip, who transacted business for the Squire of Hartington, and also for old Lady Rounce and Squire West, knew the exact shade of deference due to so great a lady as Lady Patience Gascoyne. He stood at the door of the parlour and had the honour of bowing to her as she followed Mistress Pottage quickly along the passage to the inner room beyond, her long cloak flying out behind her, owing to the draught caused by the open doors.

Alone in the small, dingy room, Patience almost fell upon the sofa in a stupor of intense fatigue. When Mistress Pottage brought the meagre, ill-cooked food, she felt at first quite unable to eat. She lay back against the hard pillows with eyes closed, and hands tightly clutching that bundle of precious letters.

Betty tried to make her comfortable. She took off her mistress's shoes and stockings and began rubbing the cold, numb feet between her warm hands.

But by-and-by youth and health reasserted themselves. Patience, realising all the time how much depended upon her own strength and energy, roused herself with an effort of will. She tried to eat some of the food, "the mess of pottage" as she smilingly termed it, but her eyes were for ever wandering to the clock which ticked the hours—oh! so slowly!—that separated her from her journey.

As for buxom little Betty, she had fallen to with the vigorous appetite of youth and a happy heart, and presently, like a tired child, she curled herself up at the foot of the couch and soon dropped peacefully to sleep.

After awhile, Patience too, feeling numb and drowsy with the weariness of this long afternoon, closed her eyes and fell into a kind of stupor. She lay on the sofa like a log, tired out, dreamless, her senses numbed, in a kind of wakeful sleep.

How long she lay there she could not have told, but all of a sudden she sat up, her eyes dilated, her heart beating fast; she was fully awake now.

Something had suddenly roused her. What was it? She glanced at the clock; it was just half-past three. She must have slept nearly half an hour. Betty, on the floor beside her, still slumbered peacefully.

Then all her senses woke. She knew what had aroused her: the rumbling of wheels, a coach pulling up, the shouts of the driver. And now she could hear men running, more shouting, the jingle of harness and horses being led round the house to the shed beyond.

The small lattice window gave upon the side of the house, she could not see the coach or who this latest arrival at the Moorhen was; but what mattered that? she knew well enough.

For a moment she stopped to think; forcibly conquering excitement and alarm, she called to her reason to tell her what to do.

Sir Humphrey Challoner's presence here might be a coincidence, she had no cause to suspect that he was purposely following her. But in any case she wished to avoid him. How could that best be done?

Mittachip, the lawyer, had seen and recognised her. Within the next few moments the Squire would hear of her presence at the inn. He too, obviously, had come to rest his horses here. How long would he stay?

She roused Betty.

"Betty! child!" she whispered. "Wake up! We must leave this place at once."

Betty opened her eyes: she saw her mistress's pale, excited face bending over her, and she jumped to her feet.

"Listen, Betty," continued Patience. "Sir Humphrey Challoner has just come by coach. I want to leave this place before he knows that I am here."

"But the horses are not put to, my lady."

"Sh! don't talk so loud, child. I am going to slip out along the passage, there is a door at the end of it which must give upon the back of the house. As soon as I am gone, do you go to the parlour and tell Thomas to have the horses put to directly they have had sufficient rest, and to let the coach be at the cross-roads as soon as may be after that."

"Yes, my lady."

"Then as quickly as you can, slip out of the house and follow the road that leads to the forge. I'll be on the lookout for you. I'll not have gone far. You quite understand?"

"Oh, yes! my lady!"

"You are not afraid?"

Mistress Betty shrugged her plump shoulders.

"In broad daylight? Oh, no, my lady! and the forge is but a mile."

Even as she spoke Patience had wrapped her dark cloak and hood round her. She listened intently for a few seconds. The sound of voices seemed to come from the more remote bar-parlour: moreover, the narrow passage at this end was quite dark: she had every chance of slipping out unperceived.

"Sh! sh!" she whispered to Betty as she opened the door.

The passage was deserted: almost holding her breath, lest it should betray her, Patience reached the door at the further end of it, Betty anxiously watching her from the inner room. Quickly she slipped the bolt, and the next instant she found herself looking out upon a dingy unfenced yard, which for the moment was hopelessly encumbered with the two huge travelling coaches: beyond these was a long wooden shed whence proceeded the noise of voices and laughter, and the stamping and snorting of horses: and far away the Moor to the right and left of her stretched out in all the majesty of its awesome loneliness.

The wind caught her cloak as she stepped out into the yard: she clutched it tightly and held it close to her. She hoped the two coaches, which stood between her and the shed, would effectively hide her from view until she was past the house. The next moment, however, she heard an exclamation behind her, then the sound of firm steps upon the flagstones, and a second or two later she stood face to face with Sir Humphrey Challoner.

CHAPTER VIII

THE REJECTED SUITOR

Whether he was surprised or not at finding her there, she could not say: she was trying with all her might to appear astonished and unconcerned.

He made her a low and elaborate bow, and she responded with the deep curtsey the fashion of the time demanded.

"Begad! the gods do indeed favour me!" he said, his good-looking, jovial face expressing unalloyed delight. "I come to this forsaken spot on God's earth, and find the fairest in all England treading its unworthy soil."

"I wish you well, Sir Humphrey," she said gently, but coldly. "I had no thought of seeing you here."

"Faith!" he laughed with some bitterness, "I had no hope that the thought of seeing me had troubled your ladyship much. I am on my way to Derby and foolishly thought to take this shorter way across the Moor. Odd's life! I was well-nigh regretting it. I was attacked and robbed last evening, and the heavy roads force me to spend the night in this unhallowed tavern. But I little guessed what compensation the Fates had in store for me."

"I was in a like plight, Sir Humphrey," she said, trying to speak with perfect indifference.

"You were not robbed, surely?"

"Nay, not that, but I hoped to reach Derby sooner by taking the short cut across the Heath, and the state of the roads has so tired the horses, I was forced to turn off at the cross-roads and to put up at this inn."

"Your ladyship is on your way to London?"

"On a visit to my aunt, Lady Edbrooke."

"Will you honour me by accepting my protection? 'Tis scarce fit for your ladyship to be travelling all that way alone."

"I thank you, Sir Humphrey," she rejoined coldly. "My man, Timothy, is with me, besides the driver. Both are old and trusted servants. I meet some friends at Wirksworth. I shall not be alone."

"But..."

"I pray you, sir, my time is somewhat short. I had started out for a little fresh air and exercise before re-entering my coach. The inn was so stifling and..."

"Surely your ladyship will spend the night here. You cannot reach Wirksworth before nightfall now. I am told the road is well-nigh impassable."

"Nay! 'tis two hours before sunset now, and three before dark. I hope to reach Wirksworth by nine o'clock to-night. My horses have had a good rest."

"Surely you will allow me to escort you thus far, at least?"

"Your horses need a rest, Sir Humphrey," she said impatiently, "and I beg you to believe that I have sufficient escort."

With a slight inclination of the head she now turned to go. From where she stood she could just see the road winding down towards Stich's forge, and she had caught sight of Betty's trim little figure stepping briskly along.

Sir Humphrey, thus obviously dismissed, could say no more for the present. To force his escort upon her openly was unfitting the manners of a gentleman. He bit his lip and tried to look gallantly disappointed. His keen dark eyes had already perceived that in spite of her self-control she was labouring under strong excitement. He forced his harsh voice to gentleness, even to tenderness, as he said,—

"I have not dared to speak to your ladyship on the subject that lay nearest my heart."

"Sir Humphrey..."

"Nay! I pray you do not misunderstand me. I was thinking of Philip, and hoped you were not too unhappy about him."

"There is no cause for unhappiness just yet," she said guardedly, "and every cause for hope."

"Ah! that's well!" he said cheerfully. "I entreat you not to give up hope, and to keep some faith and trust in your humble servant, who would give his life for you and yours."

"My faith and trust are in God, Sir Humphrey, and in my brother's innocence," she replied quietly.

Then she turned and left him standing there, with a frown upon his good-looking face, and a muttered curse upon his lips. He watched her as she went down the road, until a sharp declivity hid her from his view.

CHAPTER IX

SIR HUMPHREY'S FAMILIAR

Mistress Pottage, sad-eyed, melancholy, and for ever sighing, had been patiently waiting to receive Sir Humphrey Challoner's orders. She had understood from his man that his Honour meant to spend the night, and she stood anxiously in the passage, wondering if he would consider her best bedroom good enough, or condescend to eat the meals she would have to cook for him.

It was really quite fortunate that Lady Patience had gone, leaving the smaller parlour, which was Mistress Pottage's own private sanctum, ready for the use of his Honour.

Sir Humphrey's mind, however, was far too busy with thoughts and plans to dwell on the melancholy landlady and her meagre fare, but he was glad of the private room, and was gracious enough to express himself quite satisfied with the prospect of the best bedroom.

Some ten minutes after his brief interview with Lady Patience he was closeted in the same little dingy room where she had been spending such weary hours. With the healthy appetite of a burly English squire, he was consuming large slabs of meat and innumerable tankards of small ale, whilst opposite to him, poised on the extreme edge of a very hard oak chair, his watery, colourless eyes fixed upon his employer, sat Master Mittachip, attorney-at-law and man of business to sundry of the quality who owned property on or about the Moor.

Master Mittachip's voice was thin, he was thin, his coat looked thin: there was in fact a general air of attenuation about the man's whole personality.

Just now he was fixing a pair of very pale, but very shrewd eyes upon the heavy, somewhat coarse person of his distinguished patron.

"Her ladyship passed me quite close," he explained, speaking in a low, somewhat apologetic voice. "I was standing in the door of—er—the parlour, and she graciously nodded to me as she passed."

"Yes! yes! get on, man," quoth Sir Humphrey, impatiently.

"The door was open, your Honour," continued Master Mittachip in a weak voice, "there was a draught; her ladyship's cloak flew open."

He paused a moment, noting with evident satisfaction the increasing interest in Sir Humphrey's face.

"Beneath her cloak," he continued, speaking very slowly, like an actor measuring his effects, "beneath her cloak her ladyship was holding a bundle of letters, tightly clutched in her hand."

"Letters, eh?" commented Sir Humphrey, eagerly.

"A bundle of them, your Honour. One of them had a large seal attached to it. I might almost have seen the device: it was that of..."

"Charles Edward Stuart, the Pretender?"

"Well! I could not say for certain, your Honour," murmured Master Mittachip, humbly.

There was silence for a few moments. Sir Humphrey Challoner had produced a silver tooth-pick, and was using it as an adjunct to deep meditation. Master Mittachip was contemplating the floor with rapt attention.

"Harkee, Master Mittachip," said Sir Humphrey at last. "Lady Patience is taking those letters to London."

"That was the impression created in my mind, your Honour."

"And why does she take those letters to London?" said Sir Humphrey, bringing his heavy fist crashing down upon the table, and causing glasses and dishes to rattle, whilst Master Mittachip almost lost his balance. "Why does she take them to London, I say? Because they are the proofs of her brother's innocence. It is easy to guess their contents. Requests, admonitions, upbraidings on the part of the disappointed rebels, obvious proofs that Philip had held aloof."

He pushed his chair noisily away from the table, and began pacing the narrow room with great, impatient strides.

But while he spoke Master Mittachip began to lose his placid air of apologetic deference, and a look of alarm suddenly lighted his meek, colourless eyes.

"Good lack," he murmured, "then my Lord Stretton is no rebel?"

"Rebel?—not he!" asserted Sir Humphrey. "His sympathies were thought to be with the Stuarts, but he went south during the rebellion—'twas I who advised him—that he might avoid being drawn within its net."

But at this Master Mittachip's terror became more tangible.

"But your Honour," he stammered, whilst his thin cheeks assumed a leaden hue, and his eyes sought appealingly those of his employer, "your Honour laid sworn information against Lord Stretton ... and ... and ... I drew up the papers ... and signed them with my name as your Honour commanded..."

"Well! I paid you well for it, didn't I?" said Sir Humphrey, roughly.

"But if the accusation was false, Sir Humphrey ... I shall be disgraced ... struck off the rolls ... perhaps hanged..."

Sir Humphrey laughed; one of those loud, jovial, laughs which those in his employ soon learnt to dread.

"Adsbud!" he said, "an one of us is to hang, old scarecrow, I prefer it shall be you."

And he gave Master Mittachip a vigorous slap on the shoulder, which nearly precipitated the lean-shanked attorney on the floor.

"Good Sir Humphrey..." he murmured piteously, "b ... b ... b ... but what was the reason of the information against Lord Stretton, since the letters can so easily prove it to be false?"

"Silence, you fool!" said his Honour, impatiently, "I did not know of the letters then. I wished to place Lord Stretton in a perilous position, then hoped to succeed in establishing his innocence in certain ways I had in my mind. I wished to be the one to save him," he added, muttering a curse of angry disappointment, "and gain *her* gratitude thereby. I was journeying to London for the purpose, and now..."

His language became such that it wholly disconcerted Master Mittachip, accustomed though he was to the somewhat uncertain tempers of the great folk he had to deal with. Moreover, the worthy attorney was fully conscious of his own precarious position in this matter.

"And now you've gained nothing," he moaned; "whilst I ... oh! oh! I..."

His condition was pitiable. His Honour viewed him with no small measure of contempt. Then suddenly Sir Humphrey's face lighted up with animation. The scowl disappeared, and a shrewd, almost triumphant smile parted the jovial, somewhat sensuous lips.

"Easy! easy! you old coward," he said pleasantly, "things are not so bad as that.... Adsbud! you're not hanged yet, are you? and," he added significantly, "Lord Stretton is still attainted and in peril of his life."

"B ... b ... b ... but..."

"Can't you see, you fool," said Sir Humphrey with sudden earnestness, drawing a chair opposite the attorney, and sitting astride upon it, he viewed the meagre little creature before him steadfastly and seriously; "can't you see that if I can only get hold of those letters now, I could *force* Lady Patience into accepting my suit?"

"Eh?"

"With them in my possession I can go to her and say, 'An you marry me, those proofs of your brother's innocence shall be laid before the King: an you refuse they shall be destroyed.'"

"Oh!" was Master Mittachip's involuntary comment: a mere gasp of amazement, of terror at the enormity of the proposal.

He ventured to raise his timid eyes to the strong florid face before him, and in it saw such a firm will, such unbendable determination, that he thought it prudent for the moment to refrain from adverse comment.

"Truly," he murmured vaguely, as his Honour seemed to be waiting for him to speak, "truly those letters mean the lady's fortune to your Honour."

"And on the day of my marriage with her, two hundred guineas for you, Master Mittachip," said Challoner, very slowly and significantly, looking his man of business squarely in the face.

Master Mittachip literally lost his head. Two hundred guineas! 'twas more than he earned in four years, and that at the cost of hard work, many kicks and constant abuse. A receiver of rents has from time immemorial never been a popular figure. Master Mittachip found life hard, and in those days two hundred guineas was quite a comfortable little fortune. The attorney passed his moist tongue over his thin, parched lips.

The visions which these imaginary two hundred guineas had conjured up in his mind almost made his attenuated senses reel. There was that bit of freehold property at Wirksworth which he had long coveted, aye, or perhaps that partnership with Master Lutworth at Derby, or...

"'Twere worth your while, Master Mittachip, to get those letters for me, eh?"

His Honour's pleasant words brought the poor man back from the land of dreams.

"I? I, Sir Humphrey?" he murmured dejectedly, "how can I, a poor attorney-at-law...?"

"Zounds! but that's your affair," said his Honour with a careless shrug of his broad shoulders, "Methought you'd gladly earn two hundred guineas, and I offer you a way to do it."

"But how, Sir Humphrey, how?"

"That's for you to think on, my man. Two hundred guineas is a tidy sum. What? I have it," he said, slapping his own broad thigh and laughing heartily. "You shall play the daring highwayman! put on a mask and stop her ladyship's coach, shout lustily: 'Stand and deliver!' take the letters from her and 'tis done in a trice!"

The idea of that meagre little creature playing the highwayman greatly tickled Sir Humphrey's fancy, for the moment he even forgot the grave issues he himself had at stake, and his boisterous laugh went echoing through the old silent building.

But as his Honour spoke this pleasant conceit, Master Mittachip's thin, bloodless face assumed an air of deep thought, immediately followed by one of eager excitement.

"The idea of the highwayman is not a bad one, Sir Humphrey," he said with a quiet chuckle, as soon as his patron's hilarity had somewhat subsided, "but I am not happy astride a horse, and I know nought of pistols, but there's no reason why we should not get a footpad to steal those letters for you. 'Tis their trade after all."

"What do you mean? I was but jesting."

"But I was not, Sir Humphrey. I was thinking of Beau Brocade."

"The highwayman?"

"Why not? He lives by robbery and hates all the quality, whom he plunders whene'er he has a chance. Your Honour has had experience, only last night ... eh?"

"Well? What of it? Curse you, man, for a dotard! Why don't you explain?"

"'Tis simple enough, your Honour. You give him the news that her ladyship's coach will cross the Heath to-night, tell him of her money and her jewels, offer him a hundred guineas more for the packet of letters.... He! he! he! He'll do the rest, never fear!"

Master Mittachip rubbed his bony hands together, his colourless eyes were twinkling, his thin lips quivering with excitement, dreams of that freehold bit of property became tangible once more.

Sir Humphrey looked at him quietly for a moment or two: the little man's excitement was contagious and his Honour had a great deal at stake: a beautiful woman whom he loved and her large fortune to boot. But reason and common-sense—not chivalry—were still fighting their battle against his daring spirit of adventure.

"Tush, man!" he said after awhile, with the calmness of intense excitement, "you talk arrant nonsense when you say I'm to give a highwayman news of her ladyship's coach and offer him money for the letters. Where am I to find him? How speak with him?"

Mittachip chuckled inwardly. His Honour then was not averse to the plan. Already he was prepared to discuss the means of carrying it out.

"'Tis a lawyer's business to ferret out what goes on around him, Sir Humphrey. You can send any news you please to Beau Brocade within an hour from now."

"How?"

"John Stich, the blacksmith over at the crossroads, is his ally and his friend. Most folk think 'tis he always gives news to the rogue whene'er a coach happen to cross the Moor. But that's as it may be. If your Honour will call at the forge just before sunset, you'll mayhap see a chestnut horse tethered there and there'll be a stranger talking to John Stich; a stranger young and well-looking. He's oft to be seen at the forge. The folk about here never ask who the stranger is, for all have heard of the chivalrous highwayman who robs the rich and gives to the poor. He! he! he! Do you call at the forge, Sir Humphrey, you can arrange this little matter there.... Your news and offer of money will get to Beau Brocade, never fear."

Sir Humphrey was silent. All the boisterous jollity had gone out of his face, leaving only a dark scowl behind, which made the ruddy face look almost evil in its ugliness. Mittachip viewed him with ill-concealed satisfaction. The plan had indeed found favour with his Honour; it was quick, daring, sure: the fortune of a lifetime upon one throw. Sir Humphrey, even before the attorney had finished speaking, had resolved to take the risk. He himself was safe in any case, nothing could connect his name with that of the notorious highwayman who had cut his purse but the night before.

"I'd not have her hurt," was the first comment he made after a few minutes' silent cogitation.

"Hurt?" rejoined Mittachip. "Why should she be hurt? Beau Brocade would not hurt a pretty woman. He'll get the letters from her, I'll stake my oath on that."

"Aye! and blackmail me after that to the end of my days. My good name would be at the mercy of so damned a rascal."

"What matter, Sir Humphrey, once Lady Patience is your wife and her fortune in your pocket? Everything is fair in love, so I've been told."

Sir Humphrey ceased to argue. Chivalry and honour had long been on the losing side.

"Moreover, Sir Humphrey," added the crafty attorney, slily, "once you have the letters, you can denounce the rogue yourself, and get him hanged safely out of your way."

"He'd denounce me."

"And who'd believe the rascal's word against your Honour's flat denial? Not Squire West, for sure, before whom he'd be tried, and your Honour can have him kept in prison until after your marriage with Lady Patience."

It seemed as if even reason would range herself on the side of this daring plan. There seemed practically no risk as far as Sir Humphrey himself was concerned, and every chance of success, an that rascal Beau Brocade would but consent.

"He would," asserted Mittachip, "an your Honour told him that the coach, the money, and the letters belonged to Lady Rounce, and the young lady travelling in the coach but a niece of her ladyship. Lady Rounce is a hard woman who takes no excuse from a debtor. He! he! he! she has the worst reputation in the two counties, save your Honour!"

The lawyer chuckled at this little joke, but Sir Humphrey was too absorbed to note the impertinence. He was pacing up and down the narrow room in a last agony of indecision.

Mittachip evidently was satisfied with his day's work. The two hundred guineas he looked upon as a certainty already. After a while, noting the look of stern determination upon his Honour's face, he turned the conversation to matters of business. He had been collecting some rents for Sir Humphrey and also for Squire West and Lady Rounce, and would have to return to Wirksworth to bank the money.

Since Sir Humphrey Challoner was occupying the only available bedroom at the Moorhen, there would be no room for Master Mittachip and Master Duffy, his clerk. He hoped to reach Brassington by the bridle path before the footpads were astir, thence at dawn on to Wirksworth.

He had shot his poisonous arrow and did not stop to ascertain how far it had gone home. He bade farewell to his employer, with all the deference which many years of intercourse with the quality had taught him, and never mentioned Beau Brocade, Lady Patience or John Stich's forge again. But when he had bowed and scraped himself out of his Honour's presence, and was sitting once more beside Master Duffy in the bar-parlour, there was a world of satisfaction in his pale, watery eyes.

CHAPTER X

A STRANGER AT THE FORGE

In the meanwhile Lady Patience, with Betty by her side, had been walking towards the forge as rapidly as the state of the road permitted.

A sudden turn of the path brought her within sight of the cross-ways and of the old gallows, on which a fragment of rain-spattered rag still fluttered ghostlike in the wind.

But here, within a few yards of her goal, she stopped suddenly, with eyes dilated, and hands pressed convulsively to her heart, in an agony of terror. Walking quickly on the road from Wirksworth towards Stich's cottage were some half-dozen red-coated figures, the foremost man amongst them wearing three stripes upon his sleeve.

Soldiers with a sergeant at the forge! What could it mean but awful peril for the fugitive?

Her halt had been but momentary, the next instant she was flying down the pathway closely followed by Betty, and had reached the shed just as the soldiers were skirting the cottage towards it.

She glanced within, and gave a quick sigh of relief: there was no sign of her brother, and John was busy at his anvil.

Already the smith had caught sight of her.

"Hush!" he whispered reassuringly, "have no fear, my lady. I've had soldiers here before."

"But they'll recognise me, perhaps ... or guess..."

"No, no! my lady! Do you pretend to be a waiting wench. They are men from Derby mostly, and not like to know your face."

There was not a moment to be lost. Patience realised this, together with the certainty that her own coolness and presence of mind might prove the one chance of safety for her brother.

"Halt!" came in loud accents from the sergeant outside.

"The lock, Master Stich," said Patience, loudly and carelessly, as the sergeant stepped into the doorway, "is it ready? Her ladyship's coach is following me from Aldwark, and will be at the cross-roads anon."

"Quite ready, mistress," replied the smith, casting a rapid glance at the soldier, who stood in the entrance with hand to hat in military salute.

The latter took a rapid survey of the interior of the forge, then said politely,—

"Your pardon, ladies!"

"Well, and what is it now, Sergeant?" queried John, with affected impatience.

"I have heard that there's a stranger at your forge, smith," replied the soldier. "My corporal came down from Aldwark early this afternoon and told me about him. I'd like just to have a talk with him."

"One moment, Sergeant," said John, interposing his burly figure between Patience and the prying eyes of the young soldier.

"I think you'll find the lock quite secure now, mistress," he said, trying, good, honest fellow that he was, to put as much meaning into the careless sentence as he dared. She mutely thanked him with her eyes, took the padlock from his hands, and gave him over some money for his pains, the while her heart was nearly bursting with the agony of suspense.

"No stranger, Sergeant," rejoined the smith, once more turning with well-assumed indifference to the soldier, "only my nephew out o' Nottingham. Your corporal was a Derby man, and knew the lad's mother, my sister Hannah!"

"Quite so, quite so, smith," quoth the Sergeant, pleasantly; "then you won't mind my searching your forge and cottage just for form's sake."

Even then Patience did not betray herself either by a look or a quiver of the voice.

"Lud! how tiresome be those soldiers," she said with an affected pout. "I'd hoped to wait here in peace, friend smith, until the arrival of her ladyship's coach."

"Nay, mistress, you need not be disturbed," said the smith, jovially, "the Sergeant is but jesting, eh, friend?" he added, turning to the soldier. "There! I give you my word, Master Sergeant, that there is nought here for you to find."

"I've my orders, smith," said the Sergeant, more curtly.

"Nay, friend," interposed Lady Patience, "surely you overstep your orders. John Stich is honest and loyal, you do him indignity by such unjust suspicions."

"Your pardon, ma'am, but I know my duty. There's no suspicion against the smith, but there are many rebels in hiding about here, and I've strict orders to be on the lookout for one in particular, Philip Gascoyne, Earl of Stretton, who is known to be in these parts."

John Stich interrupted him with a loud guffaw.

"Lud, man!" he said, "there's no room for a noble lord in a wayside smithy; you waste your time."

"My orders say I've the right to search," quoth the Sergeant, firmly, "and search I'm going to."

Then he turned to his squad, who were standing at attention outside.

"Follow me, men," he said, as he stepped forward into the forge.

Fortunately the remote corners of the shed were dark, and Patience still had her hood and cloak wrapped closely round her, or her deathlike pallor, the wild, terrified look in her eyes, would at this moment have betrayed her in spite of herself.

But honest John was standing in the way of the Sergeant.

"Look'ee here, Sergeant," he said quietly, "I'm a man of few words, but I'm a free-born Englishman, and my home is my castle. It's an insult to a free and loyal citizen for soldiers to search his home, as if he were a felon. I say you *shall not* enter, so you take yourself off, before you come by a broken head."

"Smith, you're a fool," commented the Sergeant with a shrug of the shoulders, "and do yourself no good."

"That's as it may be, friend," quoth John. "There are fools in every walk in life. You be a stranger in these parts and don't know me, but folk'll tell you that what John Stich once says, that he'll stick to. So forewarned is forearmed, friend Sergeant. Eh?"

But to this the Sergeant had but one reply, and that was directed to his own squad.

"Now then, my men," he said, "follow me! and you, John Stich," he added loudly and peremptorily, "stand aside in the name of the King!"

The men were ranged round the Sergeant with muskets grasped, ready to rush in the next moment at word of command. John Stich stood between them and a small wooden door, little more than a partition, behind which Philip, Earl of Stretton, was preparing to sell his life dearly.

That death would immediately follow capture was absolutely clear both to him and to his devoted sister, who with almost superhuman effort of will was making heroic efforts to keep all outward show of alarm in check. Even amongst these half-dozen soldiers any one of them might know Lord Stretton by sight, and was not likely to forget that twenty guineas—a large sum in those days—was the price the Hanoverian Government was prepared to pay for the head of a rebel.

Philip was a man condemned to death by Act of Parliament. If he were captured now, neither prayer, nor bribes, nor even proofs of innocence would avail him before an officious magistrate intent on doing his duty. A brief halt at Brassington court-house, an execution in the early dawn!... these were the awesome visions which passed before Patience's eyes, as with a last thought of anguish and despair she turned to God for help!

No doubt John Stich was equally aware of the imminence of the peril, and, determined to fight for the life of his lord, he brandished his mighty hammer over his head, and there was a look in the powerful man's eyes that made even the Sergeant pause awhile ere giving the final word of command.

Thus there was an instant's deadly silence whilst so many hearts were wildly beating in tumultuous emotion. Just one instant—a few seconds, mayhap, whilst even Nature seemed to stand still, and Time to pause before the next fateful minute.

And then a voice—a fresh, young, happy voice—was suddenly heard to sing, "My beautiful white rose."

It was not very distant: but twenty yards at most, and even now seemed to be making for the forge, drawing nearer and nearer.

Instinctively—what else could they do?—soldiers and Sergeant turned to look out upon the Heath. There was such magic in that merry, boyish voice, clear as that of the skylark, singing the quaint old ditty.

They looked and saw a stranger dressed in elegant, almost foppish fashion, his brown hair free from powder, tied with a large bow at the nape of the neck, dainty lace at his throat and wrists, scarce a speck of mud upon his fine, well-cut coat. He was leading a beautiful chestnut horse by the bridle and had been singing as he walked.

Patience, too, catching at this happy interruption like a drowning man does at a straw, turned to look at the approaching stranger.

Her eyes were the first to meet his as he reached the entrance of the forge, and with an elaborate, courtly gesture he raised his three-cornered hat and made her a respectful bow.

Then he burst out laughing.

"Ho! ho! ho! but here's a pretty to-do. Why, John Stich, my friend, you look a bit out of temper."

He stood there framed in the doorway, with the golden light of the afternoon sun throwing into bold silhouette his easy, graceful stature, and the pleasant picture of him, with one arm round the beautiful horse's neck and his slender fingers gently fondling its soft, quivering nose.

John Stich, at first sound of the stranger's voice, had relaxed from his defiant attitude, and a ray of hope had chased away the threatening look in his eyes.

"So would you be, Captain," he said gruffly, "with these red coats inside your house, and all their talk of rebels."

"Captain?" murmured the Sergeant.

"Aye, Captain Bathurst, my man, of His Majesty's White Dragoons," said the stranger, carelessly, as without more ado he led his horse within the forge and tethered it close to the entrance. Then he came forward and slapped the Sergeant vigorously on the back.

"And I'll go bail, Sergeant, that John Stich is no rebel. He's far too big a fool!" he added in an audible whisper, and with a merry twinkle in his grey eyes.

Patience still stood rigid, expectant, terrified in the darker corner of the shed. She had not yet realised whether she dared to hope, whether this young stranger, with his pleasant, boyish voice and debonnair manner, would have the power to stay the hand of Fate, which was even now raised against her brother.

Betty, behind her mistress, was too terrified to speak.

But already the Sergeant had recovered from his momentary surprise. At mention of the stranger's military rank he had raised his hand to his tricorne hat. Now he was ready to perform his duty, and gladly noted the smith's less aggressive attitude.

"At your service, Captain," he said, "and now I have my orders. I've a right o' search and..."

But like veritable quicksilver, Captain Bathurst was upon him in a moment.

"A right o' search!" he said excitedly. "A right o' search, did you say, Sergeant? Odd's my life, but I'm in luck! Sergeant, you're the very man for me."

And he pulled the Sergeant by the sleeve.

"I pray you, sir..." protested the latter.

But the young man was not to be denied.

"Sergeant," he whispered significantly, "would you like to earn a hundred guineas?"

"One hundred guineas," rejoined the soldier readily enough; "that I would, sir, if you'll tell me how."

He kept an eye on the little wooden door behind John Stich, but his ear leaned towards the stranger; the bait was a tempting one, a hundred guineas was something of a fortune to a soldier of King George II.

"Listen then," said Bathurst, mysteriously. "You've heard of Beau Brocade, the highwayman, haven't you?"

"Aye, aye," nodded the Sergeant, "who hasn't?"

"Well then you know that there is a price of a hundred guineas for his capture, eh? ... Think of it, Sergeant! ... A hundred guineas! ... a little fortune, eh?"

The Sergeant's eyes twinkled at the thought. The soldiers too listened with eager interest, for the stranger was no longer talking in a whisper. A hundred guineas! three little words of wondrous magic, which had the power to rouse most men to excitement in those days of penury.

Lady Patience's whole soul seemed to have taken refuge in her eyes. Her body leaning forward, her lips parted with a quick-drawn breath, she gazed upon the stranger, wondering what he would do. That he was purposely diverting the Sergeant's attention from his purpose she did not dare to think, that he was succeeding beyond her wildest hopes was not in doubt for a moment.

And yet there did not seem much gained by averting the fearful catastrophe for the span of a few brief minutes.

"Aye! a fortune indeed!" sighed the Sergeant, with obvious longing.

"And I have sworn to lay that dare-devil highwayman by the heels," continued the young man. "I know where he lies hidden at this very moment, but, by Satan and all his crew, I cannot lay hands upon the rascal."

"How so?"

"The house is private! worse luck! *I* have no right of search!"

The Sergeant gave a knowing wink.

"Hm!" he said. "I understand."

Then he added significantly,—

"But the reward?"

"Odd's life! you shall have the whole of that, Sergeant, and, if your men will help me, there shall be another hundred to divide between them. I have sworn to lay the rogue by the heels for my honour's sake. Would you believe me, Sergeant, 'tis but a week ago that rascally highwayman robbed me in broad daylight! ... fifty guineas he took from me. Now I've a bet with Captain Borrowdale, five hundred guineas aside, that I'll bring about the rogue's capture."

There was no doubt now that the Sergeant's interest was fully aroused; the soldiers, at mention of the reward which was to be theirs, hung upon their Sergeant's lips, hoping for the order to march on this very lucrative errand.

"Hm!" muttered the latter, with a knowing wink, "perhaps that highwayman is a personal enemy of yours as well, sir!"

"Aye!" sighed Captain Bathurst, pathetically, "the worst I ever had."

"And you'd be mightily glad to see him hanged, an I mistake not. What?"

"Zounds! but I wouldn't say that exactly, Sergeant, but ... I have no love for him ... 'tis many an ill turn he has done me of late."

"I understand! Then the reward?"

"You shall have every penny of it, friend, and a hundred guineas for your men. What say you, gallant soldiers?" And he turned gaily to the little squad, who had stood at very close attention all this while.

But there was no need to make this direct appeal. The men were only too ready to be up and doing, to earn the reward and leave John Stich and the very problematical rebel to look after themselves.

"Now, quick's the word," said the young man, briskly, "there's not a moment to be lost."

"At your service, Captain," replied the Sergeant, turning once more towards the inner door before which John Stich still held guard, "as soon as I've searched this forge..."

"Nay, man, an you waste a minute, you and your men will miss Beau Brocade and the hundred guineas reward. Quick, man!" he added hurriedly, seeing that the soldier had paused irresolute, "quick! with your fellows straight up the road that leads northward. I'm on horseback—I'll overtake you as soon as may be."

"But..."

"You'll see a lonely cottage about half a mile from here, then a bridle path on the left; follow that, you'll come to a house that was once an inn. The rascal is there. I saw him not half an hour ago."

"But the rebel, Captain..." feebly protested the Sergeant, "my duty..."

"Nay, Sergeant, as you will," said Bathurst, coolly, with a great show of complete indifference; "but while you parley here, Beau Brocade will slip through your fingers. He is at the house now: he may be gone by sunset. Odd's life! search for your rebels! go on! waste time! and the hundred guineas are lost to you and your men for ever."

It was obvious that both sergeant and men were determined not to lose this opportunity of a bold bid for fortune.

"Done with you, sir," he said resolutely. "After all," he added, as a concession to his own sense of duty, "I can always come back and search the forge afterwards."

All the soldiers seemed as one man to be uttering a sigh of relief and eager anticipation, and even before the Sergeant had spoken the word, they turned to go.

"You are a wise man, Sergeant," said Bathurst, jovially. "Off with you! straight along that road you see before you. The cottage is just beyond that clump of distant firs, there you'll see the bridle path. But I'll overtake you before then, never fear. Time to give my horse a handful of oats..."

But even while he spoke the Sergeant had called "Attention!"

"I'll not fail you, sir," he shouted excitedly. "A hundred guineas! odd's my life! 'tis a fortune! Left turn! Quick march!"

The young man stood in the doorway and watched the little squad as, preceded by their Sergeant, they plodded their way northwards in quest of fortune. John Stich too followed them with his eyes, until the bend in the road hid the red coats from view. Then both turned and came within.

But Lady Patience through it all never looked at the soldiers; her eyes, large, glowing, magnetic, were fixed upon the stranger in the forge, as if in a trance of joy and gratitude.

CHAPTER XI

THE STRANGER'S NAME

Mistress Betty was the first to recover from terror and surprise. She too had fixed a pair of large and wondering eyes upon the stranger.

"'Tis the gentleman who brought the letter from his lordship last night," she whispered to her mistress.

Patience closed her eyes for a moment: her spirit, which had gone a-roaming into the land of dreams, where dwell heroes and proud knights of old, came back to earth once more.

"Then he must have guessed my brother was here," she murmured, "and did it to save him."

But the tension being relaxed, already the bright and sunny nature, which appeared to be the chief characteristic of the stranger, quickly re-asserted itself, and soon he was laughing merrily.

"Oh! ho! gone, by my faith!" he said to John. "Odd's life! but he swallowed that, clean as a mullet after bait, eh, friend Stich?"

It seemed as if he purposely avoided looking at Patience: perhaps, with the innate delicacy of a kindly nature, he wished to give her time to recover her composure. But now she came forward, turning to him with a gentle smile that had an infinity of pathos in it.

"Sir," she said, "I would wish to thank you..."

He put up his hand, with a gesture of self-deprecation.

"To thank me, madam?" he said, with profound deference. "Nay! you do but jest. I have done nothing to deserve so great a favour."

He bowed to her with perfect courtly grace, but she would not be gainsaid. She wished to think that he had acted thus for her.

"Sir, you wrong your own most noble deed," she said. "Will you not allow me to keep the sweet illusion, that what you did just now, you did from the kindness of your heart, and because you saw that we were all anxious ... and that ... I was unhappy..."

She looked divinely fair as she stood there beside him, with the rays of the slanting September sun touching the halo of her hair with a wand of gold. Her voice was musical and low, and there was a catch in her throat as she held out one tiny, trembling hand to him.

He took it in his own strong grasp, and kept it a prisoner therein for awhile, then he bent his slim young figure and touched her finger-tips with his lips.

"Faith, madam!" he said, "by that sweet illusion, an it dwell awhile in your memory, I am more than repaid."

In the meanwhile John had pushed open the small door which led to the inner shed.

"Quite safe, my lord!" he shouted gaily, "only friends present."

Brother and sister, regardless of all save their own joy in this averted peril, were soon locked in each other's arms. Captain Bathurst had heard her happy cry: "Philip!" had seen the look of gladness brighten her tear-dimmed eyes, and a curious feeling of wrath, which he could not explain, caused him to turn away with a frown and a sigh.

Patience was clinging to her brother, half hysterical, nervous, excited.

"You are safe, dear," she murmured, touching with trembling motherly hands the dear head so lately in peril, "quite safe ... let me feel your precious hands ... oh! it was so horrible! ... another moment and you were discovered! ... Sir!" she added once more, turning to the stranger with the sweet impulse of her gratitude, "my thanks just now must have seemed so poor ... I was nervous and excited ... but see! here is one who owes you his life, and who, I know, would wish to join his thanks to mine."

But there was a change in his manner now. He bowed slightly before her and said very coldly,—

"Nay, madam! let me assure you once again that I have done naught to deserve your thanks. John Stich is my friend, and he seemed in trouble ... if I have had the honour to serve you at the same time, 'tis I who should render thanks."

She sighed, somewhat disappointed at his coldness. But Philip, with boyish impulse, held out both hands to him.

"Nay, sir," he said, "I know not who you are, but I heard everything from behind that door, and I know that I owe you my life..."

"I beg you, sir..."

"Another moment and I had rushed out and sold my life dearly. Your noble effort, sir, did more than save that life," he added, taking Patience's hand in his, "it spared a deep sorrow to one who is infinitely dear to me ... my only sister."

"Your ... your sister?"

"Aye! my sister, Lady Patience Gascoyne, I am the Earl of Stretton, unjustly attainted by Act of Parliament. The life you have just saved, sir, is henceforth at your command."

"Indeed, Philip," added Patience, gently, "we already are deeply in this gentleman's debt. Betty, who saw him, tells me that it was he who brought me your letter yester night."

"You, sir!" exclaimed Stretton in profound astonishment, "then you are..."

He paused instinctively, for he had remembered his conversation with John Stich earlier in the day; he remembered the anger, the wonder, which he had felt when the smith told him that he had entrusted the precious letter for Lady Patience to Beau Brocade, the highwayman ...

"Then you are...?" repeated Philip, mechanically.

Patience was clinging to her brother, with her back towards the stranger, so she did not see the swift look of appeal the slender finger put up in a mute, earnest prayer for silence. But now she turned and looked inquiringly at him, her eyes asking for a name by which she could remember him.

"Captain Jack Bathurst," he said, bowing low, "at your command."

CHAPTER XII

THE BEAUTIFUL WHITE ROSE

But of course there was no time to be lost. Captain Jack Bathurst was the first to give the alarm.

"Those gallant lobsters won't be long in finding out that they've been hoodwinked," he said, "an I mistake not, they'll return here anon with a temper slightly the worse for wear. They must not find your lordship here at anyrate," he added earnestly.

"But what's to be done?" asked Patience, all her anxiety returning in a trice, and instinctively turning for guidance to the man who already had done so much for her.

"For the next hour or two at anyrate his lordship would undoubtedly be safer on the open Moor," said Bathurst, decisively. "'Tis nigh on sunset, and the shepherds are busy gathering in their flocks. There'll be no one about, and 'twould be safer."

"On the open Moor?"

"Aye! 'tis not a bad place," he said, with a touch of sadness in his fresh young voice. "I myself..."

He checked himself and continued more quietly,—

"Your lordship could return here after sundown. You'd be safe enough for the night. After that, an you'll grant me leave, my friend Stich and I will venture to devise some better plan for your safety. For the moment, I pray you, be guided by this good advice, and seek the protection of the open Moor."

He had spoken so earnestly, with such obvious heartfelt concern, and at the same time with such quiet firmness, that instinctively Philip felt inclined to obey; the weaker nature turned for support to the stronger one, to whose dominating influence it felt compelled to yield. He turned to Patience, and her eyes seemed to tell him that she was ready to trust this stranger.

"Aye! I'll go, sir!" he sighed wearily.

He kissed his sister with all the fondness of his aching heart. All his hopes for the future were centred in her and in the long journey she was about to undertake for his sake.

Bathurst discreetly left brother and sister alone. He knew nothing of their affairs, of their plans, their hopes. Stich was too loyal to speak of his lord, even to a man whom he trusted and respected as he did the Captain. The latter knew that a hunted man was in hiding in the smith's forge, he had taken a message from the man to the lady at Stretton Hall, now he knew for certain that the fugitive was the Earl of Stretton. But that was all.

Being outside the pale of the law himself, his sympathies at once ranged themselves on the side of the fugitive. Whether the latter were guilty or innocent mattered little to Jack Bathurst; what did matter to him was that the most beautiful woman he had ever set eyes on was unhappy and in tears.

Philip, seeing that he could talk to his sister unobserved, whispered eagerly,—

"The letters, dear, have a care; how will you carry them?"

"In the drawer underneath the seat of the coach," she whispered in reply. "I'll not leave the coach day or night until I've reached London. From Wirksworth onwards I'll be travelling with relays: I need neither spare horses nor waste a moment's time. I can be in town in less than six days."

"When will your coach be ready?"

"In a few minutes now, and I'll start at once: but go, go now, dear," she urged tenderly, "since Captain Bathurst thinks it better that you should."

She kissed him again and again, her heart full of hope and excitement at thought of what she could do for him, yet aching because of this parting. It was terrible to leave him in this awful peril, to be far away if danger once again became imminent!

When at last he had torn himself away from her, he made quickly for the door, where Bathurst had been waiting for him.

"Ah, sir!" sighed Philip, bitterly, "'tis a sorry plight for a soldier and a gentleman to hide for his life like a coward and a thief."

But Bathurst before leaving was looking back at the beautiful picture of Patience's sweet face bathed in tears.

"Like a thief?" he murmured. "Nay, sir, thieves have no angels to guard and love them: methinks you have no cause to complain of your fate."

There was perhaps just a thought of bitterness in his voice as he said this, and Patience turned to him, and gazed at him in tender womanly pity through her tears. At once the electrical, sunny nature within him again gained the upper hand. Laughter and gaiety seemed with him to be always close to the surface, ready to ripple out at any moment, and calling forth hope and confidence in those around.

"An you'll accept my escort, sir," he said cheerfully to Philip, "I'll show you a sheltered spot known only to myself ... and to Jack o' Lantern," he added, giving a passing tender tap to his beautiful horse. "He and I are very fond of the Moor, eh, Jack, old friend? ... We are the two Jacks, you see, sir, and seldom are seen apart. Together we discovered the spot which I will show you, sir, and where you can lie *perdu* until nightfall. 'Tis safe and lonely and but a step from this forge."

Philip accepted the offer gratefully. Like his sister, he too felt that he could trust Jack Bathurst. As he walked by his side along the unbeaten track on the Heath, he viewed with some curiosity, not unmixed with boyish admiration, the tall, well-knit figure of his gallant rescuer. He tried to think of him as the notorious highwayman, Beau Brocade, on whose head the Government had put the price of a hundred guineas.

A hero of romance he was in the hearts of the whole country-side, yet a felon in the eyes of the law. Philip could just see his noble profile, with the well-cut features, the boyish, sensitive mouth, firm chin and straight, massive brow, over which a mass of heavy brown curls clustered in unruly profusion.

A brave man, surely—Philip had experienced that; a wise one too in spite of his youth. Stretton guessed his companion to be still under thirty years of age, and yet there was at times, in spite of the inherently sunny disposition below, a look of melancholy, of disappointment, in the deep, grey eyes, which spoke of a wasted life, of opportunities lost perhaps, or of persistent adverse fate.

Through it all there was that quaint air of foppishness, the manners and appearance of a dandy about the Court. The caped coat was dark and serviceable, but it was of the finest cloth and of the latest, most fashionable cut, and beneath it peeped a dainty silk waistcoat, delicately embroidered.

The lace at throat and wrists was of the finest Mechlin, and the boots, though stout and heavy, betrayed the smallness and the arch of the foot. Though Jack Bathurst had obviously been riding, he carried neither whip nor cane.

All that Philip observed in this rapid walk to the place of shelter which Bathurst had thought out for him, Patience, with a woman's quick perception, had noted from the first. To her, of course, the Captain was but a gallant stranger, good to look at and replete with all the chivalrous attributes this troublous century called forth in the hearts of her sons. She knew naught of Beau Brocade the highwayman, and probably would have recoiled in horror at thought of connecting the name of a thief with that of her newly-found hero of romance.

She stood in the doorway for some time, watching with glowing eyes the figures of the two men, until they disappeared behind a high clump of gorse: then with a curious little sigh she turned and went within.

John Stich and Mistress Betty were carrying on an animated conversation in a remote corner of the forge. Patience did not wish to disturb them: she was deeply grateful to John, and felt kindly disposed towards the suggestion of romance conveyed by the smith's obvious appreciation of pretty Mistress Betty.

She crossed the shed, and opening the door at the further end of it, she found that it gave upon a small yard which separated the forge from the cottage, and in which Stich and his mother, who kept house for him, had with tender care succeeded in cultivating a few flowers: only one or two tall hollyhocks, some gay-looking sunflowers, and a few sweet-scented herbs. And on the south aspect a lovely trail of creeping white rose, the kind known as "Five Sisters," threw its delicate fragrance over this little oasis in the wilderness of the Moor.

And, almost mechanically, whilst her fancy once more went a-roaming in the land of dreams, Patience began to hum the quaint old ditty: "My beautiful white rose."

Suddenly—at a quick thought mayhap—her eyes grew dim, her cheeks began to burn: she drew towards her a cluster of snowy blossoms, on which the earlier rains had left a mantle of glittering diamonds, and buried her glowing face in its pure, cool depths. Then she detached one lovely white rose from the parent bough, and, sighing, pinned it to her belt.

CHAPTER XIII

A PROPOSAL AND A THREAT

Sir Humphrey Challoner had not been long in making up his mind to take Master Mittachip's pernicious advice. He twisted the old adage that "everything is fair in love" to a justification of his own evil purpose. He was not by any means a bad man. Save for his somewhat inordinate love of money, he had none of the outrageous vices which were looked upon with leniency in the quality in those days.

He drank hard, and exacted his pound of flesh equally from all his tenants, but neither of these characteristics was unusual in an English squire of the early eighteenth century: a great many of them were impecunious, and all were fond of good cheer. Originally he had meant no harm to the young Earl of Stretton. His plan, as he clumsily conceived it, was to get Philip into trouble first, then to extricate him from it, for the sake of earning the gratitude of the richest heiress in the Midlands and the most beautiful woman in England to boot.

Sir Humphrey Challoner was not a diplomatist: he was a rough country gentleman of that time, with but scant notions of abstract right and wrong where his own desires were at stake.

His original plan had failed through that very Act of Parliament which placed Philip's life in immediate and imminent peril. Sir Humphrey did not desire the lad's death: of course not. He had nothing to gain thereby, and only wished for the sister's hand in marriage. He started for London posthaste, hoping still to use what influence he had, and also what knowledge he possessed of Philip's attitude at the time of the rebellion, in order to bring about the boy's justification and release.

That Patience had evidently found a means of proving her brother's innocence without his help was a bitter disappointment to Sir Humphrey. He knew that she would never marry him of her own free will, but only on compulsion or from gratitude.

The latter was now out of the question. He could do nothing to earn it. Compulsion was the only course, and Mittachip, with crafty persuasion, had shown him the possible way; therefore he went to the forge of John Stich to carry through the plan to that end.

It was close on sunset. On the Moor, gorse, bramble and heather were bathed in ruddy gold, the brilliant aftermath of this glowing September afternoon.

Sir Humphrey had walked over from the Moorhen; as soon as he entered the forge, the first thing he noticed was the beautiful chestnut horse tethered against the door-post, the same which he himself had declared that very day to be worth a small fortune. Fate was obviously playing into his hands. Mittachip had neither deceived him nor lured him with false hopes.

Otherwise the shed was empty: there was no sign of John Stich, or of the stranger who rode the chestnut horse. Sir Humphrey went within and, as patiently as he could, set himself to wait.

When therefore Jack Bathurst returned to the forge some few minutes later, he found that her ladyship, Betty and Stich had gone, whilst, sitting on the edge of the rough deal table, and impatiently tapping his boot with a riding-whip, was no less a personage than the Squire of Hartington.

Jack had caught a glimpse of his Honour the night before on the Heath, under circumstances which even now brought a smile to his lips, and which incidentally had made the poor of Brassington richer by fifty guineas.

For a moment he hesitated whether he would go in or no. He had been masked during that incident, of course, and knew not even the ABC of fear. His dare-devil spirit of fun and adventure quickly gained the upper hand, and the next moment he had greeted his Honour with all the courtly grace he had at command.

Sir Humphrey looked at him keenly for a moment or two. Young and well-looking! Oft to be seen at the forge at sundown! ... Odd's life but...

"Your servant, sir!" he said, returning the salutation.

Sir Humphrey was in no hurry. He firmly believed that Fate had decided to be kind to him in this matter, but he feared to brusque the situation, and thereby to imperil the successful issue of his scheme.

Therefore he passed the time of day with this well-looking stranger, he talked of the weather and the rains on the Moors, the bad state of the roads and the insufficiency of police in the county, of the late rebellion and the newest fashion in coats.

Jack Bathurst seemed to fall into his mood. He was shrewd enough to perceive that Sir Humphrey Challoner was in his own estimation playing a diplomatic game of cat and mouse, and it much intrigued Bathurst to know what his ultimate purpose might be. He had not long to wait; after some five minutes of casual conversation, Sir Humphrey went straight for his goal.

"Odd's life!" he said suddenly, interrupting his own flow of small talk, "it wonders me how long that rascally smith'll stay away from his work. Adsbud! but he's a lazy vagabond. What say you, sir?"

"Nay! you, sir, wrong an honest man," replied Bathurst. "John Stich is a steady worker. Shall I call him for you? I know my way about his cottage."

"Nay, I thank you, sir! my purpose can wait. Truth to tell," added his Honour, carelessly, "'twas not the blacksmith's work I needed, but his help in a trifling matter of business."

"Indeed?"

"You'll be surprised perhaps at my question, sir, but have you ever heard mention of that fellow, Beau Brocade?"

"Oh! ... vaguely..."

"A highwayman, sir, and a consummate rogue, yet your honest John Stich is said to be his friend."

"Indeed?"

"Now, an you'll believe me, sir, I have a mind to speak with the rascal."

"Indeed? then you are bolder than most, sir," said Jack, cheerfully. He was really beginning to wonder what the Squire of Hartington was driving at.

"It seems strange, doesn't it? but to be frank with you, I'm in two minds about that rogue."

"How so?"

"Well! I have a score to settle with him, and a business to propose; and I cannot decide which course to adopt."

"You, sir, being so clever, might perhaps manage both," said Bathurst with a touch of sarcasm.

"Hm! I wonder now," continued Sir Humphrey, not wishing to notice the slight impertinence. "I wonder now what an independent gentleman like yourself would advise me to do. I have not the honour of knowing who you are," he added with grave condescension, "but I can see that you *are*, like myself, a gentleman."

Bathurst bowed in polite acknowledgment.

"I should be proud to serve you with advice, sir, since you desire it."

"Well! as I have said, I have a score to settle with the rogue. He stole fifty guineas from me last night."

"Ah me!" sighed Jack, with a melancholy shake of the head, "then I fear me he'll never haunt the Heath again."

"What mean you, sir?"

"Nay! I can picture the rascal now, after you, sir, had punished him for his impudence! A mangled, bleeding wreck! But there! I have no pity for him! Daring to measure his valour against your noted prowess!"

"Quite so! quite so!" quoth his Honour, whilst smothering a curse at this more obvious piece of insolence.

"But I entreat your pardon. I was interrupting the story."

"I saw the rogue, sir," said Sir Humphrey, glancing significantly at the young man, "saw him clearly by the light of my carriage lanthorns. He was masked, of course, but I'd know him anywhere, and could denounce him to-morrow."

He had risen to his feet, and with legs apart, standing face to face with Bathurst, he spoke every word as if he meant them to act as a threat.

"There are plenty of soldiers about these parts now, even if the country folk won't touch their vaunted hero of romance. I could get him hanged, sir, within a week. A cordon of soldiers round this Heath, my word to swear his identity, and.... But there!" he added with a jovial laugh, "'tis no concern of yours is it, sir? You were kind enough to promise me your advice. This is one of my alternatives, the score I'd wish to settle; there's still the business I could offer the rogue."

Sir Humphrey had looked the young man squarely in the face whilst he uttered his threat, but had seen nothing there, save the merriest, the most light-hearted of smiles.

"I can scarce advise you, sir," said Bathurst, still smiling, "unless I know the business as well."

"Well, sir, you know of old Lady Rounce, do you not? the meanest, ugliest old witch in the county, eh? Well! she is on her way to London, and carries with her a mass of money, wrung from her miserable tenants."

"Faith, sir! you paint a most entrancing picture of the lady."

"Now, an that rascal Beau Brocade were willing to serve me, he could at one stroke save his own neck from the gallows, enrich himself, right the innocent and confound a wicked old woman."

"And how could this galaxy of noble deeds be accomplished at one stroke, sir?"

"Her ladyship's coach will pass over the Heath to-night. It should be at the cross-roads soon. There will be all the old harridan's money and jewels to be got out of it."

"Of course."

"And also a packet of love-letters, which doubtless will be hidden away in the receptacle beneath the seat."

"Letters?" queried Bathurst. "Hm! I doubt me if love-letters would tempt a gentleman of the road."

"Nay, sir," replied his Honour, now dropping his voice to a confidential whisper, "these are letters which, if published, would compromise an artless young lady, whom old Lady Rounce pursues with her hatred and spite. Now I would give a hundred guineas to any person who will bring me those letters at the Moorhen to-morrow. Surely to a gentleman of the road the game would be worth the candle. Lady Rounce carries money with her besides, and her diamonds. What think you of it, sir?"

"'Tis somewhat difficult to advise," said Bathurst, meditatively.

"Ah well!" said Sir Humphrey with affected indifference, "'tis really not much to me. On the whole perhaps I would prefer to deliver the rascal into the hands of my friend Squire West at Brassington. Anyway, I have the night to think the matter over; 'tis too late now to wait for that lout, John Stich. I would have preferred to have had your advice, sir. I daresay 'tis difficult to give. And you a stranger too. I would have liked to save a young girl from the clutches of that old witch, Lady Rounce, and if Beau Brocade rendered me that service, I'd be tempted to hold my tongue about him.... He should have the hundred guineas to-morrow and have nought to fear from me, if he brought me those letters. If not ... well! ... well! ... we shall see.... The old gallows here have long been idle ... we shall see ... we shall see.... Good-day to you, sir ... proud to have met you.... No ... I'll not wait for John Stich. Is this your horse? ... pretty creature! ... Good-day, sir ... good-day."

His Honour was extremely condescending and pleasant. He bowed very politely to Bathurst, patted the beautiful chestnut horse, and showed no further desire to talk with John Stich.

Bathurst, with a frown on his handsome face, watched the Squire of Hartington's burly figure disappear round the bend in the road.

"I wonder now," he mused, "what mischief he's brewing. He seemed to me up to no good. I suppose he guessed who I was."

While he stood there watching, John Stich quickly entered the forge from the rear.

"I was in the cottage, Captain," he said, "my mother was serving the ladies with some milk. But just now I saw Sir Humphrey Challoner walking away from the forge. I feared he might see you."

"He did see me, honest friend," said Jack, lightly. "His Honour and I have just had a long and animated conversation together."

"Great Heavens! the man is furious with you, Captain!" said the smith, with genuine anxiety in his gruff voice, "he saw you distinctly on the Heath last night. He may have recognised you to-day."

"He did recognise me."

"And may be brewing the devil's own mischief against you."

"Oh, ho!" laughed the young man, with a careless shrug of the shoulders, "against me? ... Well! you know, honest John, I am bound to end on the gallows..."

"Sooner or later! Sooner or later!" he added merrily, noting John's look of sorrowful alarm. "They've not got me yet, though there are so many soldiers about, as that piece of underdone roast-beef said just now."

"You'll not tell me what Sir Humphrey Challoner spoke to you about?"

"No, friend, I will not," said Jack, with a look of infinite kindness and placing a slender white hand on the smith's broad shoulder. "You are my friend, you know, you shoe and care after my horse, you shelter and comfort me. May Heaven's legions of angels bless you for that. Of my life on the Heath I'll never tell you aught, whatever you may guess. 'Tis better so. I'll not have you compromised, or implicated in my adventures. In case ... well! ... if they do catch me, you know, friend, 'tis better for your sake that you should know nothing."

"But you'll not go on the Heath to-night, Captain," pleaded the smith, with a tremor in his voice.

"Aye! that I will, John Stich," rejoined Bathurst, with a careless laugh, which now had an unmistakable ring of bitterness in it, "to stop a coach, to lift a purse! that's my business.... Aye! I'll to the Heath, friend, 'tis my only home, you know, ere I find a resting-place on the gallows yonder."

John sighed and turned away, and thus did not hear the faint murmur that came of a great and good heart over-full with longing and disappointment.

"My beautiful white rose! ... how pale she looked ... and how exquisitely fair! ... Ah! me ... if only.... Jack! Jack! don't be a fool!" he added with a short, deep sigh, "'tis too late; remember, for Beau Brocade to go galloping after an illusion!"

CHAPTER XIV

THE FIGHT IN THE FORGE

John Stich ventured no further opposition, well knowing the reckless spirit which his own quiet devotion was powerless to keep in check; moreover, Lady Patience, closely followed by the ever-faithful Betty, had just entered by the door that gave from the yard.

"I was wondering, honest Stich," she said, "if my coach were yet in sight. Meseems the horses must have had sufficient rest by now."

"I'll just see, my lady," said John.

At first sound of her low, musical voice, Bathurst had turned to her, and now his eyes rested with undisguised admiration on her graceful figure, dimly outlined in the fast-gathering shadows. She too caught sight of him, and sorely against her will a vivid blush mounted to her cheeks. She pulled her cloak close to her, partly to hide the bunch of white roses that nestled in her belt.

Thus there was an instant's silent pause, during which two hearts, both young, both ardent, and imbued with the spirit of romance, beat—unknown to one another—in perfect unison.

And yet at this supreme moment in their lives—supreme though they themselves knew it not—neither of them had begun to think of love. In her there was just that delightful feeling of feminine curiosity, mingled with the subtle homage of a proud woman for the man who, in her presence, and for her sake, had proved himself brave, resourceful, full of invention and of pluck: there was also an unexplainable sense of the magnetism caused by the real *personality*, by the unmistakable *vitality* of the man. He lived, he felt, he thought differently to anyone else, in a world quite apart and entirely his own, and she felt the magic of this sunny nature, of the merry, almost boyish laugh, overlying as it were the undercurrent of disappointment and melancholy which had never degenerated into cynicism.

But in him? Ah! in him there was above all a wild, passionate longing! the longing of an intensely human, aching heart, when it is brought nigh to its own highest ideal, and knows that that ideal is infinitely beyond his reach.

The broken-down gentleman! the notorious hero of midnight adventures! highwayman! robber! thief! what right had he even to look upon her, the perfect embodiment of exquisite womanhood, the beautiful realisation of man's tenderest dreams?

Perhaps at this one supreme moment in his reckless career the wild adventurer felt the first pang of humbled pride, of that pride which had defied existing laws and built up a code of its own. He understood then all at once the stern, iron-bound rule which makes of man—free lord of creation though he be—the slave of those same laws which he himself has set up for his own protection.

Beau Brocade, the highwayman, closed his eyes, and no longer dared to look on his dream.

He turned to his horse, and with great tenderness began stroking Jack o' Lantern's soft, responsive nose.

The next moment Stich, who had been busy with his work, looked up in sudden alarm.

"The soldiers!" he said briefly, "all running ... the Sergeant's at the head o' them, and some of the shepherds at their heels."

At first Patience did not understand where the actual danger lay.

"My brother!" she gasped, terrified.

But a look from Bathurst reassured her.

"Absolutely safe," he said quickly and decisively, "a hiding-place known to no one but me. I give your ladyship my word of honour that there is not the remotest danger for him."

She felt all her terrors vanishing. But these few words spoken to comfort her went nigh to costing Bathurst dear. In those few brief seconds he had lost the opportunity of jumping on Jack o' Lantern's back and getting well away before the soldiers had reached the entrance of the forge, and had effectually barred his chance of escape.

As it was, he had only just undone the halter, and before he had time to lead Jack o' Lantern out, the voice of the Sergeant was heard quite close to the doorway, shouting breathlessly,—

"Forward! quick! Arrest that man!"

"My sword, John! for your life!" was Bathurst's ready answer to the challenge.

Stich darted to a corner of the forge. Lady Patience gave a quick, short gasp, she had suddenly realised that for some reason which she could not quite fathom, the man who had so pluckily saved her brother from the soldiers an hour ago, was now himself in imminent danger.

Jack snatched the sword eagerly which the smith was holding out to him, and resting the point of the blade on the ground before him, he tested with evident satisfaction the temper of the steel. Not a moment too soon this, for already the Sergeant, running, panting, infuriated by the trick played upon him, had appeared in the doorway, closely followed by two of his men.

Caught like a rat in a hole, Jack was prepared to fight. Perhaps at bottom he was glad that circumstances had not compelled him to show a clean pair of heels before this new danger to himself. Alone, he might have liked to flee, before *her* he preferred to fight.

"Odd's my life!" he said merrily, "'tis my friend, the Sergeant."

"You sent me on a fool's errand," shouted the latter as loudly as his scant breath would allow, "and 'tis my belief you are one of them rebel lords yourself: at anyrate you shall give an account of yourself before the magistrate. And if the smith dares to interfere, he does so at his peril," he added, seeing that John Stich had seized his hammer, and was handling it ominously, fully prepared to resist the established authority on behalf of his friend.

But whilst the Sergeant parleyed, Jack, with the rapid keen eye of a practised fencer, and the wary glance of a child of the Moor, had taken note of every advantage, however slight, which his present precarious position had left him.

The Sergeant and two men were in the doorway, momentarily pausing in order to recover their breath. Three more of the squad were running forward along the road, but were still some little distance off, and would be a few minutes before they reached the smithy.

Further on still there were the others, at present only appearing as scarlet dots on the Heath. Close on the heels of the Sergeant, two or three shepherds, with Jock Miggs in their rear, had come to see what was happening in the forge.

It had taken Jack Bathurst only a couple of seconds to note all these details. Luck so far favoured him that, for the next minute or two at least, he would only have to deal with the Sergeant and two soldiers.

"Into it, my men! Arrest him in the name of the King!" shouted the Sergeant, and the two soldiers, grasping their bayonets, made a rush for the interior of the shed, ready to surround Jack and his horse.

But quick as a lightning flash, Bathurst gave Jack o' Lantern a slight prick in the ribs with his sword; the nervous creature, already rendered restive by the sudden noise, began to plunge and rear, and thus, as his master had hoped, scattered the compact group of assailants momentarily away from the vicinity of his hoofs.

This gave the young man the desired opportunity. Nimble as a fox when hotly pursued, he stepped back and with one bound took up a position on the top of a solid oak table, which stood in the deep shadow caused by the doorway, thus, for the moment, leaving Jack o' Lantern as a barrier between himself and his enemies.

"Friend Stich," he shouted from this exalted height, "do you stand by the ladies. Stir not from their side whatever happens, nor interfere 'tween me and the soldiers at your peril."

The lust of battle was upon him now. He was satisfied with his position and longed to begin the fight. On his left was the outside wall of the shed, and guarding his right was the huge furnace of the smithy, out of which the burning embers cast fitful flickering lights upon his tall, slim figure, and drew from his blade sparks of blood-red gold.

He had wrapped the thick capes of his heavy cloth coat round his left arm: the folds of it hung down to his feet, forming a shield round the lower part of his figure.

Already the soldiers had recovered from the short panic caused by Jack o' Lantern's timely rearing. One of them now seized the horse by the bridle and led him out into the open, thus exposing Bathurst more fully to the onslaught of their bayonets.

Jack was fully prepared for them, and as soon as the Sergeant had given the order to attack, his steel began to dart in and out of the gloom like some live snake, with tongue of steel; illumined by the fitful embers of the furnace fire, it seemed to give forth a thousand sparks of witch-like flame with every turn of the cunning wrist. The outline of his head and shoulders was lost in the dense shadows above, whilst his assailants stood in the full glare of the setting sun, which, hot and blinding, came streaming into the shed.

Dazed by the flickering light of the furnace and the sunset glow beyond, the soldiers made very ineffectual plunges into the dark shadow, whence, fencing and parrying, and with many a quip and sally, Jack had at first an easy task in keeping them at bay.

This was mere child's play to him; already one of the men had an ugly gash in his cheek, and the next moment saw the Sergeant reeling backwards, with a well-directed thrust through his right arm.

But easy and exciting as was this brilliant sword-play, it could not in the long run be of much avail. Hardly had the Sergeant fallen back than three more soldiers, also hot and furious, came rushing in to reinforce their comrades. Bathurst had in his day been counted the finest fencer in England, his wrist was as fresh and strong as the steel which he held, but the odds were beginning to accumulate against him.

Five men in the shed, and the others could not be very far away!

John Stich felt his muscles nearly cracking with the vigorous effort to maintain his quiescent position and not to come to the rescue of his hard-pressed friend.

Suddenly one of the soldiers levelled his musket.

Patience saw it and gave a cry of horror. Stich, throwing prudence to the winds, would have rushed forward, to prevent this awful thing at any cost, but the Sergeant, though wounded, had lost none of his zest, and his eye had been fixed on the smith.

"Keep back the smith!" he shouted, "use your bayonets! quick!"

And as two of his men obeyed him, he himself threw his full weight against John, and together the three men succeeded in rendering the worthy fellow momentarily powerless.

"Captain! Captain!" he shouted desperately, "have a care!"

Of course Jack had realised his danger. The group of his assailants stood out in every detail before him, like a clear-cut sunlit picture. But against the musket levelled at him he could do nothing, it was Luck's chance to do him a good turn; he himself was hard pressed by two men close to his knees.

Patience felt as if her heart would cease to beat, her impulse was to rush blindly, stupidly forward, when suddenly a piping voice, vague and uncertain, was heard above the click of Jack's sword.

"Don't 'ee let 'em get 'ee, sir!" and Jock Miggs, with trembling, yet determined hands, gave a vigorous tug to the coat tails of the soldier, who was even now pulling the trigger of his musket. The latter, who had been aiming very deliberately for the one bright patch on Jack's person caused by the red glow of the furnace, lost his aim: there was a loud report, and a bullet went whizzing high above Bathurst's head, and buried itself in the woodwork above him.

This was the signal for a new phase of this curious and unequal struggle. The shepherds, at first, knowing nothing of the cause of this quarrel, had stood open-mouthed, somewhat frightened and awaiting events, at a short distance from the scene of the scuffle.

But when the chestnut horse had been led out into the open, they suddenly had an inkling as to who its owner was. Jack o' Lantern, bearing the masked highwayman on his back, was well known to the poor folk on Brassing Moor.

Beau Brocade, who but yesterday had left fifty guineas in the Brassington poor box! Beau Brocade, the hero of the Heath! He! to be caught by a parcel of red coats?

Never! Jock Miggs but voiced the feeling of the majority.

"Noa! Noa!" they shouted lustily. "Don't 'ee let 'em get 'ee, sir!"

"Not if I can help it, friends!" rejoined Bathurst in gay response.

They did not resist the soldiers; not they! Your Derbyshire yokel is too cautious an individual to run absolutely counter to established authority, but they saw their friend, their helper and benefactor, in trouble and they did what they could to help him. They got in the way, jostled the soldiers when they dared, kept the attention of one or two occupied, preventing a general onslaught on the oak table, on which Bathurst, still alert, still keen, was holding his own against such terrible odds.

"There's for you, my gallant lobster," quoth Jack, gaily.

He was standing far back on the table, entrenched between the wall on one side and the furnace on the other, and every time one of the soldiers ventured too near, his sword would dart out of the gloom: it seemed like a living creature of fire and steel, so quick and bold were his feints and parries, his sudden attacks in quarte and sixte, and all the while he kept one eye on the open Moor, where Jack o' Lantern, quivering with impatience, stood pawing the ground, and sniffing the keen evening air, ready to carry his master away, out upon the Heath, out of sight and out of danger.

Obviously the unequal contest could not last much longer. Jack knew that as well as any one. Already the red dots in the far distance had drawn considerably nearer, the next few minutes would bring this fresh reinforcement to the wearied, exhausted assailants.

The Sergeant too was ready to seize his best opportunity. He still kept two men on guard over the smith, but he soon saw that the two, who were storming Bathurst's improvised citadel, were no match with their clumsy bayonets against a brilliant fencer who, moreover, had the advantage of light and shadow, and of his elevated position.

Though he was wounded, and bleeding profusely, he had set his heart on the capture of this mysterious stranger, and having cast a glance on the open Moor beyond, he saw with renewed zest two more of his men hurrying along. With all the strength he had left he shouted to them to come on, and then turned to encourage the others.

"Take it easy, my men! Hold out a moment longer. We've got the rebel at last."

But Jack too had seen and understood. He was neither tired nor hurt, but two more men against him would inevitably prove his undoing. Already he could hear the shouts of the soldiers hurrying in response to their Sergeant's call. The next minute they would be in the forge.

A sudden change of tactics led his two assailants to venture nearer than they had done hitherto; he drew back into the shadows, and they, fired by the lust of capture, under the impression that he was at last exhausted, ventured nearer and nearer still; already they were leaning over the edge of the table, one man was thrusting at Bathurst's legs, when the latter, with a rapidity that seemed quicker than a flash of lightning, disengaged his left arm from his heavy coat, and with both hands threw it right over the heads of the two men. Before they had time to release themselves from its folds, Jack, with one bound was off the table, and the next instant he had torn open the door of the furnace and dragged out the huge iron poker with which the smith raked his fire, and with a cry of triumph slung this new and formidable weapon high over his head.

The effect of this sudden move was one of uncontrollable panic: the red-hot metal, as he swung it over his head, dropped a far-reaching shower of burning sparks; soldiers and Sergeant all drew back instinctively, and Jack, still brandishing his weapon, reached the entrance and was out in the open before any one dared to stop him.

There he flung the great glowing thing in the direction of his assailants, who even now were rallying to the attack.

But the moment had been precious to Bathurst, and Jack o' Lantern was a king among horses. Without use of stirrup or rein, Jack, like the true child of the wild Moor that he was, flung himself upon the beautiful creature's back.

Thus Patience saw him for one brief second, framed in the doorway of the forge, the last rays of the setting sun forming a background of crimson and gold for his slim, upright figure, and the brown curls on his head.

It was but a moment's vision, but one she would carry enshrined in her memory through all the years to come. His eyes, large, glowing, magnetic, met hers in a flash, and hers, bright with unshed tears, met his in quick response.

"Soldiers!" he shouted, as he rode away, "an you think I am a rebel lord, then after me, quick! whilst I ride towards the sunset."

PART II THE HEATH

CHAPTER XV

THE OUTLAW

Beau Brocade drew rein on the spur of the hill. He had galloped all the way from the forge, out towards the sunset, then on, ever on, over gorse and bracken, on red sandy soil and soft carpet of ling, on, still on!

Overhead, on the blue-green dome of the evening sky, a giant comet, made up of myriads of tiny, rose-tipped clouds, formed a fairy way, ever diminishing, ever more radiant, pointing westwards to the setting sun, where orange and crimson and blue melted in one glorious mist of gold.

Out far away, the distant Tors glowed in the evening light, like great barriers to some mystic elusive land beyond.

Jack o' Lantern had responded to his master's mood. The reins falling loosely on his neck, needing neither guide nor spur, save the excitement of his own mad career, he had continued his wild gallop on the Heath, until a sudden jerk of the reins brought him to a standstill on the very edge of a steep declivity, with quivering flanks and sensitive nerves all a-tremble, even as the last ruddy glow died out in the western sky.

One by one the myriads of rose-tipped clouds now put on their grey cloaks of evening. From the rain-soaked ground and dripping branches of bramble or fern, a blue mist was rising upwards, blending deep shadows and tender lights in one hazy monotone.

Gradually every sound died out upon the Heath, only from afar came intermittently the mournful booming of a solitary bittern, astray from its nest, or now and then the sudden quaking of a tuft of grass, a tremor amidst the young fronds of the bracken, there, where a melancholy toad was seeking shelter for the night.

Awesome, silent, majestic, the great Moor was at peace. The passions, the strife, the turmoil of mankind seemed far, very far away: further than that twinkling star which peeped down, shy and solitary, from across the rolling billows of boundless universe.

Beau Brocade stretched out both arms, and sighed in an agony of longing. Fire was in his veins, a burning thirst in his heart, for something he dared not define.

How empty seemed his life! how wrecked! how hopelessly wasted!

Yet he loved the Moor, the peace, the solitude: he loved the sunset on the Heath and every sound of animal life in this lonesome vastness.

But to-night!...

One smile from a woman's lips, a glow of pride in her eyes, just one cluster of snow-white roses at her breast, and all the glories of Nature in her most lavish mood seemed tame, empty, oh! unutterably poor.

Nay! he would have bartered his very soul at this moment to undo the past few years. To be once more Jack Bathurst of His Majesty's regiment of Guards, before one evening's mistake ruined the whole of his life. A quarrel over a game of cards, a sudden blind, unreasoning rage, a blow against his superior officer, and this same Jack Bathurst, the dandy about town, the gallant, enthusiastic, promising young soldier, was degraded from his military rank and thrown, resourceless, disgraced, banished, upon a merciless world, that has neither pity nor pardon for failures or mistakes.

But, quite unlike the young Earl of Stretton, Jack Bathurst indulged in no morbid self-condemnation. Fate and he had thrown the dice, and he had lost. But there was too much of the untamed devil in him, too much spirit of wild adventure, to allow him to stoop to the thousand and one expedients, the shifts, the humiliations which the world holds in store for the broken-down gentleman.

Moneyless, friendless, with his career irretrievably ruined, he yet scorned the life of the outcast or the pariah, of that wretched fragment of humanity that hangs on the fringe of society, envying the pleasures it can no longer share, haunting the gambling booths or noisy brothels of the towns, grateful for a nod, a handshake, from some other fragment less miserable than itself.

No! a thousand times no!

Jack Bathurst looked the future that was before him squarely in the face, then chose the life of the outlaw with a price upon his head. Aye! and forced that life to yield to him its full measure of delights: the rough, stormy nights on the Moor! the wild gallops over gorse and bramble, with the keen nor'-wester lashing his face and whipping up his blood, and with a posse of soldiers at his heels! the devil-may-care, mad, merry existence of the outlaw, who cuts a purse by night, and carries his life on his saddle-bow!

That he chose and more! for he chose the love of the poor for miles around! the blessings spoken by suffering and patient lips upon the name of the highwayman, of Beau Brocade, who took from the rich at risk of his life in order to give to the needy.

And now at even, on Brassing Moor, when a lonely shepherd caught sight of a chestnut horse bearing a slim, masked figure on its back, or heard in the distance a young voice, fresh as a skylark, singing some half-sad, half-lively ditty, he would turn his weary eyes in simple faith upwards to the stars and murmur gently,—

"God bless Beau Brocade!"

Perhaps He had!

The stars knew, but they did not tell!

CHAPTER XVI

A RENCONTRE ON THE HEATH

Master Mittachip, on his lean nag, with his clerk, Master Duffy, on the pillion behind him, was on his way to Brassington.

Sir Humphrey Challoner had not returned to the Moorhen after his visit to the forge until the sun was very low down in the west. He had bidden the attorney to await him at the inn, and Master Mittachip had not dared to disobey.

Yet the delay meant the crossing of the Heath along the bridle path to Brassington, well after the shadows of evening had lent the lonely Moor an air of awesome desolation. There were the footpads, and the pixies, the human and fairy midnight marauders, who all found the steep declivities, the clumps of gorse and bracken, the hollows and the pits, safe resting-places by day, but who were wont to emerge from their lair after dark for the terror and better undoing of the unfortunate, belated traveller.

Then there was Beau Brocade!

Master Duffy too was very timid, and clung with trembling arms to the meagre figure of the attorney.

"Nay! Master Duffy!" quoth Mittachip, with affected firmness, "why do you pry about so? Are you afraid?"

"Nay! nay! Master Mittachip," replied the clerk, whose teeth were chattering audibly, "I am ... n ... n ... not af ... f ... f ... fraid."

"Tush, man, you have me near you," rejoined Mittachip, boldly. "See! I am armed! Look at my pistols!"

And he leant back in the saddle, so as to give Master Duffy a good view of a pair of huge pistols that protruded ostentatiously from his belt.

Yet all around the air was still, the solitary Heath was at peace, even the breezy nor'-wester, that had blustered throughout the day, seemed to have lain down to rest.

Far out eastwards, the moon, behind a fast dispersing bank of clouds, was casting a silver radiance that was not yet a light, but only a herald of the glittering radiance to come.

The Moor was silent and at peace: only at times there came the sound of a gentle flutter, a moorhen perhaps within its nest, or a belated lizard seeking its home.

Whenever these slight sounds occurred, Master Mittachip's hands that held the reins trembled visibly, and his clerk clung more closely to him.

"What was that?" said the attorney in an awed whisper, as his frightened ears caught a more distinct noise.

"W ... w ... why don't you draw your p ... p ... pistols, Master Mittachip?" murmured Duffy, in mad alarm.

The noise was hushed again, but to the overwrought nerves of the two men in terror, there came the certain, awful perception that someone was on the Heath besides themselves, someone not far off, whom the mist hid from their view, but who knew that they were travelling along the bridle path, who could see and perhaps hear them.

"Truth to tell, Master Duffy," whispered the attorney, whose teeth too had begun to chatter. "Truth to tell, it's no use my drawing them ... they ... they are not loaded."

Master Duffy nearly fell off the pillion in his fright.

"What?"

"There's neither powder nor shot in them," continued Master Mittachip, ruefully.

"Th ... th ... then we are lost!" was Master Duffy's ejaculation of woe.

"Eh?—what?" quoth Mittachip, "but your pistols are charged."

And his pointed elbow sought behind it for the handles of two formidable weapons, which were stuck in Master Duffy's belt.

"N ... n ... nay!" whispered the clerk, who now was blue with terror. "I dared not carry the weapons loaded.... I trusted to your valour, Master Mittachip, to protect us."

"What was that?"

Again that noise! this time a good deal nearer, and it seemed to Master Mittachip's affrighted eyes as if he saw something moving on the bridle path before him. But he would not show too many signs of fear before his own clerk.

"Tush, man!" he said with as much boldness as he could command. "'Tis only a lizard in the grass mayhap. We'll ride on quite boldly. We can't be far from Brassington now, and no footpads would dare to attack two lusty fellows on horseback, with pistols showing in their belts! ... Lord!" he added with a shudder, "how lonely this place appears!"

"And that rascal, Beau Brocade, haunts this Heath every night, I'm told," murmured Master Duffy, who felt more dead than alive.

"Sh! sh! sh! speak not of the devil, Master Duffy, lest he appear!..."

"Hark!!!"

The two men now clung trembling to one another; not ten paces from them there came the sound of a horse's snorting, then suddenly a voice rang out clearly through the mist-laden air,—

"Hello! who goes there!"

"The Lord have mercy upon us!" whispered Mittachip.

"It must be Beau Brocade himself," echoed the clerk.

The next moment a horse and rider came into view. Master Mittachip and his clerk were too terrified even to look. The former had jerked the reins and brought his lean nag to a standstill, and both men now sat with eyes closed, teeth chattering, their very faces distorted with fear.

Beau Brocade had reined his horse quite close to them, and was peering through his black mask at the two terror-stricken faces. Evidently they amused him vastly, for he burst out laughing.

"Odd's my life! here's a pretty pair of scarecrows! ... Well! I see you can stand, so now let's see what you've got to deliver!"

At this Master Mittachip contrived to open his eyes for a second; but the black mask, and the heavily cloaked figure looked so ghostlike, so awful in the mist, that he promptly closed them again, and murmured with a shudder.—

"Mercy, oh, noble sir! We ... we are poor men!..."

"Poor-spirited men, you mean?" quoth Beau Brocade, giving the trembling figure a quick, vigorous shake. "Now then! off that nag of yours! Quick's the word!"

But even before this word of command Master Mittachip, dragging his clerk after him, had tumbled, quaking, off his horse. They now stood clinging to each other, a miserable bundle of frightened humanity.

"Come!" said Beau Brocade, looking down with some amusement at the spectacle. "I'm not going to hurt you—I never shoot at snipe! But you'll have to turn out your pockets and sharp too, an you want to resume your journey to-night."

He had seized Master Duffy by the collar. The clerk was an all too-ready prey for any highwayman, and stooping from his saddle, Beau Brocade had quickly extracted a leather bag from the pocket of his coat.

"Oho! guineas, as I live!"

"Kind sir," began Duffy, tremblingly.

"Now, listen to me, both of you," said Beau Brocade, trying to hide his enjoyment of the scene under an air of great sternness. "I know who you are. I know what work you've been doing this afternoon. Extorting rents barely due from a few wretched people, for your employers as hard-hearted as yourselves."

"Kind sir..."

"Silence! or I shoot! Besides, 'twere no use to tell me lies. The people about here know me. They call me Beau Brocade. I know them and their troubles. I happened to hear, for instance, that you extracted two guineas from the Widow Coggins, threatening her with a process for dilapidations unless she gave you hush money."

"'Twas not our fault, kind sir..."

"Then there was Mistress Haddakin, from whom you extracted fifty shillings for a new gate, which you don't intend to put up for her: and this, although she has only just buried her husband, and had a baby sick at home. You put on finer airs with the poor people than you do with me, eh?"

"'Tis not our money, sir," protested Master Mittachip, humbly.

"Some of it goes into your own pockets. Hush money, blood money, I call it. That's what I want from you, and then a bit over for the poor box on behalf of your employers."

He weighed the leather bag which he had taken out of Master Duffy's pocket.

"This'll do for the poor box. Now I want the five pounds you extorted from Widow Coggins and Mistress Haddakin. The poor women'll be glad of it on the morrow."

"I haven't a penny more than that bagful, sir," protested Master Mittachip. "My employers took all the money from me. 'Twere their rents I was collecting. I swear it, sir, kind sir! on my word of honour! And I am an honest man!"

"Come here!"

And Beau Brocade reined his horse back a few paces.

"Come here!" he repeated.

Mittachip was too frightened to disobey. He came forward, limping very perceptibly.

"Why do you walk like that?" asked Beau Brocade.

"I'm a feeble old man and rheumatic," whined Mittachip, despondently.

"Then 'twere better to ease the load out of your boot, friend. Sit down here and take it off."

And he pointed to a piece of boulder projecting through the shallow earth.

But this Master Mittachip seemed very loth to do.

"Kind sir..." he protested again.

"Sit down and take off the right boot!" repeated Beau Brocade more peremptorily, and with a gay laugh and mock threatening gesture he pointed the muzzle of his pistol at the terror-stricken attorney.

There was naught to do but to obey: and quickly too. Master Mittachip cursed the rascally highwayman under his breath, and even consigned him to eternal damnation, before he finally handed him up his boot.

Beau Brocade turned it over, shook it, and a bag of jingling guineas fell at Jack o' Lantern's feet.

"Give me that bag!"

"Sir! kind sir!" moaned Master Mittachip, as he obediently handed up the bag of gold to his merciless assailant. "Have pity! I am a ruined man! 'Tis Sir Humphrey Challoner's money. I've been collecting it for him ... and he's a hard man!"

"Oh!" said Beau Brocade, "'tis Sir Humphrey Challoner's money, is it? Nay! you old scarecrow, but 'tis his Honour himself sent me on the Heath to-night. Oho!" he added, whilst his merry, boyish laugh went echoing through the evening air, "methinks Sir Humphrey will enjoy the joke. Do you tell him, friend—an you see him in the morn—that you've met Beau Brocade and that he'll do his Honour's bidding."

He counted some of the money out of the bag and put it in his pocket: the remainder he handed back to the astonished lawyer.

"There!" he said with sudden earnestness, "I'll only make restitution to the poor whom you have robbed. You may thank your stars that an angel came down from heaven to-day and cast eyes of tender pity upon me, so that I care not to rob you, save for those in dire want. You may mount that nag of yours now, and continue your journey to Brassington. No turning aside, remember, and answer me when I challenge your good-night."

Master Mittachip and his clerk had no call to be told twice. They mounted with as much agility as their trembling limbs would allow. Truly they considered themselves lucky in having saved some money out of the clutches of the rogue, and did not care to speculate on the cause of their good fortune.

A few minutes later their lean horse was once more on its way, bearing its double burden. At first they had both looked back, attracted—now that their terror was gone—by the sight of that tall, youthful figure on the beautiful thoroughbred standing there on the crest of the hill and gradually growing more and more dim in the fast-gathering mist.

The bridle path at this point dips very suddenly and a sharp declivity leads thence, straight on to Brassington.

Beau Brocade's sharp eyes, accustomed to the gloom, watched horse and riders until the mist enveloped them and hid them from his view. Then he called loudly,—

"Good-night!"

And faintly echoing came the quaking reply,—

"Good-night!"

After that there was silence again. The outlaw was alone upon the Heath once more, the Heath which had been his home for so long.

For him it had no cruelty and held no terror: the tall gorse and bracken oft sheltered him from the rain! Wrapped in his greatcoat, he had oft watched the tiny lizards darting to and fro in the grass, or listened to the melancholy cry of moorhen or heron. The tiny rough branches of the heather had been a warm carpet on which he had slept on lazy afternoons.

The outlaw found a friend in great and lonely Nature, and when he was aweary he laid his head on her motherly breast, and like a child found rest.

CHAPTER XVII

A FAITHFUL FRIEND

How long he stood there on the spur of the hill he could not afterwards have told. It may have been a few seconds, perhaps it was an eternity.

During those few seconds or that eternity, the world was re-created for him: for him it became more beautiful than he had ever conceived it in his dreams. A woman's smile had changed it into an earthly paradise. A new and strange happiness filled his being, and set brain and sinews on fire. A happiness so great that his heart well nigh broke with the burden of it, and the bitter longing for what could never be.

The cry of a moorhen thrice repeated at intervals roused him from his dreams.

"John Stich," he murmured, "I wonder now what brings him out tonight!"

And with a final sigh of deep regret, a defiant toss of the head, Beau Brocade turned Jack o' Lantern's head northwards whence the cry had come.

There a rough track, scarce perceptible amongst the bracken, led straight up to the forge of John Stich. Horse and rider knew every inch of the way, although for the moment the fitful moon still hid her light behind a bank of clouds, and the mist now enveloped the Moor in a thick mantle of gloom.

Soon the sensitive ears of the highwayman, accustomed to every sound, had perceived heavy footsteps on the unbeaten track, and presently a burly figure detached itself from the darkness beyond and came rapidly forward.

"Odd's my life! but it's friend John!" said Beau Brocade, with a great show of severity. "Zounds! but this is rank insubordination! How dare you follow me on the Heath, you villain, and leave your noble guest unprotected? What?"

"His lordship is safe enough, Captain," said the smith, who at sight of the young man had heaved an obvious sigh of relief, "and I could not rest until I'd seen you again."

"Faith! you can't do that in this confounded mist, eh, John?" quoth Bathurst, lightly. But his fresh young voice had softened with a quaint tenderness, whilst he looked down, smiling, at the upturned face of his devoted friend.

"Well! what about my friend, the Sergeant and the soldiers, eh?" he added gaily.

"Oh! the Sergeant is too sick to speak," rejoined the smith, earnestly, "but the men vow you're a rebel lord. Those that were fit walked down to Brassington directly after you left: one man, who was wounded in the arm, started for Aldwark: they've gone to get help, Captain; either more soldiers, or loafers from the villages who may be tempted by the reward. They'll scour this Heath for you, from Aldwark to the cross-roads, and from Brassington to Wirksworth, and..."

"And so much the better, friend Stich, for while they hunt for me his lordship will be safe."

"But have a care, Captain! they're determined men, now, for you've fooled them twice. Be gy! but you've never been in so tight a corner before."

"Pshaw!" quoth Beau Brocade, lightly, "life is none too precious a boon for me that I should make an effort to save it."

"Captain..." murmured Stich, reproachfully.

"There, friend John," added the young man, with that same touch of almost womanly tenderness, that had endeared him to the heart of honest Stich, "there! there! have no fear for me! I tell thee, man, they'll not get me on this Heath! Think you the furze and bracken, the heron or peewit would betray me? Me, their friend! Not they! I am safe enough!" he continued, while a strange ring of excitement made his young voice quiver. "Let them after me, and leave *her* brother in peace! And then, John! when he is safe ... perhaps I may see her smile once more! ... Heigh-ho! A fool am I, friend! A fool, I tell thee! fit for the gallows-tree outside thy forge!"

John said nothing: he could not see Jack's face in the gloom, and did not understand his wild, mad mood, but his faithful heart ached to hear the ring of bitter longing in the voice of his friend.

There was a moment's pause, whilst Bathurst made a visible effort to control his excitement. Then he said more calmly,—

"Here, John! take this money, friend!"

He dived in the pocket of his big caped coat and then placed in John's hand the two bags of money he had extracted from Master Mittachip and his clerk.

"I've just got it from a blood-sucking agent of Sir Humphrey Challoner's: 'tis money wrung from poor people, who can ill afford it."

"Aye! aye!" quoth John, with a sigh.

"I want two guineas to go to Mistress Haddakin, who has just lost her husband: the poor wretch is nigh to starving. Then thirty shillings are for the Widow Coggins, up Hartington way: those blood-suckers took her last shilling yesterday. Wilt see to it, friend John?"

"Aye! aye!"

"The rest is for the poor box at Aldwark this time. Perhaps there'll be more before the morn."

"Captain..."

"Hush! don't begin to lecture, John!" said Beau Brocade, with curious earnestness. "I tell thee, friend, there's madness in my veins to-night. I pray thee go back home, and leave me to myself."

"Don't send me away, Captain," pleaded John, "I ... I ... am uneasy, and..."

"Dear, kind, faithful John," murmured Bathurst. "Zounds! but I'm an ungrateful wretch, for I vow thou dost love me, friend."

"You know I do, Captain. I ... I ... I'd give..."

"Nay ... nothing!" interrupted Jack, quickly, "give me nothing but that love of thine, friend ... it is more precious than life ... but I pray thee, let me be to-night ... I swear to thee I'll do no harm.... I'll see thee in the morn, John.... I'll be safe ... never fear!"

John Stich sighed. He knew that further protest was useless. Already Beau Brocade had turned Jack o' Lantern's head once more towards the crest of the hill. The smith waited awhile, listening while he could to the sound of the horse's hoofs on the rain-sodden earth. His honest heart was devoured with anxiety both for his friend and for the brave young lady who was journeying townwards to-night.

Suddenly it seemed to him as if far away he could hear the creaking of wheels on the distant Wirksworth road. The air was so still, that presently he could hear it quite distinctly. 'Twas her ladyship's coach, no doubt, plying its slow, wearying way along the quaggy road.

It would be midway to the little town by now. The narrow track on which John stood cut the road at right angles, about a mile and a half away. The smith took to blaming himself that he had kept her ladyship's journey a secret from Beau Brocade. The latter was a monarch on the Heath: he would have kept footpads at bay, watched and guarded the coach, and seen it, mayhap, safely as far as Wirksworth.

Never for a moment did the slightest fear cross the smith's mind that the notorious highwayman would stop Lady Patience's coach. Still, a warning would not have come amiss. Perhaps it was not too late. The road wound in and out a good deal, skirting bogland or massive boulders. John hoped that on the path he might yet come across Jack o' Lantern and his master, before they had met the coach.

He started to run and had covered nearly a mile when suddenly he heard a shout, which made his honest heart almost stop in its beating, a shout, followed by two pistol shots in rapid succession.

The shout had rung out clear and distinct in the fresh, lusty voice of Beau Brocade.

"Stand and deliver!"

John dared not think what the pistol shots had meant.

With elbows now pressed to his sides, he began running at a wild gallop along the rough, unbeaten track, towards the point whence shots and shout had come.

CHAPTER XVIII

MOONLIGHT ON THE HEATH

The jolting of the carriage along the quaggy road had been well nigh unendurable. Mistress Betty was groaning audibly. But Lady Patience, with her fair head resting against the cushions, was forgetting all bodily ailments, whilst absorbed in mental visions that flitted, swift and ever-changing, before her excited brain.

There was the dear brother in peril of his life, his young face looking wan and anxious, then Sir Humphrey Challoner, the man she instinctively, unreasonably dreaded, and John Stich, the faithful retainer, brave and burly, guarding his lord's life with his own. These faces and figures wandered ghostlike before her eyes, and then vanished, leaving before her mental vision but one form and face, a pair of merry, deep-set grey eyes, that at times looked so inexpressibly sad, a head crowned with a mass of unruly curls, a figure, lithe and active, sitting upon a chestnut horse and riding away towards the sunset.

It was a pleasant picture: no wonder Patience allowed her mind to dwell on it, and in fancy to hear that full-toned voice either in lively song or gay repartee, or at times with that ring of tenderness in it, which had brought the tears of pity to her eyes.

The hours sped slowly on, the cumbrous vehicle jostled onwards, plunging and creaking, whilst Thomas urged the burdened horses along.

Suddenly a jerk, more vigorous than before, roused Patience from her half-wakeful dreams. The heavy coach had seemed to take a plunge on its side, there was fearful creaking, and much swearing from the driver's box, a shout or two, panting efforts on the part of the horses, and finally the vehicle came to a complete standstill.

Mistress Betty had started up in alarm.

"Lud preserve us!" she shouted, putting a very sleepy head out of the carriage window, "what's the matter now, Thomas?"

"We be stuck in a quagmire," muttered the latter worthy, vainly trying to smother more forcible language, out of respect for her ladyship's presence.

Timothy, the groom, had dismounted: lanthorn in hand, he was examining the cause of the catastrophe.

"Get the other lanthorn, Thomas!" he shouted to the driver, "and come and give me a hand, else we'll have to spend the night on this God-forsaken heath."

"Is it serious, Timothy?" queried Lady Patience, anxiously.

"I hope not, my lady. The axle is caked with mud on this side, and we do seem stuck in some kind of morass, but if Thomas'll hurry himself..."

The latter, with many more suppressed oaths, had at last got down from his box, and had brought a second lanthorn round to the back of the coach, where Timothy had already started scraping shovelfuls of inky mud from the axle of the off-wheel.

It was at this moment, and when the two men were intent upon their work, that a voice, loud and distinct, suddenly shouted behind them,—

"Stand and deliver!"

Thomas, who was of a timorous disposition, dropped the lanthorn he held, and in his fright knocked over the other which was on the ground. He was a man of peace, and knew from past experience that 'tis safer not to resist these gentlemen of the roads.

When therefore the highwayman's well-known challenge rang out in the night, he threw up both hands in order to testify to his peaceful intentions; but Timothy, who was younger and more audacious, drew a couple of pistols from his belt, and at all hazards fired them off, one after the other, in the direction whence had come the challenge. The next moment he felt a vigorous blow on his wrists and the pistols flew out of his hand.

"Hands up or I shoot!"

Thomas was already on his knees. Timothy, thus disarmed, thought it more prudent to follow suit.

From within the coach could be heard Mistress Betty's shrill and terrified voice,—

"Nay! nay! your ladyship shall not go!" followed by her ladyship's peremptory command,—

"Silence, child! Let me go! Stay you within an you are afraid!"

There was a moment's silence, for at sound of her voice Beau Brocade had started, then he leaned forward on his horse, listening with all his might, wondering if indeed his ears had not misled him, if 'twas not a dream-voice that came to him out of the gloom.

"Have I the honour of addressing Lady Rounce?" he murmured mechanically.

At this moment the darkness, which up to now had been intense, began slowly to give place to a faint, silvery light. The moon, pale and hazy, tried to pierce the mist that still enveloped her as with a cold, blue mantle, and one by one tipped blackthorn and gorse with a cluster of shimmering diamonds.

Like a ghostly panorama the heath revealed its thousand beauties, its many mysteries: the deep, dark tangle of bramble and ling, beneath which hide the gnomes and ghouls, the tiny blue cups of the harebells, wherein the pixies have their home; the fairy rings in the grass, where the sprites dance their wild saraband on nights such as this, with the crickets to play the tunes, and the glow-worms to light them in their revels.

But to Beau Brocade the dim radiance of the moon, shy and golden through her veil of mist, only revealed one great, one wonderful picture: that of his dream made real, of his heavenly vision come down to earth, the picture of *her* stepping out of the coach that she might speak to him.

She came forward quickly, and the hood flew back from her face. She was looking at him with a half-puzzled, half-haughty expression in her eyes, and Beau Brocade thought he had never seen eyes that were so deeply blue. He murmured her name,—

"The Lady Patience!"

"Nay, sir, since you know my name," she said, with a quaint, almost defiant toss of her small, graceful head. "I pray you, whoever you may be, to let me depart in peace. See," she added, holding a heavy purse out to him, "I have brought you what money I have. Will you take it and let me go?"

But he dared not speak. He longed to turn Jack o' Lantern's head and to gallop away quickly out of her sight, before she had recognised him and learnt that the man on whom she had looked with such tender pity, and with such glowing admiration, was the highway robber, the outlaw, the notorious thief. Yet so potent was the spell of her voice, the moist shimmer of her lips, the depth and glitter of her blue eyes, that he felt as if iron fetters held him fast to the ground, there enchained before her, until at least she should speak again.

He dismounted and she stepped a little closer to him, so close now that, had he stretched out his hand, he might have touched her cloak, or even those white finger-tips which...

"Believe me, sir," she said a little impatiently, seeing that he did not speak, "I give you all I have freely an you molest me no more. I have urgent, very urgent business in London, which brooks of no delay. Kindly allow my men to go free."

She was pleading now, all the haughtiness vanished from her face. Her voice, too, shook perceptibly; the tall, silent figure before her was beginning to frighten her.

Yet he dared not trust himself to speak, lest by a word he should dispel this dream. This golden vision of paradise that heaven had so unaccountably sent to him this night! it might vanish again amidst the stars and leave the poor outlaw to his loneliness.

This moment was so precious, so wonderful.

Madly he longed for the god-like power to stop Time in its relentless way, to make sun, moon and stars, the earth and all eternity pause awhile, whilst he looked upon her, as she stood there, with the pleading look in her eyes, the honey-coloured moon above throwing a dim and flickering light upon her upturned face ... her golden hair ... that tiny hand stretched out to him.

She seemed to wait for his reply, and at last in a low voice, which he tried to disguise, he murmured,—

"Madam, I entreat you, have no fear! Believe me, I would sooner never see the sun set again than cause you even one short moment's anxiety."

Again that quaint puzzled look came into her eyes, she looked at the black mask that hid his face, as if she would penetrate the secret which it kept.

"Will you not take this purse?" she asked.

"Nay! I will not take the purse, fair lady," he said, still speaking very low, "but I would fain, an you would permit it, hold but for one instant your hand in mine. Will you not let me?"

The impulse was irresistible, the desire to hold her hand so strong that he had no power to combat it. She seemed puzzled and not a little frightened, but neither haughty nor resentful at his presumption: perhaps she felt the influence of the mystery which surrounded the dark, cloaked figure before her, or the more subtle spell of the mist-covered moon. She made no movement towards him, her hand which he craved to hold had dropped to her side.

There was magic in the vast stillness of the Moor; on each dew-tipped point of grey-green gorse, from every frond of emerald bracken, there glistened a tiny crystal. Timothy and Thomas had retreated to a safer position, out of sight behind the huge vehicle, and inside the coach Betty was cowering in terror. They stood alone, these two, away from all the world, in a land all their own, a land of dreams, of poetry, and romance, where men died for a look from women's eyes, and conquered the universe for a smile.

How silent was the Heath while he looked at her, and she returned his gaze half-trembling, wholly puzzled.

"Will you not let me?" he pleaded. And instinctively his voice trembled in the pleading, and there came back to her mind the memory of this same voice, young and tender, as she had heard it in the forge. But she would not let him know that she had guessed.

"Sir," she said with sudden, unaccountable shyness, "you have overpowered my men, they are but loutish cowards, and you are heavily armed. I am a defenceless woman.... How can I refuse if you command?"

He took the pistols from his belt and laid them on the ground at her feet.

"Nay, fair lady!" he said, "there is no question of command. See! I am unarmed now, and your men are free. Give them the word and I'll not stir hand or foot till you have worked your will with me. You see, 'tis I am at your mercy ... yet I still crave to hold your hand ... for one moment ... in mine..."

For one second more she hesitated: not because she was afraid, but because there was a subtle sweetness in this moment of suspense, a delicious feeling of expectancy for the joy that was to come.

Then she gave him her hand.

"Why! ... how it trembles," he said, "like some tiny frightened bird. See how white it looks in my rough brown hand. You are not afraid?"

"Afraid? ... oh, no! ... but ... but the hour is late ... I pray you let me depart ... I must not tarry ... for so much depends upon my journey.... I pray you let me go."

"No, no! don't go," he pleaded, clinging to the little hand whose cool touch had made his very senses reel, "don't go ... not just yet.... See how glorious is the moon above those distant hills ... and the mist-laden air which makes your hair glisten with a thousand diamonds, whilst I, poor fool, holding your cool, white hand in mine, stand here gazing on a vision that whispers to me of things which can never, never be.... No! no, don't go just yet ... let the moon hide her light once more behind the mist ... let the Heath sink into darkness ... let me live in my dream one moment longer ... it will be dispelled all too soon."

He had spoken so low, she scarce could hear, but she could feel his hand scorching hers with its fever-heat, and when he ceased speaking she heard a sigh, like a sob, a sigh of bitter longing, of hopeless regret, that made her heart ache with a new pain which was greater, more holy than pity.

A strange excitement seemed to pervade him. Madness was in his veins. He longed to seize her, to lift her up on Jack o' Lantern's back and gallop away with her over the Moor, far, far out beyond bracken and heather, over those distant Tors, on, on to the mountains of the moon, to the valley of the shadows, she lying passive in his arms, whilst he looked for ever into the clear blue depths of her eyes. Perhaps she too felt this excitement gradually creeping over her; she tried to withdraw her hand, but he would not let it go. To her also there came the sense of unreality, of a vision of dreamland, wherein no one dwelt but she and this one man, where no sound came save that of his voice, rugged and tender, which brought tears of joy and pity to her eyes.

In the grass at her feet a cricket began to chirp, and suddenly from a little distance there came the quaint, sweet sound of a shepherd's pipe, playing an old-time rigadoon.

"Hark!" she whispered.

The sound came nearer and nearer: she loved to hear the faint, elusive echo, the fairy accompaniment to her own dreamlike mood.

"What a sweet tune," she murmured, as instinctively her foot began tapping the measure on the ground. "I mind it well! How oft have I danced to it beneath the Maypole!"

"Will you then dance it with me to-night?"

"Nay, sir ... you do but jest..."

But his excitement was at fever-point now. The outlaw at least could work his will upon this Heath, of which he alone was king. He could not carry her away on Jack o' Lantern's back, but he could make her stay with him a while longer, dance with him, here in the moonlight, her hand in his, his arm at times round her waist in the mazes of the dance, her cheeks flushed, her eyes bright, her breath panting, aye! for she should feel too that reckless fire that scorched him. All the fierce, untamed blood in him ran like molten lava in his veins. Aye! for one more brief half-hour he—the lonely dweller on the Moor—the pariah, the outcast, would taste the joys of the gods.

"I was never more earnest in my life!" he vowed, with that gay, mad, merry laugh of his, "a dance with you here in the moonlight! Aye! a dance in the midst of my dreams!"

"But indeed, indeed, sir," she pleaded, "the hour is late and my business in London is very urgent."

"Nay, ten minutes for this dance will not much delay your journey, and I swear by your sweet eyes that after that you shall go unmolested."

"But if I refuse?"

"An you refuse," he said, bending the knee before her, and bowing humbly at her feet, "I will entreat you on my knees..."

"And if I still refuse?" she murmured.

"Then will I uproot the trees, break the carriage that bears you away, tear up the Heath and murder yon knaves! God in heaven only knows what I would *not* do an you refuse."

"No, no, sir, I pray you..." she said, alarmed at his vehemence, puzzled, fascinated, carried away by his wild, reckless mood and the potent spell of the witching moon. "Nay! how can I refuse? ... I am in your power ... and must do as you bid me.... An you really wish for a dance..."

She allowed him to lead her away to a short distance off the beaten track, there, where a carpet of ling and grass, and walls of bramble and gorse formed a ball-room fit for gods and goddesses to dance in. At the further end of this clearing the quaint, shrivelled figure of Jock Miggs, the shepherd, had just come into view. At a little distance to the left, and close to the roadside, there was a small wooden shed, and beyond it a pen, used by the shepherds as a shelter on rough nights when tending their sheep on the Heath.

For the moment the pen was empty, and Jock Miggs was evidently making his way to the hut for a few hours' sleep, and had been playing his pipe for the sake of company.

"Aye! a dance here!" said Beau Brocade, "with the moon and stars to light us, a shepherd to play the tune, and the sprites that haunt the Heath for company! What ho! there! friend shepherd!" he shouted to Miggs.

The worthy Jock caught sight of the two figures standing in the centre of the clearing, not twenty paces away from him.

"Lud have mercy upon me!" he gasped. "Robbery! Violence! Murder!"

"Nay, friend! only merry-making," quoth Beau Brocade, gaily. "We want to dance upon this Heath, and you to play the tune for us."

"Eh? what?" muttered the shepherd, in his vague, apologetic way, "dancing at this hour o' the night?"

"Aye!"

"And me to play for a parcel of mad folk?"

"Well said, honest shepherd! Let us all be mad to-night! but you shall play for us, and here!—here is the wherewithal to set your pipe in tune."

He threw a heavy purse across to Miggs, who, still muttering something about lunatics on the Heath, slowly stooped and picked it up.

"Guineas!" he muttered, weighing it in his hand, "guineas, as I live! Guineas for playing a dance tune. Nay, sir, you're mad, sure enough."

"Wilt play the tune, shepherd?" shouted Beau Brocade in wild impatience.

Jock Miggs shook his head with a determined air.

"Nay! your madness is nought to me. You've paid for a tune, and you shall have the tune. But, Lordy! Lordy! these be 'mazing times."

He settled himself down on a clump of grass-covered earth, and stolidly began piping the same old-time rigadoon. These were a pair of lunatics, for sure, but since the gentleman had paid for this extraordinary pleasure, 'twas not for a poor shepherd to refuse to earn a few honest guineas.

Beau Brocade bowed to his lady with all the courtly grace of a town gallant.

"Madam! your most humble, and most obedient servant."

As in a dream Patience began to tread the measure. It was all so strange, so unreal! surely this was a dream, and she would wake anon.

She turned and twisted in the mazes of the dance, gradually the intoxication of it all had reached her brain; she seemed to see round her in the grass pixie faces gazing curiously upon her. All the harebells seemed to tinkle, the shepherd's pipe sounded like fairy bells. Through the holes in the black mask she could see a pair of burning eyes watching her as if entranced.

She felt like a creature of some other world, a witch mayhap, dancing a wild saraband with this man, her lord and master, a mad, merry sprite who had arranged this moonlight Sabbath.

Her cheeks began to glow, her eyes were sparkling with the joy of this dance. Her breath came panting through her parted lips.

Aye! mad were they both! what else? Their madness was the intoxication which man alone can feel when his joy equals that of the gods! Quicker, shepherd! quicker! let thy pipe wake all the fairy echoes of this mystic, ghostlike Moor! Let all the ghouls and gnomes come running hither, let the stars pale with envy, let fairies and sprites clap their hands for joy, since one man in all this world was happier than all the spirits in heaven!

How long it lasted neither of them could tell. The honey-coloured moon lighted them all the while, the blue mist wrapped them as in a mystic veil. Still they danced on; at times she almost lay in his arms, hot, panting, yet never weary, then she would slip away, and with eyes aglow, cheeks in rosy flame, beckon to him, evade, advance, then once more put her hand in his and madden him with the touch.

Oh! that heaven-born hour! why did it ever cease?

A wild shriek, twice repeated, brought them both to a standstill.

She, with heart beating, and hand pressed to her panting bosom, was unable to stir. Whilst the excitement kept her up she had danced, but now, with that piercing shriek, the dream had vanished and she was back on earth once more.

"What was that?"

Thomas and Timothy, attracted by the strange spectacle, had gradually crept up to the clearing, and through a clump of gorse and bracken had been watching the weird, midnight dance. On the further side, and close to Jock Miggs, John Stich had been standing in the shadow of a thorn bush. He had been running all the way, ever since he heard the two pistol-shots. Amazed at the strange sight that met his honest eyes, he had not dared to interfere. Perhaps his honest faithful heart felt with, even if it did not altogether comprehend, the wayward, half-crazy mood of his friend.

Betty alone, terrified and not a little sulky, had remained in the coach. It was her shriek that roused the spectators and performers of this phantasy on the Heath.

"My lady! my lady!" screamed Betty once more at the top of her voice.

Then, all of a sudden, Patience understood. Fairyland had indeed vanished. The awful reality came upon her with appalling cruelty.

"My letters!" she gasped, and started running towards the coach.

But already Jack Bathurst had bounded across the clearing, closely followed by John Stich. Patience's cry of mad, terror-stricken appeal had gone straight to his brain, and dissipated in the fraction of a second the reckless excitement of the past hour.

The wild creature of one moment's wayward mood was in that same fraction of time re-transformed into the cool and daring dweller of the Moor, on whose head the law had set a price, and who in revenge had made every law his slave.

His keen, quick eye had already sighted the smith.

"After me, John!" he commanded, "and run for your life."

When the two men had fought their way through the clumps of gorse and bracken which screened the clearing from the road, they were just in time to see a man quickly mounting a dark brown horse, which stood some twenty yards in front of the coach.

The carriage door nearest to them was open, and poor Mistress Betty lay on the ground close beside it, still screaming at the top of her voice.

With one bound Beau Brocade had reached Jack o' Lantern, who, accustomed to his unfettered life on the Heath, had quietly roamed about at will, patiently waiting for his master's call. The young man was unarmed, since he had placed his pistols awhile ago at Patience's feet, but Jack o' Lantern was swift-footed as the deer, and would overtake any strange horseman easily.

Beau Brocade's hand was on his horse's bridle and there were barely a few yards between him and the mysterious horseman, who was preparing to gallop away, when the latter turned, and suddenly pointing a pistol at his pursuer, fired two shots in rapid succession.

The young man did not stop at once. He clutched Jack o' Lantern's bridle and tried to mount, but he staggered and almost fell.

"After him, John," he cried in a hoarse voice, as, staggering once more, he fell upon one knee. "After him! quick! take Jack o' Lantern, don't mind me!"

John had no need to be told twice. He seized the horse's bridle and swung himself into the saddle as quickly as he could.

But these few seconds had given the horseman a sufficient start. Although the moon was bright the mist was thick, and the bracken and thorn bushes very dense on the other side of the road. Already he had disappeared from view, and John's ears and eyes were not so keen as those of Beau Brocade, the highwayman, the wounded monarch of the Heath.

CHAPTER XIX

HIS OATH

Patience's first thought as soon as she reached the road was for Betty; she helped the poor girl to her feet and tried to get some coherent explanation from her.

"I was listening to the tune, my lady, and leaning my head out of the window," moaned Mistress Betty, who was more frightened than hurt, "when suddenly the carriage door was torn open, I was dragged out and left screaming on the ground.... That's all I know."

But one glance at the interior of the coach had revealed the whole awful truth. It had been ransacked, and the receptacle beneath the cushions, where had lain the all-important letters, was now obviously empty.

"The letters! oh, the letters!" moaned Patience in an agony of misery and remorse. "Philip, my dear, dear one, you entrusted your precious life in my hands, and I have proved unworthy of the trust."

Her spirit wholly broken by the agony of this cruel thought, she cowered on the step of the carriage, her head buried in her hands, in a passion of heart-broken tears.

"My lady..."

She looked down, and by the dim light of the moon she saw a figure on its knees, dragging itself with a visibly painful effort slowly towards her.

In a moment she was on her feet, tall, haughty, a world of scorn in her eyes; she looked down with horror at the prostrate figure before her.

"Nay, sir," she said with icy contempt, "an you have a spark of honour left in you, take off that mask, let me at least see who you are."

The agony of shame was more than she could bear. She who had deemed herself so proud, so strong, that she should have been thus fooled, duped, tricked, and by this man! this thief! this low class robber who had dared to touch her hand! All the pride of race and caste rose in revolt within her. Who was he that he should dare to have spoken to her as he did? Her cheeks glowed with shame at the memory of that voice which she had loved to hear, the tender accent in it, and oh! she had been his plaything, his tool, for this infamous trick which had placed her dear, dear brother's life in peril worse than before.

Meekly he had obeyed her, his own proud spirit bent before her grief. His face—ashy pale now and drawn with pain and weakness—looked up in mute appeal for forgiveness.

"A poor wretch," he murmured feebly, "whose mad and foolish whim..."

But she turned from him in bitter loathing, drawing herself up to her full height, trying by every means in her power to show the contempt which she felt for him. So absorbed was she in her grief and humiliation, in her agony of remorse for her broken trust, that she did not realise that he was hurt, and fainting with loss of blood.

"You ... you..." she murmured with horror and contempt. "Nay! I pray you do not speak to me.... You ... you have duped and tricked me, and I ... I ... Oh!" she added with a wealth of bitter reproach, "what wrong had I or my dear brother done to you that you should wish to do him so much harm? What price had his enemies set upon his head that you should *sell* it to them?"

He tried to interrupt her, for her words hurt him ten thousand times more than the wound in his shoulder: with almost superhuman effort he dragged himself to his feet, clinging to the bracken to hold himself upright. He would not let her see how she made him suffer. She! his beautiful white rose, whom unwittingly he had, it seemed, so grievously wronged. Her mind was distraught, she did not understand, and oh! it was impossible that she *could* realise the cruelty of her words, more hard to endure than any torture the fiendish brain of man could devise.

"I'd have given you gold," she continued, whilst heavy sobs choked the voice in her throat, "if 'twas gold you wanted.... Here is the purse you did not take just now! Two hundred guineas for you, sir, an you bring me back those letters!"

And with a last gesture of infinite scorn she threw the purse on the ground before him.

A cry escaped him then: the terrible, heart-rending cry of the wild beast wounded unto death. But it was momentary; that great love he bore her helped him to understand. Love is never selfish—always kind. Love *always* understands.

He could scarcely speak now, and the seconds were very precious, but with infinite gentleness he contrived to murmur faintly,—

"Madam! I swear by those sweet lips of yours now turned in anger against me that you do me grievous wrong. My fault, alas! is great! I cannot deny it, since in this short, mad hour of the dance my eyes were blind and mine ears deaf to all save to your own dear presence."

"Aye! 'twas a clever trick," she retorted, lashing herself to scorn, wilfully deaf to the charm of that faint voice, turning away from the tender appeal of his eyes: "a trick from beginning to end! Your chivalry at the forge! your *rôle* of gallant gentleman of the road! the while you plotted with a boon companion to rob me of the very letters that would have saved my brother's life."

"Letters? ... that would have saved your brother's life? ... What letters?..."

"Nay, sir! I pray you fool me no further. Heaven only knows how you learnt our secret, for I'll vouch that John Stich was no traitor. Those letters were stolen, sir, by your accomplice, whilst you tricked me into this dance."

He pulled himself together with a vigorous effort of will, forcing himself to speak quietly and firmly, conquering the faintness and dizziness which was rapidly overpowering him.

"Madam!" he said gently, "dare I hope that you will believe me when I say that I know naught of those letters? ... John Stich, as you know, is loyal and true ... not even to me would he have revealed your secret ... nay, more! ... it seems that I too have been tricked to further a villain's ends. Will you not try and believe that had I known what those letters were I would have guarded them, for your sweet sake, with my last dying breath?"

She did not reply: for the moment she could not, for her tears choked her, and there was the magic of that voice which she could not resist. Still she would not look at him.

"Sir!" she said a little more calmly, "Heaven has given you a gentle voice, and the power of tender words, with which to cajole women. I would wish to believe you, but..."

She was interrupted by the sound of voices, those of Thomas and Timothy, her men, who had kept a lookout for John Stich. The next moment the smith himself, breathless and panting, came into view. He had ridden hard, for Jack o' Lantern's flanks were dripping with sweat, but there was a look of grave disappointment on the honest man's face.

"Well?" queried Beau Brocade, excitedly, as soon as John had dismounted.

"I'm feared that I've lost the scoundrel's track," muttered John, ruefully.

"No?"

"At first I was in hot pursuit, he galloping towards Brassington; suddenly he seemed to draw rein, and the next moment a riderless horse came tearing past me, and then disappeared in the direction of Aldwark."

"A riderless horse?"

"Aye! I thought at first that maybe he'd been thrown; I scoured the Heath for half a mile around, but ... the mist was so thick in the hollow, and there was not a sound.... I'd have needed a blood-hound to track the rascal down."

An exclamation of intense disappointment escaped from the lips of Lady Patience and of Beau Brocade.

"Do you know who it was, John?" queried the latter.

"No doubt of that, Captain. It was Sir Humphrey Challoner right enough."

"Sir Humphrey Challoner!" cried Patience, in accents of hopeless despair, "the man who covets my fortune now holds my brother's life in the hollow of his hand."

Excitedly, defiantly, she once more turned to Beau Brocade.

"Nay, sir," she said, "an you wish me to believe that you had no part in this villainy, get those letters back for me from Sir Humphrey Challoner!"

He drew himself up to his full height, his pride at least was equal to her own.

"Madam! I swear to you..." he began. He staggered and would have fallen, but faithful Stich was nigh, and caught him in his arms.

"You are hurt, Captain?" he whispered, a world of anxiety in his kindly eyes.

"Nay! nay!" murmured Beau Brocade, faintly, "'tis nothing! ... help me up, John! ... I have something to say ... and must say it ... standing!"

But Nature at last would have her will with him, the wild, brave spirit that had kept him up all this while was like to break at last. He fell back dizzy and faint against faithful John's stout breast.

Then only did she understand and realise. She saw his young face, once so merry and boyish, now pale with a hue almost of death; she saw his once laughing eyes now dimmed with the keenness of his suffering. Her woman's heart went out to him, she loathed herself for her cruelty, her heart, overburdened with grief, nearly broke at the thought of what she had done.

"You are hurt, sir," she said, as she bent over him, her eyes swimming in tears, "and I ... I knew it not."

The spell of her voice brought his wandering spirit back to earth and to her.

"Aye, hurt, sweet dream!" he murmured feebly, "deeply wounded by those dear lips, which spoke such cruel words; but for the rest 'tis naught. See!" he added, trying to raise himself and stretching a yearning hand towards her, "the moon has hid her face behind that veil of mist ... and I can no longer see the glory of your hair! ... my eyes are dim, or is it that the Heath is dark? ... I would fain see your blue eyes once again.... By the tender memory of my dream born this autumn afternoon, I swear, sweet lady, that your brother's life shall be safe! ... Whilst I have one drop of blood left in my veins, I will protect him."

With trembling hand he sought the white rose which still lay close to her breast: she allowed him to take it, and he pressed it to his lips.

Then, with a final effort he drew himself up once more, and said loudly and clearly,—

"By this dear token I swear that I will get those letters back for you before the sun has risen twice o'er our green-clad hills."

"Sir ... I..."

"Tell me but once that you believe me ... and I will have the strength that moves the mountains."

"I believe you, sir," she said simply. "I believe you absolutely."

"Then place your dear hand in mine," he whispered, "and trust in me."

And the last thought of which he was conscious was of her cool, white fingers grasping his fevered hand. Then the poor aching head fell back on John's shoulder, the burning eyes were closed, kindly Nature had taken the outlaw to her breast and spread her beneficent mantle of oblivion over his weary senses at last.

PART III BRASSINGTON

CHAPTER XX

A THRILLING NARRATIVE

Mr Inch, beadle of the parish of Brassington, was altogether in his element.

Dressed in his gold-laced coat, bob-tail wig and three-cornered hat, his fine calves encased in the whitest of cotton stockings, his buckled shoes veritable mirrors of shiny brilliancy, he was standing, wand of office in hand, outside the door of the tiny Court House, where Colonel West, Squire of Brassington, was sitting in judgment on the poachers and footpads of the neighbourhood.

Before Mr Inch stood no less a person than Master Mittachip, attorney-at-law. Master Mittachip desired to speak with Squire West, and the pompous beadle was in the proud position of standing between this presumptuous desire and the supreme Majesty of the Law.

"Them's my orders, sir," he said, with all the solemnity which this extraordinary event demanded. "Them's my orders. Squire West's own orders. 'Inch,' he says to me—my name being Jeremiah Inch, sir—'Inch,' he says, 'the odours which perambulate the court-room'—and mind ye, sir, he didn't use such polite language either—'the odours is more than I can endure this hot morning!' As a matter of fact, sir, truth compellates me to state that Squire West's own words were: 'Inch, this room stinks like hell! too many sweating yokels about!' Then he gave me his orders: 'The room is too full as it is, don't admit anyone else, on any pretext or cause whatsoever.'"

Master Mittachip had made various misguided efforts to interrupt Mr Inch's wonderful flow of eloquence. It was only when the worthy beadle paused to take breath, that the attorney got in a word edgewise.

"Harkee, my good man..." he began impatiently.

"I am extra-ordinarily grieved, sir," interrupted Master Inch, who had not nearly finished, "taking into consideration that I am somewhat dubersome, whether what his Honour said about the odours could apply individually to you, but orders is orders, sir, and the Squire as a legal luminosity must be obeyed in all things."

Mr Inch heaved a deep sigh of satisfaction. It was not often that he had the opportunity of showing off his marvellous eloquence and wonderful flow of language before so distinguished a gentleman as Master Mittachip, attorney-at-law. But the latter seemed not to appreciate the elegance of the worthy beadle's diction; on the contrary, he had throughout shown signs of the greatest impatience, and now, directly Mr Inch heaved this one sigh,

Master Mittachip produced a silver half-crown, and toying with it, in apparent indifference, said significantly,—

"I am sure, friend Beadle, that if you were to acquaint Squire West that his Honour, Sir Humphrey Challoner, desired to speak with him..."

Mr Inch stroked his fat, clean-shaven chin, and eyed the silver half-crown with an anxious air.

"Ah! perhaps!" he suggested with as much dignity as the new circumstance allowed, "perhaps if I did so far contravene my orders..."

"I feel sure that Sir Humphrey would see fit to reward you," suggested the attorney, still idly fingering that tempting half-crown.

But Master Inch was still "dubersome."

"But then, you understand," he said, "it is against the regulations that I should vacate my post until after the sitting is over ... so..."

"Sir Humphrey Challoner is partaking of breakfast at the Royal George, Master Inch, he would wish Squire West to know that he'll attend on him here in half an hour."

Master Inch closed one eye, and with the other keenly watched Master Mittachip's movements. The attorney turned the half-crown over in his lean hand once or twice, then he made as if he would put it back in his pocket.

This decided the beadle.

"I'll go and reconnoitre-ate," he said, "and perhaps I can despatch a menial to impart to the Squire, Sir Humphrey's wishes and cognomen."

Thus the majestic beadle felt that his dignity had not been impaired. With a magnificent turn of his portly person, and an imposing flourish of his wand of office, he disappeared within the precincts of the Court.

Master Mittachip slipped the half-crown back in his pocket, and did not wait for the beadle's return. He was quite satisfied that Sir Humphrey's wishes would be acceded to. He turned his back on the Court House and slowly crossed the green.

Opposite to him was the Royal George, where he and Master Duffy had put up for the night. In the small hours of the morning he had been aroused from peaceful slumbers by a great disturbance at the inn. Sir Humphrey Challoner, booted and spurred, but alone, on foot, and covered with mud, was peremptorily demanding admittance.

Since then Master Mittachip had had an interview with his employer, wherein his Honour had expressed the desire to speak with Squire West after he, himself, had partaken of late breakfast. That interview had been a very brief one, but it had sufficed to show to the lean attorney that Sir Humphrey's temper was none of the best this morning.

His Honour had desired Master Mittachip's presence again, and the latter was now making his way slowly back to the Royal George, his knees quaking under him, his throat dry, and his tongue parched with terror. Sir Humphrey Challoner was not pleasant to deal with when his temper was up.

The attorney found his Honour installed at breakfast in the private parlour of the inn, and consuming large mugs full of ale and several rashers of fried bacon.

"Well?" queried Sir Humphrey, impatiently, as soon as the attorney's lean, bird-like face appeared in the doorway.

"I sent word to his Honour, Squire West," explained the latter, coming forward timidly, "saying that you would wish to see him at the Court House in half an hour. And, unless your Honour would wish me to speak to the Squire for you..."

"No!" rejoined his Honour, curtly. "'Sdeath! don't stand there fidgeting before me," he added. "Sit down!"

Master Mittachip meekly obeyed. He selected the straightest chair in the room, placed it as far away from his Honour as he could, and sat down on the extreme edge of it.

"Well! you lean-faced coward," began his Honour, whose temper did not seem to have improved after his substantial breakfast, "you allowed yourself to be robbed of my money last night, eh?"

Thus much Sir Humphrey knew already, for his first inquiry on meeting Mittachip at the inn had been after his rents. Since then the attorney had had half an hour in which to reflect on what he would say when his Honour once more broached the subject. Therefore he began to protest with a certain degree of assurance.

"On my honour, Sir Humphrey, you misjudge me," he said deliberately. "As my clerk and I passed the loneliest spot on the Heath, and without any previous warning, two masked men leapt into the path in front of us, and presented pistols. A third man called to us to stand."

Here Master Mittachip made an effective pause, the better to watch the impression which his narrative was making on his employer. The latter was quietly picking his teeth, and merely remarked quietly,—

"Well? and what did you do?"

Thus encouraged Mittachip waxed more bold.

"In a flash I drew a pistol," he continued glibly, "and so did Duffy ... for I must say he bore himself bravely. We both fired and my ball knocked the hat off the fellow nearest to me, but Master Duffy's ball unfortunately missed. I was drawing my other pistol, determined to make a desperate fight, and I believe Duffy did as much.... I was amazed that the fellows did not fire upon us in return..."

He was distinctly warming up to his subject. But here he was interrupted by a loud guffaw. Sir Humphrey was evidently vastly amused at the thrilling tale, and his boisterous laugh went echoing along the blackened rafter of the old village inn.

"Odd's my life! 'tis perfect! marvellous, I call it! And tell me, Master Mittachip," added his Honour, whose eyes were streaming and whose sides were shaking with laughter, "tell me, why did they not fire? Eh?"

From past experience Master Mittachip should have known that when Sir Humphrey Challoner laughed his loudest, then was he mostly to be dreaded. Yet in this instance the attorney's delight at his own realistic story drowned the wiser counsels of prudence. He took his Honour's hilarity as a compliment to his own valour, and continued proudly,—

"The reason was not far to seek, for at that very moment we were both seized upon from behind by two big fellows. Then all five of them fell upon us and dragged us aside into the darkness; they tied scarves about our mouths, so that we could not cry out.... Aye! and had some difficulty in doing it, for believe me, Sir Humphrey, I fought like mad! Then they rifled us of everything ... despoiled us absolutely..."

At this point it struck Master Mittachip that his Honour's continued gaiety was somewhat out of place. The narrative had become thrilling surely, exciting and blood-curdling too, and yet Sir Humphrey was laughing more lustily than ever.

"Go on, man! go on," he gasped between his paroxysms of merriment. "Odd's fish! but 'tis the best story I've heard for many a day!"

"I will swear to the truth o' it in any court of law," protested the attorney with somewhat less assurance. "The fifth man was Beau Brocade. I heard the others address him so, while I was lying gagged and bound."

"Aye! you would *lie* anywhere," commented his Honour, "gagged and bound or not."

"From your observation, Sir Humphrey, I gather that you somewhat ... er ... doubt my story!" murmured Master Mittachip in a quavering voice.

"Doubt it, man? ... doubt it?" laughed his Honour, holding his sides, "nay! how can I doubt it? I saw it all..."

"You, Sir Humphrey?"

"I was there, man, on the Heath. I saw it all ... your vigorous defence, your noble valour, your ... your..."

Master Mittachip's sallow face had assumed a parchment-like hue. He passed his dry tongue over his parched lips, great drops of moisture appeared beneath his wig. That his fears were not unfounded was presently proved by Sir Humphrey's sudden change of manner.

The hilarious laugh died down in his Honour's throat, an ugly frown gathered above his deep-set eyes, and with a violent curse he brought his heavy fist down crashing upon the table.

"And now, you lying, lumbering poltroon, where's my money?"

"B ... b ... but, Sir Humphrey..." stammered the attorney, now pallid with terror.

"There's no 'but' about it. You collected some rents for me, thirty guineas in all, that money must lie to my account in the bank at Wirksworth to-morrow, or by G—— I'll have you clapped in jail like the thief that you are."

"B ... b ... but, your Honour..."

"Silence! I've said my last word. If that money is not in the bank by noon to-morrow, I'll denounce you to the Wirksworth magistrate as a fraudulent agent. Now hold your tongue about that. I've said my last word. The rest is your affair, not mine. I've more important matters to think on."

Master Mittachip, half dead with fear, dared not offer further argument or pleading. He knew his employer well enough to realise that his honour meant every word he said, and that he himself had nothing more to hope for in the matter of the money. The deficiency extracted from him by that rascal Beau Brocade would have to be made good somehow, and Master Mittachip bethought him ruefully of his own savings, made up of sundry little commissions extorted from his Honour's tenants.

No wonder the attorney felt none too kindly disposed towards the highwayman. He watched Sir Humphrey's face as a hungry dog does his master's, and noted with growing satisfaction that his Honour's anger was cooling down gradually, and giving place to harder and more cruel determination. As he watched, the look of terror died out of his bony, sallow face, and his pale, watery eyes began to twinkle with keen and vengeful malice.

CHAPTER XXI

MASTER MITTACHIP'S IDEA

He waited a little while, and gradually a smile of the deepest satisfaction spread over his bird-like countenance; he rubbed his meagre knees up and down with his thin hands, in obvious delight, and as soon as he saw his opportunity, he remarked slily,—

"An your Honour was on the Heath last night, you can help me testify to highway robbery before Squire West. There are plenty of soldiers in this village. His Honour'll have out a posse or two; the rascal can't escape hanging this time."

Sir Humphrey's florid, sensual face suddenly paled with a curious intensity of hatred.

"Aye! he shall hang sure enough," he muttered, with a loud oath.

He dragged a chair forward, facing Mittachip, and sat astride on it, drumming a devil's tattoo on the back.

"Listen here, you old scarecrow," he said more quietly, "for I've not done with you yet. You don't understand, I suppose, what my presence here in Brassington means?"

"I confess that I am somewhat puzzled, your Honour," replied the attorney, meekly. "I remarked on it to Master Duffy, just before he started off for Wirksworth this morning. But he could offer no suggestion."

"Odd's life, man! couldn't you guess that having made my proposal to that rascally highwayman I could not rest at Aldwark unless I saw him carry it through?"

"Ah?"

"I got a horse at the Moorhen, and at nightfall I rode out on the Heath. I feared to lose my way on the bridle path, and moreover, I wished to keep her ladyship's coach in view, so I kept to the road. It must have been close on midnight when I sighted it at last. It was at a standstill in the midst of a quagmire, and as I drew near I could see neither driver on the box, nor groom at the horses' heads."

"Well?"

"Well! that's all! there was a wench inside the coach; I threw her out and searched for the letters; I found them! That rascally highwayman had played me false. Some distance from the road I spied him dancing a rigadoon in the moonlight with her ladyship, whilst her men, the dolts, were watching the spectacle! Ha! ha! ha! 'twas a fine sight too, I tell you! So now the sooner I get that chivalrous highwayman hanged, the better I shall like it."

"Then ... am I to understand that your Honour has the letters?"

"Aye! I have the letters right enough!" said Sir Humphrey, with an oath between his clenched teeth, "but I fear me her ladyship has cajoled the rogue into her service. Else why this dance? I did not know what to make of it. Madness, surely, or she never would have left the letters unprotected. He bewitched her mayhap, and the devil, his master, lent him a helping hand. I'll see him hang, I tell you.... Hang.... Hang!"

Master Mittachip's attenuated frame quaked with terror. There was so much hatred, so much lust for revenge in Sir Humphrey's half-choked voice, that instinctively the attorney cowered, as before some great and evil thing which he only half understood. After awhile Sir Humphrey managed to control himself. He was ashamed of having allowed his agent this one peep into the darkness of his soul. His love for Patience, though brutish and grasping, was as strong as his sensuous nature was capable of: his jealousy and hatred had been aroused by the strange scene he had witnessed on the Heath, and he was as conscious now of the longing for revenge, as of the desire to possess himself of Lady Patience and her fortune.

"'Sdeath!" he said more calmly, "Beau Brocade and that rascal John Stich were after me in a trice, and they'd have had the letters back from me, had I not put a bullet into the damned thief!"

"And wounded him, your Honour?" queried Mittachip, eagerly.

"Nay! I could not wait to see! but I hoped I had killed him, for 'twas John Stich who rode after me, fortunately. He was too big a fool to do me any harm and I quickly made him lose my track."

"And you've destroyed the letters, Sir Humphrey?"

"Destroyed them, you fool? Nay, it would ill suit my purpose if Stretton were to die. Can't you see that *now*," he said excitedly, "with those letters in my hand, I can force Lady Patience's acceptance of my suit? While her brother's life hangs in the balance I can offer her the letters, on condition that she consent to marry me, and threaten to destroy them if she refuse!"

"Aye! aye!" murmured the attorney, "'twere a powerful argument!"

"And remember," added his Honour, significantly, "there'll be two hundred guineas for you the day that I wed Lady Patience. That is, *if* you render me useful assistance to the end."

"Two hundred guineas!!! Good lack, Sir Humphrey, I hope you've got those letters safe!"

"Aye! safe enough for the present!"

"About your person?"

"Nay! you idiot! about my person? With so cunning a rascal as Beau Brocade at my heels!"

"Then in your valise, Sir Humphrey?"

"What? in a strange inn? Think you the fellow would be above breaking into my room? How do I know that mine host is not one of his boon companions? The rascal has many friends hereabouts."

"B ... b ... but what have you done with them, Sir Humphrey?" queried the attorney, in despair.

"In your ear, Master Mittachip," quoth his Honour, instinctively lowering his voice, lest the walls of the old inn had ears. "I thought the best plan was to hide the letters there, where Lady Patience and her chivalrous highwayman would least expect to find them."

"How so, good Sir Humphrey?"

"I was hard pressed, mind you, and had but a few seconds in which to make up my mind. I dismounted, then lashed my horse into a panic. As I expected he made straight for his own stables, at anyrate, he galloped off like mad in the direction of Aldwark, whilst I remained cowering in the dense scrub, grateful for the mist, which was very dense in the hollow. There I remained hidden for about half an hour, until all sound died away on the Heath. What happened to that damned highwayman or to John Stich I know not, but I did not feel that the letters were safe whilst they were about my person. I knew that I was some distance from this village, and still further from Aldwark, and feared that I should be pursued and overtaken. At any rate, I crept out of my hiding-place and presently found myself close to a wooden hut, not far from the roadside: and there, underneath some bramble and thorny stuff, I hid the letters well out of sight."

"Oh! but they won't be safe there, Sir Humphrey," moaned Mittachip, who seemed to see the golden vision of two hundred guineas vanishing before his eyes. "Think of it. Any moment they might be unearthed by some dolt of a shepherd!"

"'Sdeath! I know that, you fool! They're in a dry place now, but I only mean them to remain there until you can take them to your own house at Wirksworth, and put them in your strong room till I have need of them."

But this suggestion so alarmed Master Mittachip that he lost his balance and nearly fell off the edge of his chair.

"I, Sir Humphrey? .... I ... cross that lonely Heath again? ... and with those letters about my person?..."

"Tush, man! the footpads wouldn't take letters from you, and Beau Brocade will be keeping an eye on me, and wouldn't again molest you..."

"Aye! but he knows I enjoy the honour of your confidence, good Sir Humphrey! Believe me, the letters would not be safe with me."

"Adsbud!" said his Honour, firmly, "then I'll have to find someone else to take care of those letters for me, and," he added significantly, "to earn the two hundred guineas."

Master Mittachip gave an anxious gasp. That two hundred guineas!!! the ultimate ambition of his sordid, miserable existence! No! he would not miss that! ... and yet he dreaded the Heath ... and was in terror of Beau Brocade ... and he dreaded his Honour's anger ten thousand times more than either: that anger would be terrible if, having taken charge of the letters, he should be robbed of them.

The alternative was an awful one! He racked his tortuous brain for a likely issue. Sir Humphrey had risen, kicked his chair to one side, and made as if he would go.

"Now, harkee, friend Mittachip," he said firmly, "I want those letters placed somewhere in absolute safety, where neither Lady Patience's influence nor her chivalrous highwayman could possibly get at them. If you find a way and means of doing this for me, the two hundred guineas are yours. But if I have to manage this business myself, if I have to take the almost certain risk of being robbed of the letters, if I carry them about my own person, then you shall not get another shilling from me. Now you can think this matter over. I'll across to speak to Squire West, and see if I can't get that rascally highwayman captured and clapped into jail before the day is done."

He took up his hat, and threw his coat over his arm. The situation was getting desperate.

Then suddenly Master Mittachip had an idea.

"I have it, Sir Humphrey," he cried excitedly. "I have it! A perfectly safe way of conveying those letters to my strong room at Wirksworth!"

"Let's have it, then."

"I have bought some sheep of a farmer from over Aldwark way, for a client at Wirksworth. Here," he added, pulling a paper out of his pocket and handing it up to Sir Humphrey, "is the receipt and tally for them. Jock Miggs—Master Crabtree's shepherd—is taking the sheep to the town to-day. He'll most likely put up for the night on the Heath."

"Well?" queried Sir Humphrey.

"Well! Jock Miggs can neither read nor write."

"Of course not."

"Let us send *him* to Wirksworth and tell him to leave the packet of letters at my house in charge of my clerk, Master Duffy, who will put it in the strong room until you want them. Duffy started for Wirksworth at daybreak this morning, and should be there by nightfall."

"Pshaw, man! would you have me trust such valuable letters to a fool of a shepherd?"

"Nay, Sir Humphrey, but that is our safeguard. Beau Brocade never touches the poor or the peasantry, and certainly would never suspect Jock Miggs of being in your Honour's confidence, whilst the ordinary footpads would take no count of him. He is worth neither powder nor shot."

"That's true enough!"

"I should tell Miggs that the papers are accounts for the sheep, and promise him a silver crown if he delivers them safely at my door. We can put the letters in a sealed packet; no one would ever suspect him."

There was silence in the inn parlour for awhile. His Honour stood with legs apart, opposite the tiny leaded window, gazing out into vacancy, whilst Master Mittachip fixed his eyes meditatively on the broad back of his noble patron. What a deal depended on what was going on at the present moment in Sir Humphrey's active brain.

Suddenly his Honour turned on his heel.

"Odd's fish, Master Mittachip," he said, "but your plan is none so bad after all."

The attorney heaved a deep sigh of relief, and began mopping his beady forehead. The tension had been acute. This lengthy, agitating interview had been extremely trying. So much hung in the balance, and so much had depended upon that very uncertain quantity, his Honour's temper. But now the worst was over. Sir Humphrey was a man of determination, who never changed his mind once that mind was made up, and who carried any undertaking through with set purpose and unflinching will.

"Well! and when can I see that shepherd you speak of?" he asked.

"If your Honour would ride over on the Heath with me this afternoon," suggested the attorney, "I doubt not but we should come across Jock Miggs and his sheep, and in any case he would be at the hut by nightfall."

"Very good!" rejoined his Honour. "Do you see that a couple of horses be ready for us. We can start as soon as I have spoken with Squire West and laid my information against that d——d Beau Brocade. With a posse of soldiers at his heels he's less likely to worry us, eh, old scarecrow?"

"We shall not be safe, your Honour," assented worthy Master Mittachip, "until the rascal is dangling six feet above the ground. In the meanwhile," he added, seeing that Sir Humphrey was making for the door, "your Honour will be pleased to give me back that receipt and tally for the sheep I showed you just now."

But already his Honour was hurrying down the narrow passage, eager to get through the business that would lay his enemy by the heels, and render him safe in the possession of the important letters which were to secure him Lady Patience's hand and fortune.

"All right!" he shouted back lustily, "it's safe enough in my pocket. I'll give it you back on my return."

Left alone in the dingy, black-raftered parlour, Master Mittachip sat pondering for awhile, his pale, watery eyes blinking at times with the intensity of his satisfaction. Now for a little good luck—and he had no cause to fear the reverse—and that glorious vision of two hundred golden guineas would become a splendid reality. The advice he had given Sir Humphrey was undoubtedly the safest which he could offer. Beau Brocade, even with a posse of soldiers at his heels, was still a potent personality on the Heath, and it certainly looked as if her ladyship had cajoled him into her service. No one knew really who his friends and accomplices were: on and about Brassing Moor he could reckon on the help of most of the poorer villagers.

But Jock Miggs at any rate was safe, alike from the daring highwayman and the more humble footpad. The former would not suspect him, and the latter would leave a poor shepherd severely alone. The footpath from the hut by the roadside to the town of Wirksworth was but a matter of three or four miles, and for a silver crown the shepherd would be ready enough to take a sealed packet to the house of Master Mittachip in Fulsome Street.

Yes! it was all going to be for the best, in this best possible world, and as Master Mittachip thought over it all, he rubbed his thin, claw-like hands contentedly together.

CHAPTER XXII

AN INTERLUDE

The Packhorse Inn, lower down the village, was not nearly so frequented as was the Royal George. Its meagre, dilapidated appearance frightened most customers away. A few yokels only patronised it to the extent of sipping their small ale there, in the parlour when it was wet, or outside the porch when it was fine.

The few—very few—travellers, whom accident mostly brought to Brassington, invariably preferred the more solid, substantial inn on the green, but when it was a question of finding safe shelter for his wounded friend, John Stich unhesitatingly chose the Packhorse. He had improvised a rough kind of stretcher, with the help of the cushions from Lady Patience's coach, and on this, with the aid of Timothy the groom, he had carried Bathurst all the way across two miles of Heath into Brassington. The march had been terribly wearisome: the wounded man, fevered with past excitement, had become light-headed, and during intervals of lucidity was suffering acutely from his wound.

Lady Patience could not bring herself to leave him. A feeling she could not have described seemed to keep her enchained beside this man, whom but a few hours ago she had never seen, but in whom she felt now that all her hopes had centred. He had asked her to trust him, and since then had only recovered consciousness to plead to her with mute, aching eyes not to take away that trust which she had given him.

Fortunately, the noted bad state of the roads on Brassing Moor, which at any time might prove impassable for the coach, had caused her to take her own saddle as part of her equipment for her journey to London. This John Stich had fixed for her on Jack o' Lantern's back, and the faithful beast, as if guessing the sad plight of his master, carried her ladyship, with Mistress Betty clinging on behind, with lamb-like gentleness down the narrow bridle-path to Brassington.

Thomas, the driver, had been left in charge of the coach, with orders to find his way as quickly as may be along the road to Wirksworth.

It had been Bathurst's firmly-expressed wish that they should put up at Brassington, at any rate for the night. Besides being the nearest point, it was also the most central, whence a sharp lookout could be kept on Sir Humphrey Challoner's movements. Everything depended now on how serious the young man's wound turned out to be.

Patience felt that without his help she was indeed powerless to fight her cunning enemy. She was never for one moment in doubt as to the motive which prompted Sir Humphrey Challoner to steal the letters. He meant to hold them as a weapon over her to enforce the acceptance of his suit; this she knew well enough. Her instincts, rendered doubly acute by the imminence of the peril, warned her that the Squire of Harrington meant to throw all scruples to the wind, and would in wanton revenge sacrifice Philip by destroying the letters, if she fought or defied him openly.

Patience bethought her of the scene at the forge, when Bathurst's ready wit had saved her brother from the officious and rapacious soldiers: now that the terrible situation had to be met with keenness and cunning, she once more turned, with hope in her heart, to the one man who could save Philip again: but he, alas! lay helpless. And all along the weary way to Brassington she was listening with aching heart and throbbing temples to his wild, delirious words and occasional, quickly-suppressed moans.

However, they reached the Packhorse at last in the small hours of the morning: money, lavishly distributed by Lady Patience, secured the one comfortable room in the inn for the wounded man.

As soon as the day broke John Stich went in quest of Master Prosser, the leech, a gentleman famed for his skill and learning. Already the rest on a good bed, and Lady Patience's cool hand and gentle words, had done much to soothe the patient. Youth and an iron constitution quickly did the rest.

The leech pronounced the wound to be neither deep nor serious, and the extraction of the ball caused the sufferer much relief.

Within an hour after the worthy man's visit, Jack Bathurst had fallen into a refreshing sleep, and at John Stich's earnest pleading, Lady Patience had thrown herself on a bed in the small room which she had secured for herself and Mistress Betty, and had at last managed to get some rest.

The sun was already well up in the heavens when Jack awoke. His eyes, as soon as they opened, sought anxiously for her dear presence in the room.

"Feel better, Captain?" asked John Stich, who had been watching faithfully by his side.

"I feel a giant, honest friend," replied the young man. "Help me up, will you?"

"The leech said you ought to keep quiet for a bit, Captain," protested the smith.

"Oho! he did, did he?" laughed Jack, gaily. "Well! go tell him, friend, from me, that he is an ass."

"Where is she, John?" he asked quietly, after a slight pause.

"In the next room, Captain."

"Resting?"

"Aye! she never left your side since you fainted on the Heath."

"I know—I know, friend," said Jack, with a short, deep sigh; "think you I could not feel her hand..."

He checked himself abruptly, and with the help of John Stich raised himself from the bed. He looked ruefully at his stained clothes, and a quaint, pleasant smile chased away the last look of weariness and suffering from his face.

"Nay! what a plight for Beau Brocade in which to meet the lady of his dreams, eh, John? Here, help me to make myself presentable! Run down quickly to mine host, borrow brushes and combs, and anything you can lay hands on. I am not fit to appear before her eyes."

"Then will you keep quite still, Captain, until I return? And keep your arm quietly in the sling? The leech said..."

"Never mind what the leech said, run, John ... the sight of myself in that glass there causes me more pain than this stupid scratch. Run quickly, John, for I hear her footstep in the next room.... I'll not move from the edge of this bed, I swear it, if you'll only run."

He kept his word and never stirred from where he sat; but he strained his ears to listen, for through the thin partition wall he could just hear her footstep on the rough wooden floor, and occasionally her voice when she spoke to Betty.

Half an hour later, when John Stich had done his best to valet and dress him, he waited upon her ladyship at breakfast in the parlour downstairs.

She came forward to greet him, her dainty hand outstretched, her eyes anxiously scanning his face.

"You should not have risen yet, sir," she said half shyly as he pressed her finger-tips to his lips, "your poor wounded shoulder..."

"Nay, with your pardon, madam," he said lightly, "'tis well already since your sweet hand has tended it."

"'Twas my desire to nurse you awhile longer, and not allow you to risk your life for me again."

"My life? Nay! I'll trust that to mine old enemy, Fortune: she has ta'en care of it all these years, that I might better now place it at your service."

She said nothing, for she felt unaccountably shy. She, who had had half the gilded youth of England at her feet, found no light bantering word with which to meet this man; and beneath his ardent gaze she felt herself blushing like a school miss at her first ball.

"Will you honour me, sir," she said at last, "by partaking of breakfast with me?"

All cares and troubles seemed forgotten. He sat down at the table opposite to her, and together they drank tea, and ate eggs and bread and butter: and there was so much to talk about that often they would both become quite silent, and say all there was to say just with their eyes.

He told her about the Heath which he knew and loved so well, the beauty of the sunrise far out behind the Tors, the birds and beasts and their haunts and habits, the heron on the marshy ground, the cheeky robins on the branches of the bramble, the lizards and tiny frogs and toads: all that enchanting world which peopled the Moor and had made it a home for him.

And she listened to it all, for he had a deep, tender, caressing voice, which was always good to hear, and she was happy, for she was young, and the world in which she dwelt was very beautiful.

Yet she found this happiness which she felt, quite incomprehensible: she even chid herself for feeling it, for the outside world was still the same, and her brother still in peril. He, the man, alone knew whither he was drifting; he knew that he loved her with every fibre of his being, and that she was as immeasurably beyond him as the stars.

He knew what this happiness meant, and that it could but live a day, an hour. Therefore he drained the cup to its full measure, enjoying each fraction of a second of this one glorious hour, watching her as she smiled, as she sipped her tea, as she blushed when she met his eyes. And sometimes—for he was clumsy with his one arm in a sling—sometimes as she helped him in the thousand and one little ways of which women alone possess the enchanting secret, her hand would touch his, just for one moment, like a bird on the wing, and he, the poor outlaw, saw heaven open before him, and seeing it, was content.

Outside an early September sun was flooding the little village street with its golden light. They did not dare to show themselves at the window, lest either of them should be recognised, so they had drawn the thin muslin curtain across the casement, and shut out the earth from this little kingdom of their own.

Only at times the bleating of a flock of sheep, or the melancholy lowing of cattle would come to them from afar, or from the window-sill the sweet fragrance of a pot of mignonette.

CHAPTER XXIII

A DARING PLAN

It was close on ten o'clock when they came back to earth once more.

A peremptory knock at the door had roused them both from their dreams.

Bathurst rose to open, and there stood John Stich and Mistress Betty, both looking somewhat flurried and guilty, and both obviously brimming over with news.

"My lady! my lady!" cried Betty, excitedly, as soon as she caught her mistress's eye, "I have just spied Sir Humphrey Challoner at the window of the Royal George, just over the green yonder."

"Give me leave, Captain," added John Stich, who was busy rolling up his sleeves above his powerful arms, "give me leave, and I'll make the rogue disgorge those letters in a trice."

"You'd not succeed, honest friend," mused Bathurst, "and might get yourself in a devil of a hole to boot."

"Nay, Captain," asserted John, emphatically, "'tis no time now for the wearing of kid gloves. I was on the green a moment ago, and spied that ravenous scarecrow, Mittachip, conversing with the beadle outside the Court House, where Squire West is sitting."

"Well?"

"When the beadle had gone, Master Mittachip walked across the green and went straight to the Royal George. Be gy! what does that mean, Captain?"

"Oho!" laughed Jack, much amused at the smith's earnestness, "it means that Sir Humphrey Challoner intends to lay information against one Beau Brocade, the noted highwayman, and to see how nice he'll look with a rope round his neck and dangling six foot from the ground."

An involuntary cry from Lady Patience, however drowned the laughter on his lips.

"Tush, man!" he added seriously, "here's a mighty fine piece of work we're doing, frightening her ladyship..."

But John Stich was scowling more heavily than ever.

"If the scoundrel should dare..." he muttered, clenching his huge fists.

His attitude was so threatening, and his expression so menacing, that in the midst of her new anxiety Lady Patience herself could not help smiling. Beau Brocade laughed outright.

"Dare?..." he said lightly. "Why, of course he'll dare. He's eager enough in the pursuit of mischief, and must save the devil all the trouble of showing him the way. But now," he added more seriously, and turning to Mistress Betty, "tell me, child, saw you Sir Humphrey clearly?"

"Aye! clear as daylight," she retorted, "the old beast..."

"How was he dressed?"

"Just like he was yesterday, sir. A brown coat, embroidered waistcoat, buff breeches, riding-boots, three-cornered hat, and he had in his hand a gold-headed riding-crop."

"Child!—child!" cried Bathurst, joyfully, "an those bright eyes of yours have not deceived you, yours'll be the glory of having saved us all."

"What are you going to do?" asked Patience, eagerly.

"Pit my poor wits against those of Sir Humphrey Challoner," he replied gaily.

"I don't quite understand."

He came up quite close to her and tried to meet her eyes.

"But you trust me?" he asked.

And she murmured,—

"Absolutely."

"May Heaven bless you for that word!" he said earnestly. "Then will you deign to do as I shall direct?"

"Entirely."

"Very well! Then whilst friend Stich will fetch my hat for me, will you write out a formal plaint, signed with your full name, stating that last night on the Heath you were waylaid and robbed by a man, whom I, your courier, saw quite plainly, and whom you have desired me to denounce?"

"But..."

"I entreat you there's not a moment to be lost," he urged, taking pen, ink and paper from the old-fashioned desk close by, and placing them before her.

"I'll do as you wish, of course," she said, "but what is your purpose?"

"For the present to take your ladyship's plaint over to his Honour, Squire West, at the Court House."

"You'll be seen and recognised and..."

"Not I. One or two of the yokels may perhaps guess who I am, but they'd do me no harm. I entreat you, do as I bid you. Every second wasted may imperil our chance of safety."

He had such an air of quiet command about him that she instinctively obeyed him and wrote out the plaint as he directed, then gave it in his charge. He seemed buoyant and full of hope, and though her heart misgave her, she managed to smile cheerfully when he took leave of her.

"I humbly beg of you," he said finally, as having kissed her finger-tips he prepared to go, "to wait here against my return, and on no account to take heed of anything you may see or hear for the next half-hour. An I mistake not," he added with a merry twinkle in his grey eyes, "there'll be strange doings at Brassington this noon."

"But you...?" she cried anxiously.

"Nay! I pray you have no fear for me. In your sweet cause I would challenge the world, and, if you desired it, would remained unscathed."

When he had gone, she sighed, and obedient to his wish, sat waiting patiently for his return in the dingy little parlour which awhile ago his presence had made so bright.

It was at this moment that Master Mittachip, after his interview with the beadle, was in close conversation with Sir Humphrey Challoner at the Royal George.

Outside the inn, Bathurst turned to John Stich, who had closely followed him.

"How's my Jack o' Lantern?" he asked quickly.

"As fresh as a daisy, Captain," replied the smith. "I've rubbed him down myself, and he has had a lovely feed."

"That's good. You have my saddle with you?"

"Oh, aye! I knew you'd want it soon enough. Jack o' Lantern carried it for you himself, bless 'is 'eart, along with her ladyship and Mistress Betty."

"Then do you see at once to his being saddled, friend, and bring him along to the Court House as soon as may be. Hold him in readiness for me, so that I may mount at a second's notice. You understand?"

"Yes, Captain. I understand that you are running your head into a d———d noose, and..."

"Easy, easy, friend! Remember..."

"Nay! I'll not forget for whose sake you do it. But you are at a disadvantage, Captain, with only one good arm."

"Nay, friend," rejoined Bathurst, lightly, "there's many a thing a man can do with one arm: he can embrace his mistress ... or shoot his enemy."

The sleepy little village of Brassington lay silent and deserted in the warmth of the noon-day sun, as Bathurst, having parted from John Stich, hurried across its narrow streets. As he had passed quickly through the outer passage of the Packhorse he had caught sight of a few red coats at the dingy bar of the inn, and presently, when he emerged on the green, he perceived another lot of them over at the Royal George yonder.

But at this hour the worthy soldiers of His Majesty, King George, were having their midday rest and their customary glasses of ale, and were far too busy recounting their adventure with the mysterious stranger at the forge to the gaffers of Brassington, to take heed of anyone hurrying along its street.

And thus Bathurst passed quickly and unperceived; the one or two yokels whom he met gave him a rapid glance. Only the women turned round, as he went along, to have another look at the handsome stranger with one arm in a sling.

Outside the Court House he came face to face with Master Inch, whose pompous dignity seemed at this moment to be severely ruffled.

"Hey, sir! Hey!" he was shouting, and craning his fat neck in search of Master Mittachip, who had incontinently disappeared, "the Court is determinating—Squire West will grant you the interview which you seek.... Lud preserve me!" he added in noble and gigantic wrath, "I do believe the impious malapert was trying to fool me ... sending me on a fool's errand ... *me* ... Jeremiah Inch, beadle of this parish!..."

Bathurst waited a moment or two until the worst of the beadle's anger had cooled down a little, then he took a silver crown from his pocket, and pushed past the worthy into the precincts of the house.

"The interview you've arranged for, friend," he said quietly; "will do equally well for her ladyship's courier."

Master Inch was somewhat taken off his balance. Mittachip's disappearance and this stranger's impertinence had taken his breath away. Before he had time to recover it, Bathurst had pressed the silver crown into his capacious palm.

"Now tell Squire West, friend," he said with that pleasant air of authority which he knew so well how to assume, "that I am here by the command of Lady Patience Gascoyne and am waiting to speak with him."

Master Inch was so astonished that he found no word either of protest or of offended dignity. He looked doubtfully at the crown for a second or two, weighed it in his mind against the problematical half-crown promised by the defaulting attorney, and then said majestically,—

"I will impart her ladyship's cognomen to his Honour myself."

The next moment Jack Bathurst found himself alone in a small private room of the Court House, looking forward with suppressed excitement to the interview with Squire West, which in a moment of dare-devil, madcap frolic, yet with absolute coolness and firm determination, he had already arranged in his mind.

CHAPTER XXIV

HIS HONOUR, SQUIRE WEST

Squire West was an elderly man, with a fine military presence and a pleasant countenance beneath his bob-tail wig: in his youth he had been reckoned well-favoured, and had been much petted by the ladies at the county balls. Owing to this he had retained a certain polish of manner not often met with in the English country gentry of those times.

He came forward very politely to greet the courier of Lady Patience Gascoyne.

"What hath procured to Brassington the honour of a message from Lady Patience Gascoyne?" he asked, motioning Bathurst to a chair, and seating himself behind his desk.

"Her ladyship herself is staying in the village," replied Jack, "but would desire her presence to remain unknown for awhile."

"Oh, indeed!" said the Squire, a little flurried at this unexpected event, "but ... but there is no inn fitting to harbour her ladyship in this village, and ... and ... if her ladyship would honour me and my poor house..."

"I thank you, sir, but her ladyship only remains here for an hour or so, and has despatched me to you on an important errand which brooks of no delay."

"I am entirely at her ladyship's service."

"Lady Patience was on her way from Stretton Hall, your Honour," continued Bathurst, imperturbably, "when her coach was stopped on the Heath, not very far from here, and her jewels, money, and also certain valuable papers were stolen from her."

Squire West hemmed and hawed, and fidgeted in his chair: the matter seemed, strangely enough, to be causing him more annoyance than surprise.

"Dear! dear!" he muttered deprecatingly.

"Her ladyship has written out her formal plaint," said Jack, laying the paper before his Honour. "She has sent her coach on to Wirksworth, but thought your Honour's help here at Brassington would be more useful in capturing the rogue."

"Aye!" murmured the worthy Squire, still somewhat doubtfully, and with a frown of perplexity on his jovial face. "We certainly have a posse of soldiers—a dozen or so at most—quartered in the village just now, but..."

"But what, your Honour?"

"But to be frank with you, sir, I fear me that 'twill be no good. An I mistake not, 'tis another exploit of that rascal, Beau Brocade, and the rogue is so cunning! ... Ah!" he added with a sigh, "we shall have no peace in this district until we've laid him by the heels."

It was certainly quite obvious that the Squire was none too eager to send a posse of soldiers after the notorious highwayman. He had himself enjoyed immunity on the Heath up to now, and feared that it would be his turn to suffer if he started an active campaign against Beau Brocade. But Bathurst, from where he sat, had a good view through the casement window of the village green, and of the Royal George beyond it. Every moment he expected to see Sir Humphrey Challoner emerging from under the porch and entering this Court House, when certainly the situation would become distinctly critical. The Squire's hesitancy nearly drove him frantic with impatience, yet perforce he had to keep a glib tongue in his head, and not to betray more than a natural interest in the subject which he was discussing.

"Aye!" he said gaily, "an it was that rogue Beau Brocade, your Honour, he's the most daring rascal I've ever met. The whole thing was done in a trice. Odd's fish! but the fellow would steal your front tooth whilst he parleyed with you. He fired at me and hit me," he added ruefully, pointing to his wounded shoulder.

"You were her ladyship's escort on the Heath, sir?"

"Aye! and would wish to be of assistance in the recovery of her property: more particularly of a packet of letters on which her ladyship sets great store. If the rogue were captured now, these might be found about his person."

"Ah! I fear me," quoth his Honour, with singular lack of enthusiasm, "that 'twill not be so easy, sir, as you imagine."

"How so?"

"Beau Brocade is in league with half the country-side and..."

"Nay! you say you have a posse of soldiers quartered here! Gadzooks! if I had the chance with these and a few lusty fellows from the village, I'd soon give an account of any highwayman on this Heath!"

"Dear! dear!" repeated Squire West, sorely puzzled, "a very regrettable incident indeed."

"Can I so far trespass on your Honour's time," queried Bathurst, with a slight show of impatience, "as to ask you at least to take note of her ladyship's plaint?"

"Certainly ... sir, certainly ... hem! ... er.... Of course we must after the rogue ... the beadle shall cry him out on the green at once, and..."

It was easy to see that the worthy Squire would far sooner have left the well-known hero of Brassing Moor severely alone; still, in his official capacity he was bound to take note of her ladyship's plaint, and to act as justice demanded.

"'Tis a pity, sir," he said, whilst he sat fidgeting among his papers, "that you, or perhaps her ladyship, did not see the rogue's face. I suppose he was masked as usual?"

"Faix! he'd have frightened the sheep on the Heath, maybe, if he was not. But her ladyship and I noted his hair and stature, and also the cut and colour of his clothes."

"What was he like?"

"Tall and stout of build, with dark hair turning to grey."

"Nay!" ejaculated Squire West, in obvious relief, "then it was not Beau Brocade, who is young and slim, so I'm told, though I've never seen him. You saw him plainly, sir, did you say?"

"Aye! quite plainly, your Honour! And what's more," added Jack, emphatically, "her ladyship and I both caught sight of him in Brassington this very morning."

"In Brassington?"

"Outside the Royal George," asserted Bathurst, imperturbably.

"Nay, sir!" cried Squire West, who seemed to have quite lost his air of indecision, now that he no longer feared to come in direct conflict with Beau Brocade, "why did you not say this before? Here, Inch! Inch!" he added, going to the door and shouting lustily across the passage, "where is that cursed beadle? In Brassington, did you say, sir?"

"I'd almost swear to it, your Honour."

"Nay! then with a bit of good luck, we may at least lay *this* rascal by the heels. I would I could rid this neighbourhood of these rogues. Here, Inch," he continued, as soon as that worthy appeared in the doorway, "do you listen to what this gentleman has got to say. There's a d———d rascal in this village and you'll have to cry out his description at once, and then collar him as soon as may be."

Master Inch placed himself in a posture that was alike dignified and expectant. His Honour, Squire West, too, was listening eagerly, whilst Jack

Bathurst with perfect *sang-froid* gave forth the description of the supposed highwayman.

"He wore a brown coat," he said calmly, "embroidered waistcoat, buff breeches, riding-boots and three-cornered hat. He is tall and stout of build, has dark hair slightly turning to grey, and was last seen carrying a gold-headed riding-crop."

"That's clear enough, Inch, is it not?" queried his Honour.

"It is marvellously pellucid, sir," replied the beadle.

"You may add, friend Beadle," continued Jack, carelessly, "that her ladyship offers a reward of twenty guineas for that person's immediate apprehension."

And Master Inch, beadle of the parish of Brassington, flew out of the door, and out of the Court House, bell in hand, for with a little bit of good luck it might be that he would be the first to lay his hand on the tall, stout rascal in a brown coat, and would be the one to earn the twenty guineas offered for his immediate apprehension.

Squire West himself was over pleased. It was indeed satisfactory to render service to so great a lady as Lady Patience Gascoyne without interfering over much with that dare-devil Beau Brocade. The depredations on Brassing Moor had long been a scandal in the county: it had oft been thought that Squire West had not been sufficiently active in trying to rid the Heath of the notorious highwayman, whose exploits now were famed far and wide. But here was a chance of laying a cursed rascal by the heels and of showing his zeal in the administration of the county.

The Squire, in the interim, busied himself with his papers, whilst Bathurst, who was vainly trying to appear serious and only casually interested, stood by the open window, watching Master Inch's progress across the green.

Outside the Court House faithful John Stich stood waiting, with Jack o' Lantern pawing the ground by his side.

CHAPTER XXV

SUCCESS AND DISAPPOINTMENT

Thus it was that when Sir Humphrey Challoner, after his lengthy interview with Mittachip, stepped out of the porch of the Royal George on his way to the Court House, he found the village green singularly animated.

A number of yokels, including quite a goodly contingent of women and youngsters, were crowding round Master Inch, the beadle, who was ringing his bell violently and shouting at the top of his lusty voice,—

"Oyez! Oyez! Oyez! Take note that a robber, vagabond and thief is in hiding in this village."

Interested in the scene, Sir Humphrey had paused a moment, watching the pompous beadle and the crowd of gaffers and women. He still carried his riding-crop, and flicked it with a certain pleasurable satisfaction against his boot, eagerly anticipating the moment when the village crier would be giving forth in the same stentorian tones the description of Beau Brocade, the highwayman.

"Oyez! Oyez! Oyez!" continued Master Inch, with ever-increasing vigour. "Take note that this vagabond is apparelled in a brown coat, embroidered waistcoat, buff nether garments and riding-boots. Oyez! Oyez! Oyez! take note that he carried with him this morning a gold-headed riding-whip, that he is tall and slightly rotund in his corporation and has raven hair slightly attenuated with grey.

"Oyez! Oyez! Oyez! take note that if any of you observate such a person as I have just descriptioned, you are to apprise me of this instantaneously, so that I may take him by force and violence even into the presence of his Honour.

"Oyez! Oyez! Oyez!"

The gaffers were putting their heads together, whilst the young ones whispered eagerly,—

"Brown coat! ... embroidered waistcoat! ... a gold-headed whip!..."

Nay, 'twas often enough that Master Inch had to cry out the description of some wretched vagabond in hiding in the village, but it was not usual that such an one was attired in the clothes of a gentleman.

It even struck Sir Humphrey as very strange, and he pushed through the group of yokels to hear more clearly Master Inch's renewed description of the rogue.

"Oyez! Oyez! Oyez!"

At first the interest in Master Inch's pompous words was so keen that Sir Humphrey remained practically unnoticed. One or two villagers, noting that a gentleman was amongst them, respectfully made way for him, then one youngster, struck by a sudden idea, stared at him and whispered to his neighbour,—

"He's got a brown coat on..."

"Aye!" whispered the other in reply, "and an embroiderated waistcoat too."

Some of them began crowding around Sir Humphrey, so that he raised his whip and muttered angrily,—

"What the devil are ye all staring at?"

It was at this very moment that Master Inch suddenly caught sight of him, just in the very middle of a stentorian,—

"Oyez!"

He gave one tremendous gasp, the bell dropped out of his hand, his jaw fell, his round, beady eyes nearly bulged out of his head.

"'Tis him!" murmured the yokel, who stood close to his ear.

This remark brought back Master Inch to his senses and to the importance of his position. He raised his large hand above his head and brought it down with a tremendous clap on Sir Humphrey Challoner's shoulder.

"Aye! 'tis him!" he shouted lustily, "and be gy! he's got guilt writ all over his face, and 'tis a mighty ugly surface!"

Sir Humphrey, taken completely by surprise, was positively purple with rage.

"Death and hell!" he cried, clutching his riding-whip significantly. "What's the meaning of this?"

But already the younger men, full of excitement and eagerness, had closed round him, impeding his movements, whilst two more lusty fellows incontinently seized him by the collar. They felt neither respect nor sympathy for a vagabond attired in gentleman's clothes.

Sir Humphrey tried to shake himself free, whilst the beadle majestically replied,—

"You'll have it explanated to you, friend, before his Honour!"

The excitement and lust of capture was growing apace.

"Got him!" shouted most of the men.

"Showin' his ugly face in broad daylight!" commented the women.

"Hold him tight, beadle," was the universal admonition.

"You rascal! you dare!..." gasped Sir Humphrey, struggling violently, and shaking a menacing fist in the beadle's face.

"Silence!" commanded Master Inch, with supreme dignity.

"I'll have you whipped for this!"

But this aroused the beadle's most awesome ire.

"To the stocks with him!" he ordered, "he insultates the Majesty of the Law!"

"You low-born knave! Aye! you'll hang for this!"

It was all this clamour that at last aroused Master Mittachip in the parlour of the Royal George from the happy day-dreams in which he was indulging. At first he took no count of it, then he quietly strolled up to the window and undid the casement, to ascertain what all the tumult was about.

What he did see nearly froze the thin blood within his veins. He would have cried out, but his very throat contracted with the horror of the spectacle which he beheld.

There! across the village green, he saw Sir Humphrey Challoner, his noble patron, the Squire of Hartington, being clapped into the village stocks, whilst a crowd of yokels, the clumsy, ignorant d———d louts! were actually pelting his Honour with carrots, turnips and potatoes!

Oh! was the world coming to an end? There! a peck of peas hit Sir Humphrey straight in the eye. No wonder his Honour was purple, he would have a stroke of apoplexy for sure within the next five minutes.

At last Master Mittachip recovered the use of his limbs. With one bound he was out of the inn parlour, and had pushed past mine host and hostess, who, as ignorant as were all the other villagers of their guest's name and quality, were watching the scene from the porch, and holding their sides with laughter.

Jack Bathurst had watched it all from the window of the Court House: his dare-devil, madcap scheme had succeeded beyond his most sanguine hopes. When he saw Sir Humphrey Challoner actually clapped in the village stocks, with the pompous beadle towering over him, like the sumptuous Majesty of the Law, he could have cried out in wild merry glee.

But Jack was above all a man of prompt decision and quick action. For his own life he cared not one jot, and would gladly have laid it down for the sake of the woman he loved with all the passionate ardour of his romantic temperament, but with him, as with every other human being, self-preservation was the greatest and most irresistible law. He had readily imperilled his safety in order to obtain possession of the letters, which meant so much happiness to his beautiful white rose: but this done, he was ready to do battle for his own life, and to sell his freedom as dearly as may be.

He hoped that he had effectually accomplished his purpose through the arrest of Sir Humphrey Challoner, whose pockets Master Inch was even now deliberately searching, in spite of vigorous protests and terrible language from his Honour. His heart gave a wild leap of joy when he saw the beadle presently hurrying across the green and holding a paper in his hand. It looked small enough—not a packet, only a single letter: but if it were the momentous one, then indeed would all risks, all perils seem as nothing when weighed against the happiness of having rendered *her* this service.

But Jack also saw Master Mittachip darting panic-stricken out of the inn opposite. He knew of course that within the next few moments—seconds perhaps—the fraud would be discovered and Sir Humphrey Challoner liberated, amidst a shower of abject apologies from the Squire and parish of Brassington combined. What the further consequences of it all would be to himself was not difficult to foresee.

He looked behind him. The Squire was sitting at his desk, apparently taking no notice of the noise and shouting outside. Down below, John Stich, who had been watching the scene on the green with the utmost delight, stood ready, holding Jack o' Lantern by the bridle. In a moment, with a few courteous words to the Squire, Bathurst had hurried out of the Court House. He met the beadle at the door, who, paper in hand, conscious of his own importance and flurried with wrath, was hurrying to report the important arrest to Squire West.

Bathurst stopped him with a quick,—

"'Twas well done, Master Inch!"

And pressing a couple of guineas into the beadle's hand, he added,—

"Her ladyship will further repay when you've found the rest of her property. In the meanwhile, these, I presume, are the letters she lost."

"Only one letter, sir," said Master Inch, as somewhat taken off his pompous guard he allowed Jack to take the paper from him.

There was not a minute to be lost. Master Mittachip, having vainly tried to harangue the yokels, who were still pelting his Honour with miscellaneous vegetables, was now hurrying to the Court House as fast as his thin legs would carry him.

Bathurst took one glance at the paper which Master Inch had given him. A cry of the keenest disappointment escaped his lips.

"What is it, Captain?" asked John Stich, who had anxiously been watching his friend's face.

"Nothing, friend," replied Bathurst, "only a receipt and tally for some sheep."

John Stich uttered a violent oath.

"And the scoundrel'll escape with a shower of potatoes and no more punishment than the stocks. And you've risked your life, Captain, for nothing!"

"Nay! not for nothing, honest friend," said Jack, in a hurried whisper, as he mounted Jack o' Lantern with all the speed his helpless arm would allow. "Do you go back to her ladyship as fast as you can. Beg her from me not to give up hope, but to feign an illness and on no account speak to anyone about the events of to-day until she has seen me again. You understand?"

"Aye! aye! Captain!"

At this moment there came a wild cry from the precincts of the Court House, and Master Mittachip, accompanied by Squire West himself, and closely followed by the beadle, were seen tearing across the green towards the village stocks.

"The truth is out, friend," shouted Jack, as pressing his knees against Jack o' Lantern's sides, and giving the gallant beast one cry of encouragement, he galloped away at break-neck speed out towards the Moor.

CHAPTER XXVI

THE MAN HUNT

By the time Squire West and the whole of the parish of Brassington had realised what a terrible practical joke had been perpetrated on them by the stranger, the latter was far out of sight, with not even a cloud of dust to mark the way he went.

But the hue-and-cry after him had never ceased the whole of that day. Squire West, profuse and abject in his apologies, had told off all the soldiers who were quartered in the village to scour the Heath day and night, until that rogue was found and brought before him. The Sergeant, who was in command of the squad, and the Corporal too, had a score of their own to settle with the mysterious stranger, whom the general consensus of opinion declared to have been none other than that scoundrel unhung, the notorious highwayman, Beau Brocade.

Master Inch, as soon as he had recovered his breath, distinctly recollected now seeing a beautiful chestnut horse pawing the ground outside the Court House during the course of the morning: he blamed himself severely for not having guessed the identity of the creature, so closely associated in every one's mind with the exploits of the highwayman.

The yokels, however, at this juncture, entrenched themselves behind a barrier of impenetrable density. In those days, just as even now, it is beyond human capacity to obtain information from a Derbyshire countryman if he do not choose to give it. Whether some of those who had pelted Sir Humphrey Challoner with vegetables had or had not known who his Honour was, whether some of them had or had not guessed Beau Brocade's presence in the village, remained, in spite of rigorous cross-examination a complete mystery to the perplexed Squire and to his valiant henchman, the beadle.

Promises, threats, bribes were alike ineffectual.

"I dunno!" was the stolid, perpetual reply to every question put on either subject.

Her ladyship, on the other hand, overcome with fatigue, was too ill to see anyone.

The posse of soldiers, a score or so by now, had however been reinforced as the day wore on by a contingent of Squire West's own indoor and outdoor servants, also by a few loafers from Brassington itself, of the sort that are to be found in every corner of the world where there is an ale-house, the idlers, the toadies, those who had nothing to lose and something to gain by running counter to popular feeling and taking up cudgels against Beau Brocade, for the sake of the reward lavishly promised by Squire West and Sir Humphrey Challoner.

The latter's temper had not even begun to simmer down at this late hour of the day when, all arrangements for the battue after the highwayman being completed, he at last found himself on horseback, ambling along the bridle-path towards the shepherd's hut, with Master Mittachip beside him.

It had been a glorious day, and the evening now gave promise of a balmy night to come, but the Heath's majestic repose was disturbed by the doings of man. Beneath the gorse and bracken lizards and toads had gone to rest in the marshy land beyond, waterhen and lapwing were asleep, but all the while on the great Moor, through the scrub and blackthorn, along path and ravine, man was hunting man and finding enjoyment in the sport.

As Sir Humphrey Challoner and the attorney rode slowly along, they could hear from time to time the rallying cry of the various parties stalking the Heath for their big game. The hunt was close on the heels of Beau Brocade. Earlier in the afternoon his horse had been seen to make its way, riderless, towards the forge of John Stich.

The quarry was on foot, he was known to be wounded, he must fall an easy prey to his trackers soon enough: sometimes in the distance there would come a shout of triumph, when the human blood-hounds had at last found a scent, then Sir Humphrey would rouse himself from his moody silence, a look of keen malice would light up his deep-set eyes, and reining in his horse, he would strain his ears to hear that shout of triumph again.

"He'll not escape this time, Sir Humphrey," whispered Mittachip, falling obsequiously into his employer's mood.

"No! curse him!" muttered his Honour with a string of violent oaths, "I shall see him hang before two days are over, unless these dolts let him escape again."

"Nay, nay, Sir Humphrey! that's not likely!" chuckled Master Mittachip. "Squire West has pressed all his own able-bodied men into the service, and the posse of soldiers were most keen for the chase. Nay, nay, he'll not escape this time."

"'Sdeath!" swore his Honour under his breath, "but I do feel stiff!"

"A dreadful indignity," moaned the attorney.

"Nay! but Squire West was most distressed, and his apologies were profuse! Indeed he seemed to feel it as much as if it had happened to himself."

"Aye! but not in the same place, I'll warrant! Odd's life, I had no notion how much a turnip could hurt when flung into one's eye," added his Honour, with one of those laughs that never boded any good.

"A most painful incident, Sir Humphrey!" sighed Mittachip, brimming over with sympathy.

"'Twas not the incident that was painful! Zounds! I am bruised all over. But I'll have the law of every one of those dolts, aye! and make that fool West administer it on all of them! As for that ape, the beadle, he shall be publicly whipped. Death and hell! they'll have to pay for this!"

"Aye! aye! Sir Humphrey! your anger is quite natural, and Squire West assured me that that rascal Beau Brocade, who played you this impudent trick, cannot fail to be caught. The hunt is well organised, he cannot escape."

As if to confirm the attorney's words, there rose at this moment from afar a weird and eerie sound, which caused Master Mittachip's shrivelled flesh to creep along his bones.

"What was that?" he whispered, horror-struck.

"A blood-hound, the better to track that rascal," muttered Sir Humphrey, savagely.

The attorney shivered; there had been so much devilish malice in his Honour's voice, that suddenly his puny heart misgave him. He took to wishing himself well out of this unmanly business. The horror of it seemed to grip him by the throat: he was superstitious too, and firmly believed in a material hell; the sound of that distant snarl, followed by the significant yelping of a hound upon the scent, made him think of the cries the devils would utter at sight of the damned.

"The dog belongs to one of Squire West's grooms," remarked his Honour, carelessly, "a savage beast enough, by the look of him. Luck was in our favour, for our gallant highwayman had carried Lady Patience's plaint inside his coat for quite a long time, and then left it on his Honour's table ... quite enough for any self-respecting blood-hound, and this one is said to be very keen on the scent.... Squire West tried to protest, but set a dog to catch a dog, say I."

Master Mittachip tried to shut his ears to the terrible sound. Fortunately it was getting fainter now, and Sir Humphrey did not give him time for much reflection.

His Honour had stopped for awhile listening, with a chuckle of intense satisfaction, to the yelping of the dog straining on the leash, then when the sound died away, he said abruptly,—

"Are we still far from the hut?"

"No, Sir Humphrey," stammered Mittachip, whose very soul was quaking with horror.

"We'll find the shepherd there, think you?"

"Y ... y ... yes, your Honour!"

"Harkee, Master Mittachip. I'll run no risk. That d——d highwayman must be desperate to-night. We'll adhere to our original plan, and let the shepherd take the letters to Wirksworth."

"You ... you ... you'll not let them bide to-night where they are, Sir Humphrey?"

"No, you fool, I won't. They are but just below the surface, under cover of some bramble, and once those fellows come scouring round the hut, any one of them may unearth the letters with a kick of his boot. There's been a lot of talk of a reward for the recovery of a packet of letters! ... No, no, no! I'll not risk it."

Sir Humphrey Challoner had thought the matter well out, and knew that he ran two distinct risks in the matter of the letters. To one he had alluded just now when he spoke of the probability—remote perhaps—of the packet being accidentally unearthed by one of the scouring parties. Any man who found it would naturally at once take it to Squire West, in the hope of getting the reward promised by her ladyship for its recovery. The idea, therefore, of leaving the letters in their hiding-place for awhile did not commend itself to him. On the other hand, there was the more obvious risk of keeping them about his own person. Sir Humphrey thanked his stars that he had not done so the day before, and even now kept in his mind a certain superstitious belief that Beau Brocade—wounded, hunted and desperate—would make a final effort, which might prove successful, to wrench the letters from him on the Heath.

CHAPTER XXVII

JOCK MIGGS'S ERRAND

Master Mittachip had tried to utter one or two feeble protests, but Sir Humphrey had interrupted him emphatically,—

"The rascal may hope to win his pardon through the Gascoyne influence, by rendering her ladyship this service. Where'er he may be at this moment, I am quite sure that his eye is upon me and my doings."

Mittachip shuddered and closed his eyes: he dared not peer into the dark scrub beside him, and drew his horse in as close to Sir Humphrey's as he could.

"If you're afraid, you lumbering old coward," added his Honour, "go back and leave me in peace. I'll arrange my own affairs as I think best."

But the prospect of returning to Brassington alone across this awful Heath sent Master Mittachip into a renewed agony of terror: though his noble patron seemed suddenly to have become uncanny in this inordinate lust for revenge, he preferred his Honour's company to his own, and therefore made a violent effort to silence his worst fears. The Moor just now was comparatively calm: the shouts of the hunters and the yelping of the hound had altogether ceased; perhaps they had lost the scent.

Another half-hour's silent ride brought them to the spur of the hill, along the top of which ran the Wirksworth Road, and as they left the steep declivity behind them, their ears were pleasantly tickled by the welcome and bucolic sound of the bleating of sheep.

"Your friend the shepherd seems to be at his post," quoth Sir Humphrey with a sigh of satisfaction.

They were close to the point where on the previous night Lady Patience's coach had come to a halt, and the next moment brought them in sight of the shepherd's hut, with the pen beyond it, vaguely discernible in the gloom.

Sir Humphrey gave the order to dismount. Master Mittachip, feeling more dead than alive, had perforce to obey. They tied their horses loosely to a clump of blackthorn by the roadside and then crept cautiously towards the hut.

It suited their purpose well that the night was a dark one. The moon was not yet high in the heavens, and was still half-veiled by a thin film of fleecy clouds, leaving the whole vista of the Moor wrapped in mysterious grey-blue semitones.

"You have brought the lanthorn," whispered Sir Humphrey, hurriedly.

"Y ... y ... y ... yes, your Honour," stammered Mittachip.

"Then quick's the word," said his Honour, pointing to a thick clump of gorse and bramble quite close to the shed. "The letters are in the very centre of that clump, and only just below the surface. Do you creep in there and get them."

There was nothing for Master Mittachip to do but to obey, and that with as much alacrity as his terror would allow. His teeth were chattering in his head, and his hands were trembling so violently that he was some time in striking a light for the lanthorn.

Sir Humphrey suppressed an oath of angry impatience.

"Lud preserve me," murmured the poor attorney, "if that highwayman should come upon me whilst I am engaged in the task! ... You ... you'll not leave me, Sir Humphrey?..."

"I'll lay my stick across your cowardly shoulders if you don't hurry," was his Honour's only comment.

He watched Mittachip crawling on his hands and knees underneath the bramble, and his deep stertorous breathing testified to the anxiety which was raging within him. A few moments of intense suspense, and then Master Mittachip reappeared from beneath the scrub, covered with wet earth, still trembling, but holding the packet of letters triumphantly in his hand.

Sir Humphrey snatched it from him.

"Quick! find the shepherd now! Don't waste time!" he whispered, pushing the cowering attorney roughly before him. "One feels as if every blade of grass had a pair of ears on this damned Heath!" he muttered under his breath.

Jock Miggs, the shepherd, had counted over his sheep, closed the gate of the pen, and was just turning into the hut for the night, when he was hailed by Master Mittachip.

"Shepherd! hey! shepherd!"

Miggs looked about him, vaguely astonished.

Since his adventure of the previous night, when he had been made to play a tune for mad folks to dance to, he felt that nothing would seriously surprise him.

When therefore he felt himself seized by the arm without more ado and dragged into the darkest corner of the hut, he did not even protest.

"Did you wish to speak with me, sir?" he asked plaintively, rubbing his arm, for Sir Humphrey's impatient grip had been very strong and hard.

"Yes!" said the latter, speaking in a rapid whisper, "here's Master Mittachip, attorney-at-law, whom you know well, eh?"

"Aye, aye," murmured Jock Miggs, pulling at his forelock, "t' sheep belong to his Honour Oi believe."

"Exactly, Miggs," interposed Master Mittachip, spurred to activity by a vigorous kick from Sir Humphrey, "and I have come out here on purpose to see you, for it is very important that you should go at once on to Wirksworth for me, with a packet and a note for Master Duffy, my clerk."

"What, now? This time o' night?" quoth Jock, vaguely.

"Aye, aye, Miggs ... you are not afraid, are you?"

Sir Humphrey had taken up his stand outside the hut, leaving Mittachip to arrange this matter with the shepherd. He had leaned his powerful frame against the wall of the shed, and was grasping his heavily-weighted riding-crop, ready and alert in case of attack. The darkness round him at this moment was intense, and his sharp eyes vainly tried to pierce the gloom, which seemed to be closing in upon him, but his ears were keenly alive to every sound which came to him out of the blackness of the night.

And all the while he tried not to lose one word of the conversation between Mittachip and the shepherd.

"That's true, Jock," the attorney was saying. "Well! then if you'll go to Wirksworth for me, now, at once, there'll be a guinea for you."

"A guinea!" came in bewildered accents from the worthy shepherd, "Lordy! Lordy! but these be 'mazing times!"

"All I want you to do, Jock, is to take a packet for me to my house in Fulsome Street. You understand?"

But here there was a pause. Miggs was evidently hesitating.

"Well?" queried Mittachip.

"Oi'm thinking, sir..."

"What?"

"How can Oi go on your errand when Oi've got to guard this 'ere sheep for you?"

"Oh, damn the sheep!" quoth Master Mittachip, emphatically.

"Well, sir! if you be satisfied..."

"You know my house at Wirksworth?"

"Aye, aye, sir."

"I'll give you a packet. You are to take it to Wirksworth now at once, and to give it to my clerk, Master Duffy, at my house in Fulsome Street. You are quite sure you understand?"

"I dunno as I do!" quoth Jock, vaguely.

But with an impatient oath Sir Humphrey turned into the hut: matters were progressing much too slowly for his impatient temperament. He pushed Mittachip aside, and said peremptorily,—

"Look here, shepherd, you want to earn a guinea, don't you?"

"Aye, sir, that I do."

"Well, here's the packet, and here's a letter for Master Duffy at Master Mittachip's house in Fulsome Street. When Master Duffy has the packet and reads the letter he will give you a guinea. Is that clear?"

And he handed the packet of letters, and also a small note, to Jock Miggs, who seemed to have done with hesitation, for he took them with alacrity.

"Oh! aye! that's clear enough," he said, "'tis writ in this paper that I'm to get the guinea?"

"In Master Mittachip's own hand. But mind! no gossiping, and no loitering. You must get to Wirksworth before cock-crow."

Jock Miggs slipped the packet and the note into the pocket of his smock. The matter of the guinea having been satisfactorily explained to him, he was quite ready to start.

"Noa, for sure!" he said, patting the papers affectionately. "Mum's the word! I'll do your bidding, sir, and the papers'll be safe with me, seeing it's writ on them that I'm to get a guinea."

"Exactly. So you mustn't lose them, you know."

"Noa! noa! I bain't afeeard o' that, nor of the highwaymen; and Beau Brocade wouldn't touch the loikes o' me, bless 'im. But Lordy! Lordy! these be 'mazing times."

Already Sir Humphrey was pushing him impatiently out of the hut.

"And here," added his Honour, pressing a piece of money into the shepherd's hand, "here's half-a-crown to keep you on the go."

"Thank 'ee, sir, and if you think t' sheep will be all right..."

"Oh, hang the sheep!..."

"All right, sir ... if Master Mittachip be satisfied ... and I'll leave t' dog to look after t' sheep."

He took up his long, knotted stick, and still shaking his head and muttering "Lordy! Lordy!" the worthy shepherd slowly began to wend his way along the footpath, which from this point leads straight to Wirksworth.

Sir Humphrey watched the quaint, wizened figure for a few seconds, until it disappeared in the gloom, then he listened for awhile.

All round him the Heath was silent and at peace, the plaintive bleating of the sheep in the pen added a note of subdued melancholy to the vast and impressive stillness. Only from far there came the weird echo of hound and men on the hunt.

His Honour swore a round oath.

"Zounds!" he muttered, "the rogue must be hard pressed, and he's not like to give us further trouble. Even if he come on us now, eh, you old scarecrow? ... the letters are safe at last! What?"

"Lud preserve me!" sighed the attorney, "but I hope so."

"Back to Brassington then," quoth Sir Humphrey, lustily. "Beau Brocade can attack us now, eh? Ha! ha! ha!" he laughed in his wonted boisterous way, "methinks we have outwitted that gallant highwayman after all."

"For sure, Sir Humphrey," echoed Mittachip, who was meekly following his Honour's lead across the road to where their horses were in readiness for them.

"As for my Lady Patience! ... Ha!" said his Honour, jovially, "her brother's life is ... well! ... in my hands, to save or to destroy, according as she will frown on me or smile. But meseems her ladyship will have to smile, eh?"

He laughed pleasantly, for he was in exceedingly good temper just now.

"As for that chivalrous Beau Brocade," he added as he hoisted himself into the saddle, "he shall, an I mistake not, dangle on a gibbet before another nightfall."

"Hark!" he added, as the yelping of the bloodhound once more woke the silent Moor with its eerie echo.

Mittachip's scanty locks literally stood up beneath his bob-tail wig. Even Sir Humphrey could not altogether repress a shudder as he listened to the shouts, the cries, the snarls, which were rapidly drawing nearer.

"We should have waited to be in at the death," he said, with enforced gaiety. "Meseems our fox is being run to earth at last."

He tried to laugh, but his laughter sounded eerie and unnatural, and suddenly it was interrupted by the loud report of a pistol shot, followed by what seemed like prolonged yells of triumph.

Master Mittachip could bear it no longer; with the desperation of intense and unreasoning terror he dug his spurs into his horse's flanks, and like a madman galloped at breakneck speed down the hillside into the valley below.

Sir Humphrey followed more leisurely. He had gained his end and was satisfied.

CHAPTER XXVIII

THE QUARRY

Some few minutes before this the hunted man had emerged upon the road.

As, worn-out, pallid, aching in every limb, he dragged himself wearily forward on hands and knees, it would have been difficult to recognise in this poor, suffering fragment of humanity the brilliant, dashing gentleman of the road, the foppish, light-hearted dandy, whom the countryside had nicknamed Beau Brocade.

The wound in his shoulder, inflamed and throbbing after the breakneck ride from the Court House to the Heath, had caused him almost unendurable agony, against which he had at first resolutely set his teeth. But now his whole body had become numb to every physical sensation. Covered with mud and grime, his hair matted against his damp forehead, the lines of pain and exhaustion strongly marked round his quivering mouth, he seemed only to live through his two senses: his sight and his hearing.

The spirit was there though, indomitable, strong, the dogged obstinacy of the man who has nothing more to lose. And with it all the memory of the oath he had sworn to her.

All else was a blank.

Hunted by men, and with a hound on his track, he had—physically—become like the beasts of the Moor, alert to every sound, keen only on eluding his pursuers, on putting off momentarily the inevitable instant of capture and of death.

Early in the day he had been forced to part from his faithful companion. Jack o' Lantern was exhausted and might have proved an additional source of danger. The gallant beast, accustomed to every bush and every corner of the Heath, knew its way well to its habitual home: the forge of John Stich. Jack Bathurst watched it out of sight, content that it would look after itself, and that being riderless it would be allowed to wend its way unmolested whither it pleased, on the Moor.

And thus he had seen the long hours of this glorious September afternoon drag on their weary course; he had seen the beautiful day turn to late, glowing afternoon, then the sun gradually set in its mantle of purple and gold, and finally the grey dusk throw its elusive and mysterious veil over Tors and Moor. And he, like the hunted beast, crept from gorse bush to scrub, hiding for his life, driven out of one stronghold into another, gasping with thirst, panting with fatigue, determined in spirit, but broken down in body at last.

By instinct and temperament Jack Bathurst was essentially a brave man. Physical fear was entirely alien to his nature: he had never known it, never felt it. During the earlier part of the afternoon, with a score of men at his heels, some soldiers, others but indifferently-equipped louts, he had really enjoyed the game of hide-and-seek on the Heath: to him, at first, it had been nothing more. It was but a part of that wild, mad life he had chosen, the easily-endured punishment for the breaking of conventional laws.

He knew every shrub and crag on this wild corner of the earth which had become his home, and could have defied a small army, when hidden in the natural strongholds known only to himself.

But when he first heard the yelping of the bloodhound set upon his track by the fiendish cunning of an avowed enemy, an icy horror seemed to creep into his very marrow: a horror born of the feeling of powerlessness, of the inevitableness of it all. His one thought now was lest his hand, trembling and numb with fatigue, would refuse him service when he would wish to turn the muzzle of his pistol against his own temple, in time to evade actual capture.

The dog would not miss him. It was practically useless to hide: flight alone, constant, ceaseless flight, might help him for a while, but it was bound to end one way, and one way only: the scent of blood would lead the cur on his track, and his pursuers would find and seize him! bind him like a felon, and hang him! Aye! hang him like a common thief!

He had oft laughed and joked with John Stich about his ultimate probable fate. He knew that his wild, unlawful career would come to an end sooner or later, but he always carried pistols in his belt, and had not even remotely dreamt of capture.

... Until now!

But now he was tired, ill, half-paralysed with pain and exhaustion. His trembling hand crept longingly round the heavy silver handle of the precious weapon. Every natural instinct in him clamoured for death, now, at this very moment before that yelping cur drew nearer, before those shouts of triumph were raised over his downfall.

Only ... after that ... what would happen? He would be asleep and at peace ... but she? ... what would she think? ... that like a coward he had deserted his post ... like a felon he had broken his oath, whilst there was one single chance of fulfilling it ... that he had left her at the mercy of that same enemy who had already devised so much cruel treachery.

And like a beast he crept back within his lair, and watched and listened for that one chance of serving her before the end.

He had seen Sir Humphrey Challoner and Mittachip ambling up the hillside. He tried not to lose sight of them, and, if possible, to keep within earshot, but he was driven back by a posse of his pursuers, close upon his heels, and now having succeeded in reaching the road at last, he had the terrible chagrin of seeing that he was too late; the two men were remounting their horses and turning back towards Brassington.

"Methinks we have outwitted that gallant highwayman after all," Sir Humphrey was saying with one of those boisterous outbursts of merriment, which to Bathurst's sensitive ears had a ring of the devil's own glee in it.

"What hellish mischief have those two reprobates been brewing, I wonder?" he mused. "If those fellows at my heels hadn't cut me off I might have known..."

He crept nearer to the two men, but they set their horses at a sharp trot down the road: Jack vainly strained his ears to hear their talk.

For the last eight hours he had practically covered every corner of the Heath, backwards and forwards, across boulders and through morass; the hound had had some difficulty in finding and keeping the trail, but now it seemed suddenly to have found it, the yelping drew nearer, but the shouts had altogether ceased.

What was to be done? God in heaven, what was to be done?

It was at this moment that the plaintive bleating of one or two of the penned-up sheep suddenly aroused every instinct of vitality in him.

"The sheep!..." he murmured. "A receipt and tally for some sheep!..."

Fresh excitement had in the space of a few seconds given him a new lease of strength. He dragged himself up to his feet and walked almost upright as far as the hut.

There certainly was a flock of sheep in the pen: the dog was watching close by the gate, but the shepherd was nowhere to be seen.

"The sheep! ... A receipt and tally for some sheep! ... In Sir Humphrey Challoner's coat pocket! ..."

Oh! for one calm moment in which to think ... to think!

"The sheep!..." This one thought went on hammering in the poor tired brain, like the tantalising, elusive whisper of a mischievous sprite.

And with it all there was scarce a second to be lost.

The hound, yelping and straining on the leash, was not half a mile away; the next ten or perhaps fifteen minutes would see the end of this awful manhunt on the Moor. And yet there close by, behind those clumps of gorse and the thickset hedge of bramble, was the clearing, where just twenty-four hours ago he had danced that mad rigadoon, with her almost in his arms.

Instinctively, in the wild agony of this supreme moment, Beau Brocade turned his steps thither. This clearing had but two approaches, there where the tough branches of furze had once been vigorously cut into. Last night he had led her through the one whilst Jock Miggs sat beside the other, piping the quaint sad tune.

For one moment the hunted man seemed to live that mad, merry hour again, and from out the darkness fairy fingers seemed to beckon: and her face—just for one brief second—smiled at him out of the gloom.

Surely this was not to be the end! Something would happen, something *must* happen to enable him to render her the great service he had sworn to do.

Oh! if that yelping dog were not quite so close upon his track! Within the next few minutes, seconds even, he would surely think of something that would guide him towards that great goal: *her service*. Oh! for just a brief respite in which to think! a way to evade his captors for a short while—a means to hide! a disguise! anything.

But for once the Moor—his happy home, his friend, his mother—was silent, save for the sound of hunters on his trail, of his doom drawing nearer and nearer, whilst he stood and remembered his dream.

It was madness surely, or else a continuance of that fairy vision, but now it seemed to him, as he stood just there, where yesterday her foot had plied the dear old measure, that his ear suddenly caught once more the sound of that self-same rigadoon.

It was a dream of course. He knew that, and paused awhile, although every second now meant life or death to him.

The tune seemed to evade him. It had been close to his ear a moment ago, now it was growing fainter and fainter, gradually vanishing away: soon he could scarce hear it, yet it seemed something tangible, something belonging to her: it was the tune which she had loved, to which her foot had danced so gladsomely, so he ran after it, ran as fast as his weary body would take him, to the further end of the clearing, whither the sweet, sad tune was leading him with its tender, plaintive echo.

There, just where the clearing debouched upon the narrow path which leads to Wirksworth, he overtook Jock Miggs who was slowly wending his way along, and who just now must have passed quite close to him, blowing on his tiny pipe, as was his wont.

"The shepherd! ... Chorus of angels in paradise lend me your aid now!"

With a supreme effort he pulled his scattered senses together: the mighty fever of self-defence was upon him, that tower of strength which some overwhelming danger will give to a brave man once perhaps in his lifetime. The veil of semi-consciousness, of utter physical prostration, was lifted from his dull brain for this short brief while. The exhausted, suffering, hunted creature had once more given place to the keen, alert son of the Moor, the mad, free child of Nature, with a resourceful head and a daring hand. And for that same brief while the great and mighty power whom men have termed Fate, but whom saints have called God, allowed his untamed spirit to conquer his body and to hold it in bondage, chasing pain away, trampling down exhaustion, whilst disclosing to his burning eyes, amidst the dark and deadly gloom, the magic, golden vision of a newly-awakened hope.

CHAPTER XXIX

THE DAWN

A while ago, in an agony of longing, he had cried out for a moment's respite! for a disguise! and now there stood before him Jock Miggs in smock and broad-brimmed hat, with pipe and shepherd's staff. His pursuers, headed by the yelping dog, were still a quarter of a mile away. Five minutes in which to do battle for his life, for his freedom, for the power to keep his oath! The plan of action had surged in his mind at first sight of the wizened little figure of the shepherd beside the further approach to the clearing.

Beau Brocade drew himself up to his full height, sought and found in the pocket of his coat the black mask which he habitually wore; this he fixed to his face, then drawing a pistol from his belt, he overtook Jock Miggs, clapped him vigorously on the shoulder, and shouted lustily,—

"Stand and deliver!"

Jock Miggs, aroused from his pleasant meditations, threw up his hands in terror.

"The Lud have mercy on my soul!" he ejaculated as he fell on his knees.

"Stand and deliver!" repeated Beau Brocade, in as gruff a voice as he could command.

Jock Miggs was trying to collect his scattered wits.

"B ... b ... but ... kind sir!" he murmured, "y ... y ... you wouldn't harm Jock Miggs, the shepherd ... would you?"

"Quick's the word! Now then..."

"But, good sir ... Oi ... Oi ... Oi've got nowt to deliver..."

Jock Miggs was pitiful to behold: at any other moment of his life Bathurst would have felt very sorry for the poor, scared creature, but that yelping hound was drawing desperately near and he had only a few minutes at his command.

"Naught to deliver?" he said with a great show of roughness, and seizing poor Jock by the collar.

"Look at your smock!"

"My smock, kind sir?..."

"Aye! I've a fancy for your smock ... so off with it ... quick!"

Jock Miggs struggled up to his feet, he was beginning to gather a small modicum of courage. He had lived all his life on Brassing Moor and it was his first serious encounter with an armed gentleman of the road. Whether 'twas Beau Brocade or no he was too scared to conjecture, but he had enough experience of the Heath to know that poor folk like himself had little bodily hurt to fear from highwaymen.

But of course it was always wisest to obey. As to his old smock...

"He! he! he! my old smock, sir!" he laughed vaguely and nervously, "why..."

"I don't want to knock the poor old cuckoo down," murmured Bathurst to himself, "but I've just got three minutes before that cur reaches the top of the clearing and ... Off with your smock, man, or I fire," he added peremptorily, and pointing the muzzle of his pistol at the trembling shepherd.

Miggs had in the meanwhile fully realised that the masked stranger was in deadly earnest. Why he should want the old smock was more than any shepherd could conceive, but that he meant to have it was very clear. Jock uttered a final plaintive word of protest.

"Kind sir ... but if Oi take off my smock ... I sha'nt be quite d ... d ... decent ... sir ... wi' only my shirt."

"You shall have my coat," replied Bathurst, decisively.

"Lud preserve me! ... Your coat, sir!"

"Yes! it's old and shabby, and my waistcoat too.... Now off with that smock, or..."

Once more the muzzle of the pistol gleamed close to Jock Miggs's head. Without further protest he began to divest himself of his smock. The process was slow and laborious, and Jack set his teeth not to scream with the agony of the suspense.

He himself had had little difficulty in taking off his own coat and waistcoat, for earlier in the day, before he had been so hard pressed, the pain in his shoulder had caused him to slip his left arm out of its sleeve.

Moreover, the excitement of these last fateful moments kept him at fever pitch: he was absolutely unconscious of aught save of the rapid flight of the seconds and the steady approach of dog and men towards the clearing.

Even Jock Miggs, who up to now had been too intent on his own adventure to take much heed of what went on in the gloom beyond, even he perceived that something unusual was happening on the Moor.

"What's that?" he asked with renewed terror.

"A posse of soldiers at my heels," said Beau Brocade, decisively, "that's why I want your smock, my man, and if I don't get it there'll be just time to blow out your dull brains before I fall into their hands."

This last argument was sufficiently convincing. Miggs thought it decidedly best to obey; he helped his mysterious assailant on with his own smock, cap and kerchief, and not unwillingly attired himself in Beau Brocade's discarded coat and waistcoat.

"A pistol in your belt in case you need it, friend," whispered Bathurst, rapidly, as he slipped one of the weapons in Miggs's belt, keeping the other firmly grasped in his own hand.

There was no doubt that the hound was on the scent now: the men had ceased shouting but their rapid footsteps could be heard following closely upon the dog, whose master was muttering a few words of encouragement.

Anon there came a whisper, louder than the rest,—

"This way!..."

Then another,—

"There's a path here!"

"Be gy! this confounded darkness!"

"Steady, Roy! steady, old man! Eh? What?"

"This way!"

"Can't you find the trail, old Roy?"

And the gorse was crackling beneath rapid and stealthy footsteps. There was now just the width of the clearing between Beau Brocade and his pursuers.

"This way, Sergeant. Roy's got the trail again."

Neither Jock Miggs nor yet Beau Brocade could see what was going on at the further end of the clearing. The dog, wildly straining against the leash, was quivering with intense excitement, his master hanging on to him with all his might.

Miggs, scared like some sheep lost among a herd of cows, was standing half-dazed, smoothing down with appreciative fingers the fine cloth of his new apparel, terrified every time his hand came in contact with the pistol in his belt.

But Beau Brocade had crept underneath a heavy clump of gorse and bramble, and with his finger on the trigger of his weapon he cowered there, ready for action, his eyes fixed upon the blackness before him.

The next moment the outline of the hound's head and shoulders became faintly discernible in the gloom. With nose close to the ground, powerful jaws dropping and parched tongue hanging out of its mouth, it was heading straight for the clump of gorse where cowered the hunted man.

Beau Brocade took rapid aim and fired. The dog, without a howl, rolled over on its side, whilst Jock Miggs uttered a cry of terror.

Then there was an instant's pause. The pursuers, silenced and awed, had stopped dead, for they had been taken wholly unawares, and for a second or two waited, expecting and dreading yet another shot.

Then a mild, trembling voice came to them from the darkness.

"There 'e is, Sergeant! Just afore you—standing ... see!..."

The Sergeant and soldiers had no need to be told twice. Their pause had only been momentary and already they had perceived the outline of Jock Miggs's figure, standing motionless not far from the body of the dead dog.

With a shout of triumph Sergeant and soldiers fell on the astonished shepherd, whilst the same mild, trembling voice continued to pipe excitedly,—

"Hold 'un tight, Sergeant! Jump on 'im! Tie 'is legs! Sure, an' 'tis he, the rascal!"

Jock Miggs had had no chance of uttering one word of protest, for one of the soldiers, remembering a lesson learnt the day before at the smithy, had thrown his own heavy coat right over the poor fellow's head, effectually smothering his screams. Another man had picked up the still smoking pistol from the ground close to Miggs's feet.

"Pistols!" said the Sergeant, excitedly. "The pair o' them too," he added, pulling the other silver-mounted weapon out of Miggs's belt, and the black mask out of the pocket of his coat: "and silver-mounted, be gy! ... And his mask! ... Now, my men, off with him.... Tie his legs together—off with your belts, quick! ... and you, Corporal, keep that coat tied well over his head ... the rascal's like an eel, and'll wriggle out of your hands if you don't hold him tight.... Remember there's a hundred guineas reward for the capture of Beau Brocade."

Poor old Miggs, smothered within the thick folds of the soldier's coat, could scarce manage to breathe. The men were fastening his knees and ankles together with their leather belts, his arms too were pinioned behind his back.

Thus trussed and spitted like a goose ready for roasting, he felt himself being hauled up on the shoulders of some of the men and then borne triumphantly away.

"We've gotten Beau Brocade!"

"Hip! hip! hurray!"

And so they marched away, shouting lustily, whilst Beau Brocade remained alone on the Heath.

The excitement was over now. He was safe for the moment and free. But the hour of victory seemed like the hour of death; as the last shouts of triumph, the last cry of "Hurrah!" died away in the distance, he fell back against the wet earth; his senses were reeling, the very ground seemed to be giving way beneath his feet, a lurid, red film to be rising before his closing lids, blotting out the darkness of the Moor, and that faint, very faint, streak of grey which had just appeared in the east.

God, to whom he had cried out in his agony, had given him the respite for which he had craved. He was safe and free to think ... to think of her ... and yet now his one longing seemed to be to lie down and rest ... and rest ... and sleep...

Many a night he had lain thus on the open Moor, with the soft, sweet-scented earth for his bed, and the tender buds of heather as a pillow for his head. But to-night he was only conscious of infinite peace, and his trembling hands drew the worthy shepherd's smock closer round him.

His wandering spirit paused awhile to dwell on poor Miggs in his sorry plight.... Ah, well! the morning would see Jock free again, but in the meanwhile...

Then all of a sudden the spirit was back on earth, back to life and to a mad, scarce understandable hope. His hand had come in contact with a packet of letters in the pocket of Miggs's smock.

Far away in the sky the eastern stars had paled before the morning light. One by one the distant peaks of the Derbyshire hills emerged from the black mantle of the night, and peeped down on the valley below, blushing a rosy red. Upon the Heath animal life began to be astir—in the morass beyond a lazy frog started to croak.

Beau Brocade had clasped the letters with cold, numb fingers: he drew them forth and held them before his dimmed eyes.

"The letters!..." he murmured, trembling with the agony of this great unlooked-for joy. "The letters!..."

How they came there, he could not tell. He was too weary, too ill to guess. But that they were her letters he could not for a moment doubt. He had found them! God and His angels had placed them in his hands!

Ah, Fortune! fickle Fortune! the wilful jade and the poor outlaw were to be even then after all. And 'twas Beau Brocade, highwayman, thief, who was destined in a few hours to bring her this great happiness.

"Will she ... will she smile, I wonder..."

He loved to see her smile, and to watch the soft tell-tale blush slowly mounting to her cheek. Ah! now he was dreaming ... dreams that never, never could be. He would bring her back the letters, for he had sworn to her that she should have them ere the sun had risen twice o'er yon green-clad hills. And then all would be over, and she would pass out of his life like a beautiful comet gliding across the firmament of his destiny.

A moment but not to stay.

In the east, far away, rose had changed to gold. From Moor and Heath and Bogland came the sound of innumerable bird-throats singing the great and wonderful hymn of praise, hosanna to awakening Nature.

The outlaw had kept his oath; he turned to where the first rays of the rising sun shed their shimmering mantle over the distant Tors, and in one great uplifting of his soul to his Maker he prayed that sweet death might kiss him when he placed the letters at her feet.

PART IV
H.R.H. THE DUKE OF CUMBERLAND

CHAPTER XXX

SUSPENSE

Throughout the whole range of suffering which humanity is called upon to endure, there is perhaps nothing so hard to bear as suspense.

The uncertainty of what the immediate future might bring, the fast-sinking hope, the slowly-creeping despair, the agony of dull, weary hours: Patience had gone through the whole miserable gamut during that long and terrible day when, obedient to Bathurst's wishes, she had shut herself up in the dingy little parlour of the Packhorse and refused to see anyone save the faithful smith.

And the news which John Stich brought to her from time to time was horrible enough to hear.

He tried to palliate as much as possible the account of that awful battue organised against Beau Brocade, but she guessed from the troubled look on the honest smith's face, and from the furtive, anxious glance of his eyes, that the man whom she had trusted with her whole heart was now in peril, even more deadly than that which had assailed her brother.

And with the innate sympathy born of a true and loving heart, she guessed too how John Stich's simple, faithful soul went out in passionate longing to his friend, who, alone, wounded, perhaps helpless, was fighting his last battle on the Heath.

Yet the trust within her had not died out. Beau Brocade had sworn to do her service and to bring her back the letters ere the sun had risen twice o'er the green-clad hills. To her overwrought mind it seemed impossible that he should fail. He was not the type of man whom fate or adverse circumstance ever succeeded in conquering, and on his whole magnetic personality, on the intense vitality of his being, Nature had omitted to put the mark of failure.

But the hours wore on and she was without further news. Her terror for her brother increased the agony of her suspense. She could see that John Stich too had become anxious about Philip. There was no doubt that with an organised man-hunt on the Moor the lonely forge by the cross-roads would no longer be a safe hiding-place for the Earl of Stretton. The smithy was already marked as a suspected house, and John Stich was known to be a firm adherent of the Gascoynes and a faithful friend of Beau Brocade.

During the course of this eventful day the attention of the Sergeant and soldiers had been distracted, through Bathurst's daring actions, from Stich's supposed nephew out o' Nottingham, but as the beautiful September afternoon turned to twilight and then to dusk, and band after band of hunters set out to scour the Heath, it became quite clear both to Patience and to the smith that Philip must be got away from the forge at any cost.

He could remain in temporary shelter at the Packhorse, under the guise of one of Lady Patience's serving-men, at anyrate until another nightfall, when a fresh refuge could be found for him, according as the events would shape themselves within the next few hours.

Therefore, as soon as the shadows of evening began to creep over Brassing Moor, Stich set out for the cross-roads. He walked at a brisk pace along the narrow footpath which led up to his forge, his honest heart heavy at thought of his friend, all alone out there on the Heath.

The weird echo of the man-hunt did not reach this western boundary of the Moor, but even in its stillness the vast immensity looked hard and cruel in the gloom: the outlines of gorse bush and blackthorn seemed akin to gaunt, Cassandra-like spectres foreshadowing some awful disaster.

Within the forge Philip too had waited in an agony of suspense, whilst twice the glorious sunset had clothed the Tors with gold.

Driven by hunger and cold out of the hiding-place on the Moor which Bathurst had found for him, he had returned to the smithy the first night, only to find John Stich gone and no trace of his newly-found friend. His sister, he knew, must have started for London, but he was without any news as to what had happened in the forge, and ignorant of the gallant fight made therein by the notorious highwayman.

The hour was late then, and Philip was loth to disturb old Mistress Stich, John's mother, who kept house for him at the cottage. Moreover, he had the firm belief in his heart that neither Bathurst nor Stich would have deserted him, had they thought that he was in imminent danger.

Tired out with the excitement of the day, and with a certain amount of hope renewed in his buoyant young heart, he curled himself up in a corner of the shed and forgot all his troubles in a sound sleep.

The next morning found him under the care of old Mistress Stich at the cottage. She had had no news of John, who had wandered out, so she said, about two hours after sunset, possibly to find the Captain; but she thrilled the young man's ears with the account of the daring fight in the forge.

"Nay! but they'll never get our Captain!" said the worthy dame, with a break in her gentle old voice, "and if the whole countryside was after him they'd never get him. Leastways so says my John."

"God grant he may speak truly," replied the young man, fervently; "'tis shame enough on me that a brave man should risk his life for me, whilst I have to stand idly behind a cupboard door."

The absence of definite news weighed heavily upon his spirits, and as the day wore on and neither John Stich nor Bathurst reappeared, his hopes very quickly began to give way to anxiety and then to despair. Philip always had a touch of morbid self-analysis in his nature: unlike Jack Bathurst, he was ever ready to bend the neck before untoward fate, heaping self-accusation on self-reproach, and thus allowing his spirit to bow to circumstance, rather than to attempt to defy it.

And throughout the whole of this day he sat, moody and silent, with the ever-recurring thought hammering in his brain,—

"I ought not to have allowed a stranger to risk his life for me. I should have given myself up. 'Twas unworthy a soldier and a gentleman."

By the time the shadows had lengthened on the Moor, and Jack o' Lantern covered with sweat had arrived riderless at the forge, Philip was formulating wild plans of going to Wirksworth and there surrendering himself to the local magistrate. He worked himself up into a fever of heroic self-sacrifice, and had just resolved only to wait until dawn to carry out his purpose, when John Stich appeared in the doorway of his smithy.

One look in the honest fellow's face told the young Earl of Stretton that most things in his world were amiss just now. A few eager questions, and as briefly as possible Stich told him exactly how matters stood: the letters stolen by Sir Humphrey Challoner, Bathurst's determination to re-capture them and the organized hunt proceeding this very night against him.

"Her ladyship and I both think, my lord, that this place is not safe for you just now," added John, finally, "and she begs you to come to her at Brassington as soon as you can. The road is safe enough," added the smith, with a heavy sigh, "no one'd notice us—they are all after the Captain, and God knows but perhaps they've got him by now."

Philip could say nothing, for his miserable self-reproaches had broken his spirit of obstinacy. His boyish heart was overflowing with sympathy for the kindly smith. How gladly now would he have given his own life to save that of his gallant rescuer!

Obediently he prepared to accede to his sister's wishes. He knew what agony she must have endured when the letters were filched from her; he guessed that she would wish to have him near her, and in any case he wanted to be on the spot, hoping that yet he could offer his own life in exchange for the one which was being so nobly risked for him.

Quite quietly, therefore, and without a murmur, he prepared to accompany Stich back to Brassington. At the Packhorse a serving-man's suit could easily be found for him, and he would be safe enough there, for a little while at least.

John Stich, having tended Jack o' Lantern with loving care, took a hasty farewell of his mother. While his friend's fate and that of his young lord hung in the balance he was not like to get back quietly to his work.

"The Captain may come back here for shelter mayhap," he said, with a catch in his throat, as he kissed the old dame "good-bye"; "you'll tend to him, mother?"

"Aye! you may be sure o' that, John," replied Mistress Stich, fervently.

"He'll need a rest mayhap, and some nice warm water; he's such a dandy, mother, you know."

"Aye! aye!"

"And you might lay out his best clothes for him; he may need 'em mayhap."

"Aye! I've got 'em laid in lavender for him. That nice sky-blue coat, think you, John?"

"Aye, and the fine 'broidered waistcoat, and the black silk bow for his hair, and the lace ruffles for his wrists, and..."

Stich broke down, a great lump had risen in his throat. Would the foppish young dandy, the handsome, light-hearted gallant, ever gladden the eyes of honest John again?

CHAPTER XXXI

"WE'VE GOTTEN BEAU BROCADE!"

The presence of Philip at the inn had done much to cheer Patience in her weary waiting. He and John Stich had reached the Packhorse some time before cockcrow, and the landlord had been only too ready to do anything in reason to further the safety of the fugitive, so long as his own interests were not imperilled thereby.

This meant that he would give Philip a serving-man's suit and afford him shelter in the inn, for as long as the authorities did not suspect him of harbouring a rebel; beyond that he would not go.

Lady Patience had paid him lavishly for this help and his subsequent silence. It was understood that the fugitive would only make a brief halt at Brassington: some more secluded shelter would have to be found for him on the morrow.

For the moment, of course, the thoughts of everyone in the village would be centred in the capture of Beau Brocade. The highwayman had many friends and adherents in the village, people whom his careless and open-handed generosity had often saved from penury. To a man almost, the village folk hoped to see him come out victorious from the awful and unequal struggle which was going on on the Heath. So strong was this feeling that the beadle, who was known to entertain revengeful thoughts against the man who had played him so impudent a trick the day before, did not dare to show his rubicund face in the bar-parlour of either inn on that memorable night.

No one had gone to bed. The men waited about, consuming tankards of small ale, whilst discussing the possibility of their hero's capture. The women sat at home with streaming eyes, plaintively wondering who would help them in future in their distress, if Beau Brocade ceased to haunt the Heath.

Patience herself did not close an eye. Her hand clinging to that of Philip, she sat throughout that long, weary night watching and waiting, dreading the awful dawn, with the terrible news it would bring.

And it was when the first rosy light shed its delicate hue over the tiny old-world village, that the sweet-scented morning air was suddenly filled with the hoarse triumphal cry,—

"We have gotten Beau Brocade!"

"Hip! hip! hip! hurray!"

Wearied and dazed with the fatigue of her long vigil, Patience had sunk into a torpor when those shouts, rapidly drawing nearer to the village, roused her from this state of semi-consciousness.

She hardly knew what she had hoped during these past anxious hours: now that the awful certainty had come, it seemed to stun her with the unexpectedness of the blow.

"We've gotten Beau Brocade!"

The village folk turned out in melancholy groups from the parlour of the inn; they too had entertained vague hopes that their hero would emerge unscathed from the perils which encompassed him; to them too the news of his capture came as that of a sad, irretrievable catastrophe. They congregated in small, excited numbers on the village green, their stolid heads shaking sadly at sight of the squad of soldiers, who were bringing in a swathed-up bundle of humanity, smothered about the head in a scarlet coat, and with hands and legs securely strapped down with a couple of military belts. Only the fine brown cloth coat, the beautifully-embroidered waistcoat and silver-mounted pistol proclaimed that miserable, helpless bundle to be the gallant Beau Brocade.

The soldiers themselves were in a wild state of glee; they had carried their prisoner in triumph all the way from the Heath, and had never ceased shouting until they had deposited him on the green. Owing to the unusual hour, and to the absence of His Honour, Squire West, the pinioned highwayman was to be locked up in the pound until noon.

In the small private parlour of the Packhorse Patience had sat rigid as a statue, while those shouts of triumph seemed to strike her heart as with a hammer. Her fist pressed against her burning mouth, she was making desperate efforts to smother the scream of agony which would have rent her throat.

But with one bound John Stich was soon out of the Packhorse, where he, too, with aching heart and mind devoured with anxiety, had watched and waited through the night.

It did not take him long to reach the green, and using his stalwart elbows to some purpose, he quickly made a way for himself through the small crowd and was presently looking down on the huddled figure which lay helpless on the ground.

There was the Captain's fine brown coat sure enough, with its ample, silk-lined, full skirts, and rich, cut-steel buttons; there was the long, richly-embroidered waistcoat; the lace cuffs at the wrists, and the handsome sword-belt, through which the finely-chased silver handle of the pistol still protruded. But John Stich had need but to cast one glance at the hands, and another at the feet encased in rough countryman's boots, to realise with a sudden, wild exultation of his honest heart that in some way or other his Captain had succeeded in once more playing a trick on his pursuers, and that the man who lay there muffled on the ground was certainly not Beau Brocade.

But even in the suddenness of this intense joy and relief, John Stich was shrewd enough not to betray himself. Obviously every moment, during which the captors enjoyed their mistaken triumph, was a respite gained for the hunted man out on the Heath. Therefore when the Sergeant ordered the rascal to be locked up in the pound awaiting his Honour's orders, and gave Stich a vigorous rap on the shoulder, saying lustily,—

"Well, Master Stich, we've got your friend after all, you see?"

The smith quietly replied,—

"Aye! aye! you've gotten him right enough. No offence, Sergeant! Have a small ale with me before we all go to bed?"

"'Tis nowt to me," he added, seeing with intense satisfaction the heavy bolts of the pound securely pushed home on the unfortunate Jock Miggs.

The Sergeant was nothing loth, and eagerly followed Stich to the bar of the Royal George, where small ale now flowed freely until the sun was high in the heavens.

But as soon as the smith had seen the soldiers safely installed before their huge tankards, he rushed out of the inn and across the green, back to the Packhorse, to bring the joyful news to Lady Patience and her brother.

In the privacy of the little back parlour he was able to give free rein to his joy.

"They'll never get the Captain," he shouted, tossing his cap in the air, "and, saving your ladyship's presence, we was all fools to think they would."

Patience had said nothing when the smith first brought the news. She smiled kindly and somewhat mechanically at the exuberance of his joy, but when honest John once more left her, to glean more detailed account of the great man-hunt on the Heath, she turned to her brother, and falling on her knees she buried her fair head against the lad's shoulder and sobbed in the fulness of her joy as if her heart would break.

CHAPTER XXXII

A PAINFUL INCIDENT

A few hours later, when hunters and watchers had had a little rest, came the rude awakening after the hour of triumph.

Jock Miggs, still trussed and pinioned, had been hauled out of the pound. Master Inch, the beadle, resplendent in gold-laced coat and the majesty of his own importance, had taken the order of ceremony into his own hands.

His Honour, Squire West, would be round at the Court House about noon, and Inch, still smarting under the indignity put upon him through the instrumentality of the highwayman, had devised an additional little plan of revenge.

Sir Humphrey Challoner had emphatically declared that the beadle should be publicly whipped for having dared to lay hands on the Squire of Hartington's person. Master Inch remembered this possible and appalling indignity, which mayhap he would be called upon to suffer, and therefore when the bolts of the pound were first drawn, disclosing the swathed-up bundle of humanity which was supposed to be the highwayman, the beadle shouted in his most stentorian, most pompous tones,—

"To the pond with him!"

The soldiers—most of them lads recruited from the Midland counties, and a pretty rough lot to boot—were only too ready for this additional bit of horseplay.

'Twas fun enough to sit an old scold in the ducking-stool, but to carry on the same game with Beau Brocade, the notorious highwayman, who had defied the four counties and set every posse of soldiers by the ears, would be rare sport indeed.

With a shout of joy they seized Jock Miggs by the legs and shoulders, and with much laughter and many a lively sally they carried him to the shallow duck-pond at the further end of the green. Very sadly, and with many an anxious shake of the head, the village folk followed the little procession, which was headed by the Sergeant and pompous Master Inch.

At the moment when the unfortunate shepherd was being swung in mid-air, preparatory to his immersion in the water, one of the soldiers laughingly dragged away the coat which swathed poor Miggs's head and shoulders, and was near suffocating him.

"We don't want 'im to drown, do we?" he said, just as his comrades dropped the wretched man straight into the pond.

Immediately there was a loud cry from beadle and spectators,—

"Lud love us all! that bain't Beau Brocade!"

And one timid voice added,—

"Why! 'tis Jock Miggs, the shepherd!"

The beadle nearly had a fit of apoplectic rage. That cursed highwayman surely must be in league with the devil himself. The soldiers were gasping with astonishment, and staring open-mouthed at the dripping figure of Jock Miggs, who with unruffled stolidity was quietly struggling out of the water.

"Lordy! Lordy! these be 'mazing times," he muttered in his vague, fatalistic way as he shook himself dry in the sunshine, after the manner of his own woolly sheep-dog.

"Oho! ho! ha! ha! ha!" came in merry chorus from the crowd of village folk, "look at Jock Miggs, the highwayman!"

The soldiers, were absolutely speechless. Master Inch, the beadle, had said emphatically,—

"Damn!"

Truly there was nothing more to be said: those who were inclined to be superstitious felt convinced that the devil himself had had something to do with this amazing substitution.

That it was Beau Brocade who had been captured on the Heath last night none of those who were present at the time doubted for a single instant. To their minds the highwayman had been mysteriously spirited away by the agency of Satan his friend, who had quietly deposited Jock Miggs, the shepherd, in his place.

John Stich, with Mistress Betty beside him, had watched these proceedings from the other end of the green, fully prepared to come to Miggs's assistance and to disclose the latter's identity at once if the horse-play became at all too rough. He now pushed his way through the group of soldiers, and good-naturedly taking hold of the bewildered shepherd's arm, he led him to the porch of the Royal George.

"You'd like to wet your gullet after this, eh, Jock?" he said, as he ordered a tankard of steaming ale to be brought forthwith to the dripping man.

The soldiers, somewhat shamefaced, had pressed into the bar-parlour of the inn: presently there would be a few broken heads in the village as a result of the morning's work, but for the moment the yokels had not begun to chaff: 'twas Jock who was the centre of attraction outside in the porch, sitting on a bench and sipping large quantities of hot ale.

"Let's all drink a glass of ale to the health of Jock Miggs, the highwayman!" came in merry accents from one of the gaffers.

"Hurrah for Jock Miggs, the highwayman!" was the universal gleeful chorus.

"Be gy! Don't he look formidable!" quoth one of the villagers, pointing at the shepherd's scared figure on the bench.

"Let me perish!" said another in mock alarm, "but I'se mightily afeeard o' him."

Mistress Betty too had mixed with the throng, and was eyeing Jock, with irrepressible laughter dancing in her saucy little face.

"Lud! 'tis that funny bit of sheep's wool!" she said gaily. "Faith! and you do look sadly, Jock Miggs, and no mistake! Have you been in the pond?"

"How did 'e foind that out?" queried Miggs, vaguely. "Aye! they dumped Oi in t' pond, they did ... and nearly throttled Oi ... 'tis a blamed shame!"

He had sipped huge tankards of hot ale until he felt thoroughly warm, and was steaming now like a great loaf just out of the oven.

"Dumped ye in the pond?" laughed Mistress Betty. "You were no beauty before, Jock Miggs ... but now ... Oh! Gemini! ... Why, what had you done?"

"I'd done nowt!" retorted the bewildered shepherd. "A foine gentleman he took a fancy to me old smock, he did ... he put a pistol to my head ... then he give me his own beautiful coat for to make me look decent ... and I were just puttin' it on when them soldiers fell on me ... and nigh throttled me, and clapped me in the pound they did..."

"Ye seem to have had a rough time o' it, friend Miggs," said John Stich, kindly.

"Aye, that be so!" commented Jock, vaguely. "'Mazing times these be!"

"They mistook you in your fine clothes for Beau Brocade," explained one of the villagers.

"May be so!" quoth Miggs. "I dunno."

But Mistress Betty held up a rosy finger at the unfortunate shepherd, and said with grave severity,—

"Ye are not Beau Brocade, Jock Miggs, are ye?"

"I dunno!" replied Jock Miggs with imperturbable vagueness. "I don't rightly know who Oi be! I think them soldiers made a mistake, but I dunno."

He was undoubtedly the hero of the hour, and the rest of his morning was spent in pleasant conviviality with all his friends in the village, until by about noon the worthy shepherd was really hopelessly at sea as to who he really was. At one o'clock he became quite convinced that he was Beau Brocade the highwayman—or at any rate a very dangerous character—and had only escaped hanging through his reputation of supernatural cunning and bravery.

The Sergeant and soldiers were drowning their acute disappointment in the bar-parlour of the Royal George. They certainly were not in luck, for even at the very moment when egged on by the Sergeant they were planning a fresh battue of the Heath, there came into Brassington an advance guard from the Duke of Cumberland, with the news that His Royal Highness would pass through the village with his army corps on his way to the north. The Sergeant was requisitioned to arrange for His Highness's quarters at the Royal George: the men would not be allowed to go hunting after a highwayman, in case their officers had need of them for other purposes.

All thoughts of a fresh hunt after their elusive quarry would therefore have to be abandoned until after the army had passed through Brassington, and Sergeant and soldiers could but hope that they would be left behind, in order that they might make one more gigantic attempt to earn the hundred guineas reward, offered for the capture of Beau Brocade.

CHAPTER XXXIII

THE AWAKENING

John Stich could scarce contain himself for joy. Fate indeed and all the angels in heaven had ranged themselves on the side of his Captain.

That Beau Brocade should have emerged unconquered after all out of the terrible position in which he was placed last night, seemed to the worthy smith nothing short of miraculous, and only accomplished through the special agency of heaven, whose most cherished child the gallant highwayman most undoubtedly was, in his friend's enthusiastic estimation.

For the moment, therefore, the kindly smith felt tolerably happy about his friend. The presence of His Royal Highness the Duke of Cumberland with his army corps in this part of the country would do much towards keeping the Sergeant and soldiers' attention away from the Heath, at any rate for a day or two. Perhaps the squad now quartered at Brassington would be drafted to one of the regiments, and a fresh contingent, composed of men who'd have no special bone to pick with the highwayman, left behind for the still active hunt against the rebels.

But this train of thought brought the faithful smith's mind back to the Earl of Stretton and the stolen letters. Reassured momentarily as to his friend, he was still aware of the grave peril which threatened his young lord.

Neither he nor Lady Patience could conjecture what had become of the letters. Sir Humphrey Challoner, after his woeful adventure in Brassington, had condescended to accept Squire West's hospitality for the nonce. Stich had spied him in the course of the morning, walking in the direction of the village in close conversation with his familiar, Master Mittachip, attorney-at-law. In spite of the momentary respite in his anxiety, the smith felt that there lay still the real danger to Beau Brocade and to Lord Stretton. Moreover, by now he longed to see his friend and to learn how he'd fared. Vaguely in his honest heart he feared that the young man had succumbed on the Heath to pain and fatigue, and mayhap had failed to reach the forge.

When he saw the entire population of Brassington busy with Jock Miggs, and the soldiers intent on the news from the Duke of Cumberland's advance guard, he determined to set out for the crossroads, in the hopes of finding the Captain at the forge.

He had just crossed the green and turned into the narrow bridle-path which led straight to his smithy, when he spied a yokel, dressed in a long smock and wearing a broad-brimmed hat, coming slowly towards him. The man was leaning heavily on a thick knotted stick and seemed to be walking with obvious pain and fatigue.

Some unexplainable instinct caused the smith to wait awhile until the yokel came a little nearer. This corner of the village was quite deserted; the laughter of the folk assembled round the Royal George could be heard only as a distant echo from across the green. The next moment the smith uttered a quickly-suppressed cry of astonishment as he recognised Bathurst's face underneath the broad-brimmed hat.

"Sh! ... sh ... sh!" whispered the young man hurriedly—"her ladyship? ... can I see her?"

"Yes! yes!" replied John, whose honest eyes were resting anxiously on his friend's pallid face, "but you, Captain? ... you?..."

He did not like to formulate the question, and Bathurst interrupted him quickly.

"I've rested awhile at the forge, John ... your mother was an angel ... and now I want to see her ladyship."

John's honest heart misgave him. His friend's fresh young voice sounded hoarse and unnatural, there was a restless, feverish glitter in his eyes, and the slender, tapering hand which rested on the stick trembled visibly.

"You ought to be in bed, Captain," he muttered gruffly, "and well nursed too; you are ill..."

"I am sufficiently alive, friend, at any rate to serve Lady Patience to the end."

"I'll go tell her ladyship," said the smith, with a sigh.

"Say a man from the village would wish to speak with her.... Don't mention my name, John ... she'll not know me, I think.... 'Tis best that she should not.... And I look a miserable object enough, don't I?" he added with a feeble laugh.

"Her ladyship would command you to rest if she knew..."

"I don't wish her to know, friend," said Jack, smiling in spite of himself at the good fellow's vehemence, "her tender pity would try to wean me from my purpose, which is to serve her with the last breath left in me. And now, quick, John.... Don't worry about me, old friend.... I am only a little tired after that scramble on the Heath ... and the wound that limb of Satan dealt me is at times rather troublesome.... But I am very tough, you know.... All my plans are made, and I'll follow you at a little distance. Beg her ladyship to speak with me in the passage of the inn ... 'twould excite too much attention if I went up to her parlour.... No one'll know me, never fear."

John knew of old how useless it was to argue with the Captain once he had set his mind on a definite course of action. Without further protest, therefore, and yet with a heavy heart, he turned and quickly walked back through the village to the Packhorse, followed at some little distance by Bathurst.

In order to arouse as little suspicion as possible, it had been necessary for the young Earl of Stretton to mix from time to time with the servant and the barman of the inn. He was supposed to be an additional serving-man, come to help at the Packhorse in view of her ladyship's unexpected stay there. In this out-of-the-way village of Brassington no one knew him by sight, and he was in comparative safety here, until nightfall, when he meant to strike up country again for shelter.

He was standing in the shadow behind the bar, when John Stich entered the parlour, bearing the message from Beau Brocade. The room was dark and narrow, over-filled with heavy clouds of tobacco smoke and with the deafening clamour of loud discussions and exciting narratives carried on by two or three soldiers and some half-dozen villagers over profuse tankards of ale.

John Stich managed to reach Philip's ear without exciting attention. The young man at once slipped out of the room, in order to tell his sister that a yokel bearing important news would wish to speak with her privately.

Her heart beating with eagerness and apprehension, Patience hurried down the narrow stairs, and in the passage found herself face to face with a man dressed in a long, dingy smock, and whose features she could not distinguish beneath the broad brim of his hat.

He raised a respectful hand to his forelock as soon as he was in her ladyship's presence, but did not remove his hat.

"You wished to speak with me, my man?" asked Lady Patience, eagerly.

"I have a message for to deliver to Lady Patience Gascoyne," said Bathurst, whose voice, hoarse and quavering with fatigue, needed no assumption of disguise. He kept his head well bent, and the passage was very dark.

Patience, with her thoughts fixed on the gallant, upright figure she had last seen so full of vitality and joy in the little inn-parlour upstairs, scarce gave more than a passing glance to the stooping form, leaning heavily on a stick before her.

"Yes, yes," she said impatiently, "you have a message? From whom?"

"I don't rightly know, my lady ... a gentleman 'twas ... on the Heath this morning ... he give me this letter for your ladyship."

Burying his tell-tale, slender hand well inside the capacious sleeve of Jock Miggs's smock, Bathurst handed Patience a note written by himself. She took it from him with a glad little cry, and when he turned to go she put a restraining hand on his arm.

"Wait till I've read the letter," she said, "I may wish to send an answer."

She unfolded the letter slowly, very slowly, he standing close beside her and watching the tears gathering in her eyes as she began to read, murmuring the words half audibly to herself:—

"Have no fear. I have the letters, and with your permission will take them straight to London. I have a powerful friend there who will help me to place them before the King and Council without delay. To carry this safely through it is important that I should not be seen again in Brassington, as Sir Humphrey Challoner luckily has lost track of me for the moment, and I can be at Wirksworth before nightfall, and on my way to London before another dawn. Your enemy will keep watch on *you*, so I entreat you to stay in Brassington so as to engage his attention, whilst I go to London with the letters. His lordship would be safest, I think, in the cottage of old Widow Coggins at Aldwark. It has been my good fortune to do her some small service; she'll befriend his lordship for my sake. John Stich will convey him thither as soon as maybe. I entreat you to be of good cheer. A few days will see your brother a free man, and rid you for ever of your enemy. Believe me, the plan I have had the honour to set forth is safe and quick, and on my knees I beg you to allow me to carry it through in your service."

She folded the letter and then slipped it into the folds of her gown.

Through the open doorway behind her a ray of sunshine came shyly peeping in, framing her graceful figure with a narrow fillet of gold. They were alone in the passage, and she, intent upon the precious letter, was taking no notice of him: thus he could feast his eyes once more upon his dream, his beautiful white rose, drooping with the dew, the graceful silhouette outlined against the sunlit picture beyond, the queenly head, with its wealth of soft golden hair, bent with rapt attention on the letter which trembled in her hand.

His whole being ached with mad passionate longing for her, his lips burned with a desire to cover her neck and throat with kisses, yet he would have knelt on the flagstones before her and worshipped as did the saints before Our Lady's shrine. In his heart was a great joy that he could do her service, and a strange, wild hope that he might die for her.

"The gentleman who gave you this letter..." she said with a slight catch in her low, melodious voice. "You saw him? ... He was well? ... How did he look?..."

Her eyes now were swimming in tears, and Bathurst had much ado to still the mad beating of his heart, and to force his voice to a natural tone.

"Lud, my lady," he said, "but he was just like any other body Oi thought."

"Not ill?"

"Noa! noa! not that Oi could see."

"Go back to him, friend," she said, with sudden eagerness, "tell him that he must come to me at once ... I ... I would speak with him."

It required all Bathurst's firm strength of will not to betray himself before her. The tender pleading in her eyes, the gentle, womanly sympathy in her voice, set all his pulses beating. But he had made up his mind that she should not know him just then. A look, a cry, might give him away, and there was but one chance now to be of useful service to her, and that was to take the letters at once to London, whilst their joint enemy had for the nonce no thought of him.

Therefore he contrived to say quite stolidly,—

"Noa, noa, the gentleman said to Oi, 'You can bring a message, but th' lady mustn't come nigh me!'"

She gave a quick little sigh of disappointment.

"Then, my good fellow," she said, "try to remember ... tell him ... tell him ... I would wish to thank him ... tell him.... Nay! nay!" she suddenly added, pulling a faded white rose from her belt, "tell him nothing ... but give him this flower ... in token that I have received his letter ... and will act as he bids me.... You'll remember?"

He dared not trust himself to speak, but as she held out the rose to him he took it from her hand and involuntarily his finger-tips came in contact with hers just for a second ... long enough for the divine magnetism of his great love to pass from him to her.

She seized hold of his hand, for in that one magnetic touch she had recognised him. Her heart gave a great leap of joy, the joy of being near him once more, of again feeling the tender, grey eyes resting with passionate longing on her face. But she uttered neither cry nor word, for it was a great, silent and godlike moment—when at last she understood.

He had stooped still lower and rested his burning lips upon her cool fingers, and upon the rose which she had worn at her breast.

Neither of them spoke, for their hearts were in perfect unison, their whole being thrilled with the wild, jubilant echo of a divine hosanna, and around them the legions of God's angels made a rampart of snow-white wings, to shut out all the universe from them, leaving them alone with their love.

CHAPTER XXXIV

A LIFE FOR A LIFE

That moment was brief, as all such great and happy moments are.

But a few seconds had passed since both her hands had rested in his, and he forgot the world in that one kiss upon her finger-tips.

The next instant a fast-approaching noise of hurrying footsteps, accompanied by much shouting, roused them from their dream.

Both through the back and the front door a crowd of excited soldiers had pushed their way into the inn, whilst the folk in the bar-parlour, attracted by the sudden noise, pressed out into the narrow passage to see what was happening.

John Stich, foremost amongst these, made a rush for Patience's side. She found herself suddenly pressed back towards the foot of the stairs, and face to face with a noisy group of village folk, through which the Sergeant and some half-dozen soldiers were roughly pushing their way.

She looked round her, helpless and bewildered. Jack Bathurst had disappeared.

The whole thing had occurred in the brief space of a few seconds, even before Patience had had time to realise that anything was amiss.

The narrow staircase, at the foot of which she now stood, led straight up to the private parlour, where Philip was even now awaiting her return.

"Out of the way, you rascals," the Sergeant was shouting, whilst elbowing his way through the small group of gaping yokels, and pressing forward towards the stairs.

"Will your ladyship allow me the privilege of conducting you out of this crowd?" said a suave voice at Patience's elbow.

Sir Humphrey Challoner, closely followed by the obsequious Mittachip, had pushed his way into the inn, in the wake of the soldiers, and was now standing between her and the crowd, bowing very deferentially and offering her his arm, to conduct her upstairs.

But a few moments ago he had heard the startling news that Jock Miggs had been captured on the Heath, in mistake for Beau Brocade. As far as Sir Humphrey could ascertain nothing of importance had been found on the shepherd's person, and in a moment he realised that, through almost supernatural cunning, the highwayman must have succeeded in filching the letters, and by now had no doubt once more restored them to Lady Patience.

All the scheming, the lying, the treachery of the past few days had therefore been in vain; but Sir Humphrey Challoner was not the man to give up a definite purpose after the first material check to his plans. If her ladyship was once more in possession of the letters, they must be got away from her again. That was all. And if that cursed highwayman was still free to-day, 'sdeath but he'll have to hang on the morrow.

In the meanwhile Philip's momentary safety was a matter of the greatest moment to Sir Humphrey Challoner. If that clumsy lout of a Sergeant got hold of the lad, all Sir Humphrey's schemes for forcing Lady Patience's acceptance of his suit by means of the precious letters would necessarily fall to the ground.

But instinctively Patience recoiled from him; his suave words, his presence near her at this terrible crisis, frightened her more effectually than the Sergeant's threatening attitude. She drew close to John Stich, who had interposed his burly figure between the soldiers and the foot of the stairs.

"Out of the way, John Stich," shouted the Sergeant, peremptorily, "this is not your forge, remember, and by G—— I'll not be tricked again."

"Those are her ladyship's private rooms," retorted the smith, without yielding one inch of the ground. "Landlord," he shouted at the top of his voice, "I call upon you to protect her ladyship from these ruffians."

"You insult His Majesty's uniform," quoth the Sergeant, briefly, "and do yourself no good, smith. As for the landlord of this inn, he interferes 'tween me and my duty at his peril."

"But by what right do you interfere with me, Master Sergeant?" here interposed Lady Patience, trying to assume an indifferent air of calm haughtiness. "Do you know who I am?"

"Aye! that I do, my lady!" responded the Sergeant, gruffly, "and that's what's brought me here this morning. Not half an hour ago I heard that Lady Patience Gascoyne was staying at the Packhorse, and now the folks say that a new serving-man came to give a helping hand here. He arrived in the middle of the night, it seems. Strange time for a serving-man to turn up, ain't it?"

"I know nothing of any servant at this inn, and I order you at once to withdraw your men, and not to dare further to molest me."

"Your pardon, my lady, but my orders is my orders: I have been sent here by His Royal Highness the Duke of Cumberland hisself to hunt out all the rebels who are in hiding in these parts. I've strict orders to be on the lookout for Philip James Gascoyne, Earl of Stretton, who, I understand, is your ladyship's own brother, and as I've a right o' search, I mean to see who else is staying in those rooms upstairs besides your ladyship."

"This is an outrage, Sergeant!"

"Maybe, my lady," he retorted drily, "but with us soldiers orders is orders, saving your presence. I was tricked at the smithy, and again on the Heath. My belief is that we were hunting a bogey last night, There may or mayn't be any highwayman called Beau Brocade, but there was a fine young gallant at the forge the day afore yesterday, who did for me and my men, and I'll take my oath that he was none other than the rebel, Philip Gascoyne, Earl of Stretton."

"'Tis false and you talk like a madman, Sergeant."

"Maybe! but your ladyship'll please stand aside until I've searched those rooms upstairs, or I'll have to order my men to lay hands on your ladyship. Now then, John Stich, stand aside in the name of the King!"

John Stich did not move, and Lady Patience still stood defiant and haughty at the foot of the stairs. The villagers, stolid and stupid, were staring open-mouthed, not daring to interfere. But of course it was only a question of seconds, the worthy smith could not guard the staircase for long against the Sergeant and a dozen soldiers, and in any case nothing would be of any avail. Philip in the room upstairs was trapped like a fox in its lair, and nothing could save him now from falling into the soldiers' hands.

In vain she sought for Bathurst among the crowd: with wild, unreasoning agony she longed for him in this moment of her greatest need, and he was not there. She felt sure that if only he were near her he would think of something, do something, to avert the appalling catastrophe.

"I give your ladyship one minute's time to stand quietly aside," said the Sergeant, roughly. "After that I give my men orders to lay hands on you, and on any one who dares to interfere."

"Give me the letters," whispered Sir Humphrey Challoner, insinuatingly, in her ear. "I can yet save your brother."

"How?" she murmured involuntarily.

He looked up towards the top of the stairs.

"Then he *is* up there?"

She did not reply. It was useless to deny it, the next few moments would bring the inevitable.

"Stand back, Sergeant," quoth John Stich, defiantly. "I have the honour to protect her ladyship's person against any outrage from you."

"Good words, smith," retorted the Sergeant, "but I tell ye I've been tricked twice by you and I mean to know the reason why. Let her ladyship allow me to search the room upstairs and I'll not lay hands on her."

"Ye shall not pass," repeated the smith, obstinately.

"The letters," whispered Sir Humphrey, "give me the letters and I pledge you my honour that I can save him yet."

But half mad with terror and misery, scornful, defiant, she turned on him.

"Your honour!" she said, with infinite contempt.

But in her inmost heart she murmured in agonised despair,—

"What's to be done? Oh, God, protect him!"

"Stand back, John Stich," repeated the Sergeant, for the third time, "or I give my men the order to charge. Now then, my men!"

"Ye shall not pass!" was the smith's persistent, obstinate answer to the challenge.

"Forward!" shouted the soldier in a loud voice. "Into it, my men! Use your bayonets if anyone interferes with ye!"

The soldiers, nothing loth, were ready for the attack: there had already been too much parleying to suit their taste. They had been baffled too often in the last few days to be in the mood to dally with a woman, be she her ladyship or no.

With a loud cry they made a dash for the stairway, which behind Stich and Lady Patience lost itself in the gloom above.

And it was from out this darkness that at this moment a light-hearted, fresh young voice struck upon the astonished ears of all those present.

"Nay! too much zeal, friend Stich. Stand aside, I pray you. Faith! it'll give me great pleasure to converse with these gallant lobsters."

And Jack Bathurst, pushing the bewildered smith gently to one side, came down the stairs with a smile upon his face, calm, debonnair, dressed as for a feast.

He had discarded Jock Miggs's long smock, broad-brimmed hat and kerchief, and appeared in all the gorgeous finery of the beautiful lavender-scented clothes, he had donned at the forge with the kindly aid of Mistress

Stich. He was still very pale and there were a few lines of weariness and of bodily pain round the firm, sensitive mouth, but his grey eyes, deep-sunk and magnetic, glowed with the keen fire of intense excitement. The coat of fine blue cloth set off his tall, trim figure to perfection. His left hand was tucked into the opening of his exquisitely embroidered waistcoat, and dainty ruffles of delicate Mechlin lace adorned his neckcloth and wrists. As he appeared there, handsome, foppish and smiling, 'twas no wonder that the countryside had nicknamed him Beau Brocade.

"Well! my gallant friend!" he said, addressing the Sergeant, since the latter seemed too astonished to speak, "what is it you want with me, eh?"

The Sergeant was gradually recovering his breath. Fate apparently was playing into his hands. It was almost too bewildering for any bluff soldier to realise, but it certainly seemed pretty clear that the rebel Earl of Stretton and Beau Brocade the highwayman were one and the same person.

"You are Philip Gascoyne, Earl of Stretton?" he asked at last.

"Faith! you've guessed that, have you?" responded Bathurst, gaily. "Odd's life, 'tis marvellous how much penetration lies hidden beneath that becoming coat of yours."

"Then, Philip Gascoyne, Earl of Stretton, you are attainted by Parliament for high treason, and I arrest you in the name of the King!"

There were indeed many conflicting emotions raging in the hearts of all those present whilst this brief colloquy was going on.

John Stich, accustomed to implicit obedience where his Captain's actions were concerned, had not dared to speak or stir. Sir Humphrey Challoner, completely thrown off his mental balance by the unexpected appearance of Bathurst, was hastily trying to make up his bewildered mind as to what was now best to be done.

As to Patience herself, at first a great, an overwhelming joy and pride had seized her at the thought that he was near her now, that he had not deserted her in the hour of her greatest need, that once again he had interposed his magnetic, powerful personality between her and the danger which threatened her and Philip.

It was only when the Sergeant's momentous words, "I arrest you in the name of the King!" rang out clearly and decisively above the loud tumult which was beating in her heart, that she became aware of the deadly peril which threatened the man she loved.

True, he had come once more between her and danger, but once again he had done it at risk of his life, and was like at last to lay it down for her.

She had been standing a little to one side, turning, as all had done, toward the elegant, foppish figure in the fine clothes and dainty ruffles of lace, but now she stepped forward with mad, unreasoning impulse, thrusting herself between him and the Sergeant, and trying to shield him behind the folds of her cloak.

"No! no! no! no!" she said excitedly. "Sergeant, 'tis all a mistake! ... I swear..."

But already Jack Bathurst had bent forward, and had contrived to whisper, unheard by all save her,—

"Hush—sh—your brother ... remember his danger..."

"Your pardon, lady," said the Sergeant, seeing that she paused, irresolute, not knowing what to do in face of this terrible alternative which was confronting her. "Your pardon, lady, but this gentleman is Philip, Earl of Stretton, is he not?"

"For your brother's sake," whispered Bathurst once more.

"No ... yes ... Oh! my God!" murmured Patience, in the agony of this appalling misery.

Her brother or the man she loved. One or the other betrayed by one word from her, now at this moment, with no time to pray to God for help or guidance, no chance of giving her own life for both!

"Out on you, friend," said Bathurst, lightly, "do you not see her ladyship is upset. Nay! have no fear, I'll follow you quietly!" he added, seeing that the Sergeant and soldiers were making a motion to surround him, "but you'll grant me leave to say farewell to my sister?"

The Sergeant could not very well refuse. He was at heart a humane man, and now that he was sure of this important capture, he would have done a good deal to ingratiate himself, through little acts of courtesy, with Lady Patience Gascoyne.

However, he had no mind to be tricked again, and in face of an almost immediate execution for high treason, the prisoner seemed extraordinarily self-possessed and cheerful. But for her ladyship's obvious despair and sorrow, the worthy Sergeant might even now have had some misgivings.

As it was, he told off three men to mount the stairs, and to stand on guard at the top of them, in case the prisoner made a dash that way, in the hopes of reaching the roof. The Sergeant still kept an idea in his mind that some supernatural agency was at work in favour of this extraordinary man, who up to now had seemed to bear a charmed life. He had the little narrow passage and hall of the inn cleared of the gaping yokels, who went off one by one, scratching their addled polls, wondering what it all meant, and who was Beau Brocade. Was he the Earl of Stretton? was he the highwayman? or some pixie from the Heath with power to change himself at will?

Sir Humphrey Challoner retired within the shadow of the stairway. On the whole he preferred to leave the events to shape their own course. In one way Fate had befriended him. Whether hanged in his own name or in that of the Earl of Stretton, the highwayman would within the next few hours be safely out of the way, and then it would be easier no doubt to obtain possession of the letters once again.

He too like the Sergeant and soldiers, felt an instinctive dread of supernatural agency in connection with Beau Brocade. In these days there existed still a deeply-rooted belief in witchcraft, and the educated classes were not altogether proof against the popular superstitions.

Sir Humphrey had a curious, intense hatred for the man who had so chivalrously championed Lady Patience's cause. His own love for her was so selfish and lustful that overpowering jealousy formed its chief characteristic. He was frantically, madly jealous of Jack Bathurst, for with the keen eyes of the scorned suitor, he had noted the look of joy and pride in her face when the young man first appeared on the stairs, and he alone of all those present knew how to interpret her obvious despair, her terrible misery, when brought face to face with the awful alternative of giving up her brother or the man she loved.

Sir Humphrey swore some heavy oaths under his breath at thought of the scorn with which she had rejected him. Womanlike, she had yielded to the blandishments of that thief, and proud Lady Patience Gascoyne had fallen in love with a highwayman!

But now Fate meant to be kind to Sir Humphrey. With that chivalrous coxcomb out of the way, Lady Patience would be once more at his mercy. Philip was still a fugitive under the ban of attainder, and the letters could be got hold of once again, unless indeed the devil, with an army of witches and evil sprites, came to the assistance of that rascal Beau Brocade.

CHAPTER XXXV

QUITS

Hemmed in by a compact little group of soldiers at the foot of the stairs, and with three men on guard at the head of it, Bathurst and Patience had but a few minutes in which to live these last brief moments of their love.

She clung passionately to him, throwing aside all the haughty reserve of her own proud nature: conquered by her great love: a woman only, whose very life was bound up in his.

"They shall not take you!" she moaned in the agony of her despair. "They shall not.... I will not let you go!"

And he held her in his arms now, savouring with exquisite delight this happiest moment of his life, the joy of feeling her tender form clinging to him in passionate sorrow, to see the tears gathering in her blue eyes, one by one, for him and to know that her love—her great, measureless, divine love—was at last wholly his.

But the moments were brief, and the Sergeant below was already waxing impatient. He drew her gently into a dark angle of the stairs, up against the banisters, and taking the packet of letters from his pocket, he pressed them into her hand.

"The letters! quick!" he whispered. "God guard you and him!"

"The letters?" she murmured mechanically.

"Aye! I can do nothing now ... but try to see the Duke of Cumberland before you go to London, show him the letters.... He may be in this village to-day ... if not, you can see him at Wirksworth.... He has power to stay execution even if your brother is arrested ... he might use it, if he had seen the letters..."

"Yes! yes!" she murmured.

Sorrow seemed to have dazed her, she did not quite know what she was doing, but her left hand closed instinctively over the precious packet, then dropped listlessly by her side.

Neither she nor Bathurst had perceived a thin, attenuated figure hoisting itself monkey-wise over the dark portion of the banisters.

"Try and hear what those two are saying," Sir Humphrey had whispered, and the attorney, obedient and obsequious, had made a desperate effort to do as he was bid. The staircase was but partially lighted by a glimmer of daylight, which came slanting round the corner from the passage. The banisters were in complete shadow, and the Sergeant and soldiers were too intent on watching their prisoner to notice Master Mittachip or Sir Humphrey.

The next moment Patience felt a terrific wrench on all her fingers; even as she uttered a cry of pain and alarm, the packet of letters was torn out of her hand from behind, and she was dimly conscious of a dark figure clambering over the banisters and disappearing into the darkness below.

But with a mad cry of rage Jack Bathurst had bounded after that retreating figure; wholly taken by surprise, he only saw the dim outline of Mittachip's attenuated form, as the latter hastily dropped the packet of letters at Sir Humphrey Challoner's feet, who stooped to pick them up. Like an infuriated wild beast Jack fell on Sir Humphrey.

"You limb of Satan!" he gasped. "You ... you.... Give me back those letters! ... Stich! Stich! quick!..."

The force of the impact had thrown both men to the ground. Bathurst was gripping his antagonist by the throat with fingers of steel. But already the Sergeant and his men had come to the rescue, dragging Jack away from the prostrate figure of Sir Humphrey, whilst the soldiers from above had run down and were forcibly keeping John Stich in check.

Freed from his powerful antagonist, his Honour quietly picked himself up, readjusted his crumpled neckcloth and flicked the dust from off his coat. He was calmly thrusting the packet of letters in his pocket, whilst the Sergeant was giving orders to his men to bind their prisoner securely, if he offered further resistance.

"Sergeant!" said Bathurst, despairingly, "that miscreant has just stolen some letters belonging to her ladyship."

"Silence, prisoner!" commented the Sergeant. "You do yourself no good by this violence."

It seemed as if Fate meant to underline this terrible situation with a final stroke of her ironical pen, for just then the quiet village street beyond suddenly became alive with repeated joyous shouts and noise of tramping feet. In a moment the dull, monotonous air of Brassington was filled with a magnetic excitement which seemed to pervade all its inhabitants at once, and even penetrated within the small dingy inn, where the last act of a momentous drama was at this moment being played.

"It must be the Duke of Cumberland's army!" quoth the Sergeant, straining his ears to catch the sound of a fast-approaching cavalcade.

"Then you'll please His Royal Highness with the smart capture you've made, Sergeant," said Sir Humphrey, with easy condescension.

This was indeed Fate's most bitter irony. "The Duke has power to stay execution, and would use it if you showed him the letters!" These were the last words of counsel Bathurst had given Patience, and now with freedom for her brother almost within her grasp, she was powerless to do aught to save him.

"The letters, Sir Humphrey!" she murmured imploringly, "an you've a spark of honour left in you."

"Nay!" he retorted under his breath, with truly savage triumph, "an you don't close your lover's mouth, I'll hand your brother over to these soldiers too, and then destroy the letters before your eyes."

He turned, and for a moment regarded with an almost devilish sneer the spectacle of his enemy rendered helpless at last. Bathurst, like some fettered lion caught in a trap, was still making frantic efforts to free himself, until a violent wrench on his wounded shoulder threw him half unconscious on his knees.

"Ha! ha! ha!" laughed Sir Humphrey, "I think, my chivalrous friend, you and I are even at last."

"Come, prisoner, you'd best follow me quietly now," said the Sergeant, touched in spite of himself by Patience's terrible sorrow.

But at Sir Humphrey's final taunt Jack Bathurst had shaken off the deadly feeling of sickness which was beginning to conquer him. He threw back his head, and with the help of the soldiers struggled again to his feet. The clamour outside was beginning to be louder and more continuous: through it all came the inspiriting sound of a fast-approaching regimental band.

"The Duke of Cumberland, is it, Sergeant?" he said suddenly.

"Marching through the village on his way to the north," assented the Sergeant. "Now then, prisoner..."

"Nay, then, Sergeant," shouted Jack in a loud voice, as, wrenching his right arm from the grasp of the soldier who held him, he pointed to Sir Humphrey Challoner, "detain that man! ... An I am the rebel Earl of Stretton, he was my accomplice, and has all the papers relating to our great conspiracy at this moment about his person ... the door!—the door!" he added excitedly, "take care! ... he'll escape you! ... and he has papers on him now that would astonish the King."

Instinctively the soldiers had rushed for both the doorways, and when Sir Humphrey, with a shrug of the shoulders, made a movement as if to go, the Sergeant barred the way and said,—

"One moment, sir."

"You would dare?" retorted Sir Humphrey, haughtily. "Are you such a consummate fool as not to see that that man is raving mad?"

"Search him, Sergeant!" continued Bathurst, excitedly, "you'll find the truth of what I say.... Search him ... her ladyship knows he was my accomplice.... Search him!—the loss of those papers'd cost you your stripes."

The Sergeant was not a little perplexed. Already, the day before, the seizure of Sir Humphrey Challoner's person had been attended with disastrous consequences for the beadle of Brassington, and now....

No doubt the Sergeant would never have ventured, but the near approach of the Duke of Cumberland's army, and of his own superior officers, gave the worthy soldier a certain amount of confidence. He had full rights and powers of search, and had been sent to this part of the country to hunt for rebels. He had been tricked and hoodwinked more often than he cared to remember, and he knew that his superior officers would never blame him for following up a clue, even if thereby he was somewhat overstepping his powers.

"The papers," continued Bathurst, "the papers which'll prove his guilt ... the papers! or he'll destroy them."

The Sergeant gave a last look at his prisoner. He seemed secure enough guarded by three men, who were even now strapping his hands behind his back. The accusation therefore could be no trick to save his own skin, and who knows? if the Earl of Stretton was a rebel lord, then why not the Squire of Hartington?

"Seize him, and search him!" commanded the Sergeant, "in the name of the King!"

"Your pardon, sir," he added deferentially, "but the Duke of Cumberland is within earshot almost, and I should be cashiered if I neglected my duty."

"This is an outrage!" cried Sir Humphrey, who had become purple with rage.

"It's doing your Honour no harm! and if I've done wrong no doubt I shall be punished. Search him, my men!"

It was Sir Humphrey's turn now to be helpless in the hands of the soldiers. He knew quite well that the Sergeant was within his duty and would certainly not get punished for this. Worse outrages than this attempt on his august person had been committed in the Midlands on important personages, on women and even children, during this terrible campaign against fugitive rebels.

Less than five seconds had elapsed when the soldier drew the packet of letters from Sir Humphrey's pocket and handed it to his Sergeant.

"They'd best be for His Royal Highness's own inspection," said the latter, quietly, as he slipped them inside his scarlet coat.

"Aye! for His Royal Highness!" quoth Jack Bathurst in mad, wild, feverish glee. "Oh, now is it that your Honour thought you could be even with me? What?"

Sir Humphrey was speechless with the hopelessness of his baffled rage. But Patience, almost hysterical with the intensity of her relief after the terrible suspense which she had just endured, had fallen back half fainting against the stairs, and murmuring,—

"The letters! ... Before His Royal Highness! ... Thank God! ... Thank God!..."

Then suddenly she drew herself up, and laughing, crying, joyous, happy, she flew upstairs shouting,—

"Philip!—Philip!—come down!—come down! ... you are safe!..."

CHAPTER XXXVI

THE AGONY OF PARTING

About half an hour ago, when Jack Bathurst suddenly burst in upon Lord Stretton in the dingy little parlour upstairs, he gave the lad no inkling of what was happening down below. He had hastily discarded Jock Miggs's smock and hat and extracted a solemn promise from Philip not to stir from the parlour, whatever might be the tumult downstairs.

Then he had left the boy chafing like a wild beast in its cage. The heavy oak doors and thick walls of the old-fashioned inn deadened all the sounds from below, and Bathurst had taken the precaution of locking the door behind him. But for this, no doubt Philip would have broken his word, sooner than allow his chivalrous friend once more to risk his life for him.

As the noise below grew louder and louder, Stretton became more and more convinced that some such scene as had been enacted a day or two ago at the forge was being repeated in the hall of the Packhorse. He tried with all his might to force open the door which held him imprisoned, and threw his full weight against it once or twice, in a vain endeavour to break the thick oaken panels.

But the old door, fashioned of stout, well-seasoned wood, resisted all his efforts, whilst the noise he made thereby never reached the ears of the excited throng.

Like a fettered lion he paced up and down the narrow floor of the dingy inn parlour, chafing under restraint, humiliated at the thought of being unable to join in the fight, that was being made for his safety.

His sister's cry came to him in this agonising moment like the most joyful, the most welcome call to arms.

"The door! ... quick!..." he shouted as loudly as he could, "it is locked!"

She found the bolt and tore open the door, and the next instant he was running downstairs, closely followed by Patience.

The Sergeant and soldiers had been not a little puzzled at hearing her ladyship suddenly calling in mad exultation on her brother, whom they believed they were even now holding prisoner.

The appearance of Philip at the foot of the stairs, and dressed in a serving-man's suit, further enhanced their bewilderment.

But already Patience stood proud, defiant, and almost feverish in her excitement, confronting the astonished group of soldiers.

"This, Sergeant!" she said, taking hold of her brother's hand, "is Philip Gascoyne, Earl of Stretton, my brother. Arrest *him* if you wish, he surrenders to you willingly, but I call upon you to let your prisoner go free."

The Sergeant was sorely perplexed. The affair was certainly getting too complicated for his stolid, unimaginative brain. He would have given much to relinquish command of this puzzling business altogether.

"Then you, sir," he said, addressing Philip, "you are the Earl of Stretton?"

"I am Philip James Gascoyne, Earl of Stretton, your prisoner, Sergeant," replied the lad, proudly.

"But then, saving your ladyship's presence," said the soldier, in hopeless bewilderment, "who the devil is my prisoner?"

"Surely, Sergeant," quoth Sir Humphrey, with a malicious sneer, "you've guessed that already?"

Jack Bathurst, exhausted and faint after his long fight and victory, had listened motionless and silent to what was going on around him. With the letters safely bestowed in the Sergeant's wallet and about to be placed before His Royal Highness the Duke of Cumberland himself, he felt that indeed his task was accomplished.

Fate had allowed him the infinite happiness of having served his beautiful white rose to some purpose. Philip now would be practically safe; what happened to himself after that he cared but little.

At sound of Sir Humphrey's malicious taunt, an amused smile played round the corners of his quivering mouth; but Patience, with a rapid movement, had interposed herself between Sir Humphrey and the Sergeant.

"Your silence, Sir Humphrey," she commanded excitedly, "an you've any chivalry left in you."

"Aye!" he replied in her ear, "my silence now ... at a price."

"Name it."

"Your hand."

So low and quick had been questions and answers that the bewildered Sergeant and his soldiers had not succeeded in catching the meaning of the words, but Sir Humphrey's final eager whisper, "Your hand!" reached Jack Bathurst's sensitive ear. The look too in the Squire of Hartington's face had already enabled him to guess the purport of the brief colloquy.

"Nay, Sir Humphrey Challoner," he said loudly, "but 'tis not a marketable commodity you are offering to this lady for sale. I'll break your silence for you. What is the information that you would impart to these gallant lobsters? ... That besides being my mother's son I am also the highwayman, Beau Brocade!"

"No! no! no!" protested Patience, excitedly.

"Odd's my life!" quoth the Sergeant, "but methought..."

"Aye, Beau Brocade," said Sir Humphrey, with a sneer, "robber, vagabond and thief, that's what this ... *gentleman* means."

"Faith! is that what I meant?" retorted Jack Bathurst, lightly. "I didn't know it for sure!"

But with a wild cry Patience had turned to the Sergeant.

"It's a lie, Sergeant!" she repeated, "a lie, I tell you. This gentleman is ... my friend ... my..."

"Well, whichever you are, sir," quoth the Sergeant, turning to Beau Brocade decisively, "rebel, lord or highwayman, you are my prisoner, and," he added roughly, for many bitter remembrances of the past two days had surged up in his stolid mind, "and either way you hang for it."

"Aye! hang for it!" continued Sir Humphrey, savagely. "So, now methinks, my chivalrous young friend, that we can cry quits at last. And now, Sergeant," said his Honour, peremptorily, "that you've found out the true character of your interesting prisoner, you can restore me my letters, which he caused you to filch from me."

But the Sergeant was not prepared to do that. He had been tricked and hoodwinked so often, that he would not yield one iota of the advantage which he had contrived to gain.

"Your pardon, sir," he said deferentially yet firmly, "I don't exactly know the rights o' that. I think I'd best show them to His Royal Highness, and you, sir, will be good enough to explain yourself before his Honour, Squire West."

"You'll suffer for this insolence, Sergeant," retorted Sir Humphrey, purple with rage. "I command you to return me those letters, and I warn you that if you dare lay hands on me or hinder me in any way, I'll have you degraded and publicly whipped along with that ape the beadle."

But the Sergeant merely shrugged his shoulders and ordered off three of his men to surround Sir Humphrey Challoner and to secure his hands if he attempted to resist. His Honour's wild threats of revenge did not in the least frighten the soldier, now that he felt himself on safe ground at last.

The rapid approach of the army gave him a sense of security; he knew that if he had erred through excess of zeal, a reprimand would be the only punishment meted out to him, whilst he risked being degraded if he neglected his duty. Whether the Squire of Hartington had or had not been a party to the late rebellion, he neither knew nor cared, but certainly he was not going to give up a packet of letters over which there had been so much heated discussion on both sides.

The fast-approaching tumult in the street confirmed him in his resolve. He turned a deaf ear to all Sir Humphrey's protestations, and only laughed at his threats.

Already the soldiers were chafing with eagerness to see the entry of His Royal Highness with his staff: the village folk one by one had gone out to see the more joyful proceedings, and left the Sergeant and his prisoners to continue their animated discussion.

"Are you ready, my lord?" asked the Sergeant, turning to Philip.

"Quite ready!" replied the lad, cheerfully, as he prepared to follow the soldiers. He gave his sister a look of joy and hope, for he was going to temporary imprisonment only; within a few moments perhaps his safety would be assured. Lady Patience Gascoyne, in virtue of her rank and position, could easily obtain an audience of the Duke of Cumberland, and in the meanwhile the letters proving Philip's innocence would have been laid before His Royal Highness. No wonder that as the lad, marching light-heartedly between two soldiers, passed close to Jack Bathurst, he held out his hand to his brave rescuer in gratitude too deep for words.

"Are you ready, sir?" quoth the Sergeant now, as he turned to Beau Brocade.

But here there was no question of either joy or hope: no defence, no proofs of innocence. The daring outlaw had chosen his path in life, and being conquered at the last, had to pay the extreme penalty which his country demanded of him for having defied its laws.

As he too prepared to follow the soldiers out into the open, Patience, heedless of the men around her, clung passionately, despairingly to the man who had sacrificed his brave life in her service, and whom she had rewarded with the intensity, the magnitude of her love.

"They shall not take you," she sobbed, throwing her protecting arms round the dearly-loved form, "they shall not ... they shall not..."

The cry had been so bitter, so terribly pathetic in its despair, that instinctively the soldiers stood aside, awed in spite of their stolid hearts at the majesty of this great sorrow; they turned respectfully away, leaving a clear space round Patience and Bathurst.

Thus for a moment he had her all to himself, passive in her despair, half crazed with her grief, clinging to him with all the passionate abandonment of her great love for him.

"What? ... tears?" he whispered gently, as with a tender hand he pressed back the graceful drooping head, and looked into her eyes, "one ... two ... three ... four glittering diamonds ... and for me! ... My sweet dream!" he added, the intensity of his passion causing his low, tender voice to quiver in his throat, "my beautiful white rose, but yesterday for one of those glittering tears I'd gladly have endured hell's worst tortures, and to-day they flow freely for me.... Why! I would not change places with a King!"

"Your life ... your brave, noble life ... thus sacrificed for me.... Oh, why did I ever cross your path?"

"Nay, my *dear*," he said with an infinity of tenderness, and an infinity of joy. "Faith! it must have been because God's angels took pity on a poor vagabond and let him get this early glimpse of paradise."

His fingers wandered lovingly over her soft golden hair, he held her close, very close to his heart, drinking in every line of her exquisite loveliness, rendered almost ethereal through the magnitude of her sorrow: her eyes shining with passion through her tears, the delicate curve of throat and chin, the sensitive, quivering nostrils, the moist lips on which anon he would dare to imprint a kiss.

"And life now to me," she whispered 'twixt heart-broken sobs, "what will it be? ... how shall I live but in one long memory?"

"My life, my saint," he murmured. "Nay! lift your dear face up to me again! let me take away as a last memory the radiant vision of your eyes ... your hair ... your lips..."

His arms tightened round her, her head fell back as if in a swoon, she closed her eyes and her soul went out to him in the ecstasy of that first kiss.

"Ah! it is a lovely dream I dreamt," he whispered, "and 'tis meet that the awakening shall be only in death!"

He tried to let her go but she clung to him passionately, her arms round him, in the agony of her despair.

"Take me with you," she sobbed, half fainting. "I cannot bear it ... I cannot..."

Gently he took hold of both her hands, and again and again pressed them to his lips.

"Farewell, sweet dream!" he said. "There! dry those lovely tears! ... If you only knew how happy I am, you would not mourn for me.... I have spun the one thread in life which was worth the spinning, the thread which binds me to your memory.... Farewell!"

The Sergeant stepped forward again. It was time to go.

"Are you ready, sir?" he asked kindly.

"Quite ready, Sergeant."

She slid out of his arms, her eyes quite dry now, her hands pressed to her mouth to smother her screams of misery. She watched the soldiers fall into line, with their prisoner in their midst, and turn to the doorway of the inn, through which the golden sunshine came gaily peeping in.

Outside a roll of drums was heard and shouts of "The Duke! The Duke!" The excitement had become electrical. His Royal Highness, mounted on a magnificent white charger, was making his entry into the village at the head of his general staff, and followed at some distance by the bulk of his army corps, who would camp on the Heath for the night.

Squire West, his stiff old spine doubled in two, was in attendance on the green, holding a parchment in his hand, which contained his loyal address and that of the inhabitants of Brassington: the beadle, more pompous than ever, and resplendent in blue cloth and gold lace, stood immediately behind his Honour.

In the midst of all this gaiety and joyful excitement the silent group, composed of the soldiers with their three prisoners, appeared in strange and melancholy contrast. Philip and Bathurst were to be confined in the Court House, under a strong guard, pending his Honour the Squire's decision, and as the little squad emerged upon the green, 'twas small wonder that they caught His Royal Highness's eye.

He had been somewhat bored by Squire West's long-winded harangue, and was quite glad of an excuse for cutting it short.

"Odd's buds!" he said, "and what have we here? Eh?"

The Sergeant and soldiers stood still at attention, some twenty yards away from the brilliant group of His Highness's general staff. The little diversion had caused Squire West to lose the thread of his speech, and much relieved, the Duke beckoned the Sergeant to draw nearer.

"Who are your prisoners, Sergeant?" queried His Highness, looking with some interest at the two young men, one of whom was a mere lad, whilst the other had a strange look of joy and pride in his pale face, an air of aloofness and detachment from all his surroundings, which puzzled and interested the Duke not a little.

"'Tis a bit difficult to explain, your Royal Highness," replied the Sergeant, making the stiff military salute.

"Difficult to explain who your prisoners are?" laughed the Duke, incredulously.

"Saving your Highness's presence," responded the Sergeant, "one of these gentlemen is Philip Gascoyne, Earl of Stretton."

"Oho! the young reprobate rebel who was hand-in-glove with the Pretender! I mind his case well, Sergeant, and the capture does your zeal great credit. Which of your prisoners is the Earl of Stretton?"

"That's just my trouble, your Royal Highness. But I hope that these papers will explain."

And the Sergeant drew from his wallet the precious packet of letters and handed them respectfully to the Duke.

"What are these letters?"

"They were found on the person of that gentleman, sir," replied the Sergeant, indicating Sir Humphrey Challoner, who stood behind the two younger men, silent and sulky, and nursing desperate thoughts of revenge. "He is said to be an accomplice and I thought 'twas my duty to bring him before a magistrate. If I've done wrong...".

"You've done quite right, Sergeant," said the Duke, firmly. "You were sent here to rid the country of rebels, whom an Act of Parliament has convicted of high treason, and it had been gross neglect of duty not to refer such a case to the nearest magistrate. Give me the papers, I'll look through them anon. See your prisoners safely under guard, then come back to my quarters."

"Damnation!" muttered Sir Humphrey, as he saw the Duke take the packet of letters from the Sergeant's hand, and then turn away to listen to the fag end of Squire West's loyal address.

Throughout his chagrin, however, the Squire of Hartington was able to gloat over one comforting idea. He had now lost all chance of pressing his suit on Lady Patience, his actions in the past three days would inevitably cause her to look upon him with utter hatred and contempt, but the man who was the cause of his failure, the chivalrous and meddlesome highwayman, Beau Brocade, would, as sure as the sun would set this night, dangle on the nearest gibbet to-morrow.

CHAPTER XXXVII

REPARATION

It was in the middle of the afternoon when His Royal Highness, having attended to other important affairs, and partaken of a hasty meal at the Royal George, finally found leisure to look through the letters handed up to him by the Sergeant.

As he read one through, and then the other, Lord Lovat's letter urging the Earl of Stretton to join the rebellion, that of Kilmarnock upbraiding the lad for holding aloof, and finally the autograph of Charles Edward himself at the end of a long string of reproaches, calling Philip a traitor for his loyalty to King George,—

"There has been a terrible blunder here!" quoth His Royal Highness, emphatically. "Bring the Earl of Stretton to me at once," he added, speaking to his orderly.

Ten minutes later Philip, with Patience by his side, was in the presence of the Duke of Cumberland, who, on behalf of his country and its government, was tendering apologies to the Earl of Stretton for grievous blunders committed.

"It seems you have suffered unjustly, my lord," said His Highness, with easy graciousness. "It will be my privilege to keep you under my personal protection until these letters have been placed before the King and Council."

"I myself will guarantee your brother's safety, Lady Patience," he added, turning with a genial smile to her; "you will entrust him to my care, will you not? Your father and I were old friends, you know. In my young days I had the pleasure of staying at Stretton Hall, and the privilege of dandling you on my knees, for you were quite a baby then. I little thought I should have the honour of being of service to you in later years."

With courtly gallantry the Duke raised her cold finger-tips to his lips. He looked at her keenly, for he could not understand the almost dead look of hopeless misery in her face which she bravely, but all in vain, tried to hide from him. Evidently she was quite unable to speak. When her brother had been brought before His Highness she had begged for and easily obtained the favour of being present at the interview, but even at the Duke's most genial and encouraging words she had not smiled.

"It was lucky," added His Royal Highness, kindly patting her hand, "that so strange a Fate should have placed these letters in my hand."

But at these gentle, almost fatherly words, Patience's self-control entirely gave way. With a heart-broken sob she threw herself at the Duke's feet.

"Nay! not Fate, your Royal Highness," she moaned, "but the devotion of a brave man, who has sacrificed his life to save my brother and me... Save him, your Highness! ... save him! ... he is noble, brave, loyal, and you are powerful ... save him! ... save him!..."

It was impossible to listen unmoved to the heart-rending sorrow expressed in this appeal. The Duke very gently raised her to her feet.

"Nay, fair lady ... I pray you rise," he said respectfully. "Odd's my life! but 'tis not beauty's place to kneel.... There! there!" he added, leading her to a chair and sitting beside her, "you know how to plead a cause; will you deign to confide somewhat more fully in your humble servant? We owe your family some reparation at anyrate, and you some compensation for the sorrow you have endured."

And speaking very low at first, then gradually gaining confidence, Patience began to relate the history of the past few days, the treachery, of which she had been a victim, the heroic self-sacrifice of the man who was about to lay down his life because of his devotion to her and to her cause.

His Highness listened quietly and very attentively, whilst she, wrapped up in the bitter joy of memory, lived through these last brief and happy days all over again. Even before she had finished, he had sent word to the Sergeant to bring both his other prisoners before him at once.

Sir Humphrey and Jack Bathurst were actually in the room before Patience had quite completed her narrative. Bathurst ill and pale, but with that strange air of aloofness still clinging about his whole person. He seemed scarce to live, for his mind was far away in the land of dreams, dwelling on that last exquisite memory of his beautiful white rose lying passive in his arms, the memory of that first and last, divinely passionate kiss.

The Duke looked up when the prisoners entered the room; although he knew neither of them by sight, he had no need to ask whose cause the beautiful girl beside him had been pleading so earnestly.

"What do you wish to say, sir?" he said, addressing Sir Humphrey Challoner first. "You are no doubt aware of her ladyship's grievances against you. They are outside my province, and unfortunately outside the province of our country's justice. But I would wish to know why you should have pursued the Earl of Stretton and that gentleman, your fellow-prisoner, with so much hatred and malice."

"I have neither hatred nor malice against the Earl of Stretton," replied Sir Humphrey, with a shrug of the shoulders, "but no doubt her ladyship would wish to arouse your Royal Highness's sympathy for a notorious scoundrel. That gentleman is none other than Beau Brocade, the most noted footpad and most consummate thief that ever haunted Brassing Moor."

The Duke of Cumberland looked with some surprise, not altogether unmixed with kindliness, at the slim, youthful figure of the most notorious highwayman in England. He felt all a soldier's keen delight in the proud bearing of the man, the straight, clean limbs, the upright, gallant carriage of the head, which neither physical pain nor adverse circumstances had taught how to bend.

Then he remembered Lady Patience's enthusiastic narrative, and said, smiling indulgently,—

"Odd's my life! but I did not know gentlemen of the road were so chivalrous!"

"Your Royal Highness..." continued Sir Humphrey.

"Silence, sir!"

Then the Duke rose from his chair, and went up close to Bathurst, who, half-dreaming, had listened to all that was going on around him, but had scarce heard, for he was looking at Patience and thinking only of her.

"Your name, sir?" asked the Duke very kindly, for the look of love akin to worship which illumined Jack Bathurst's face had made a strong appeal to his own manly heart.

"Jack Bathurst," replied the young man, almost mechanically, and rousing himself with an effort in response to the Duke's kind words, "formerly captain in the White Dragoons."

"Bathurst? ... Bathurst?" repeated the Duke, not a little puzzled. "Ah, yes!" he added after a slight pause, "who was condemned and cashiered for striking his superior officer after a quarrel."

"The same, your Royal Highness."

"'Twas Colonel Otway, who, we found out afterwards, was a scoundrel, a liar, and a cheat," said His Highness with sudden eager enthusiasm, "and fully deserving the punishment you, sir, had been brave enough to give him."

"Aye! he deserved all he got," replied Jack, with a wistful sigh and smile, "I'll take my oath of that."

"But ... I remember now," continued the Duke, "a tardy reparation was to have been offered you, sir ... but you were nowhere to be found."

"I'd become a scoundrel myself by then, and moneyless, friendless, disgraced, had taken to the road, like many another broken gentleman."

"Then take to the field now, man," exclaimed His Highness, gaily. "We want good soldiers and gallant gentlemen such as you, and your country still owes you reparation. You shall come with me, and in the glorious future which I predict for you, England shall forget your past."

He extended a kindly hand to Bathurst, who, still dreaming, still not quite realising what had happened, instinctively bent the knee in gratitude.

CHAPTER XXXVIII

THE JOY OF RE-UNION

On the green outside, the crowd of village folk were shouting themselves hoarse,—

"Three cheers for the Duke of Cumberland!"

Already the news had gone the round that Beau Brocade, the highwayman, had been granted a special pardon by His Royal Highness.

John Stich, half crazy with joy, was tossing his cap in the air, and in the fulness of his heart was stealing a few kisses from Mistress Betty's pretty mouth.

The appearance of Sir Humphrey Challoner in the porch of the Royal George, looking as black as thunder and followed by his obsequious familiar, Master Mittachip, was the signal for much merriment and some quickly-suppressed chaff.

"Stand aside, you fool!" quoth Sir Humphrey, pushing Jock Miggs roughly out of his way.

"Nay, stand aside all of ye!" admonished John Stich, solemnly, "and mind if any of ye've got any turnips about ... be gy!..."

The Squire of Hartington raised his riding-crop menacingly.

"You dare!" he muttered.

But Mistress Betty interposed her pretty person 'twixt her lover and his Honour's wrath.

"Saving your presence, sir," she said pertly, "my intent was only going to tell the lads to keep their turnips for this old scarecrow."

And laughing all over her dimpled little face she pointed to Master Mittachip, who was clinging terrified to Sir Humphrey's coat-tails.

"Sir Humphrey..." he murmured anxiously, as Betty's sally was received with a salvo of applause, "good Sir Humphrey ... do not let them harm me.... I've served you faithfully..."

"You've served me like a fool," quoth Sir Humphrey, savagely, shaking himself free from the mealy-mouthed attorney. "Damn you," he added, as he walked quickly out of the crowd and across the green, "don't yap at my heels like a frightened cur."

"God speed your Honour," shouted Stich after him.

"Think you, John, he'll come to our wedding?" murmured Betty, saucily, at which honest John hugged her with all his might before the entire company.

"Be gy! I marvel if the old fox'll go to her ladyship's and the Captain's wedding, eh?"

"Lordy! Lordy! these be 'mazing times," commented Jock Miggs, vaguely.

―――

But within the small parlour of the Royal George all this noise and gaiety only came as a faint, merry echo.

His Royal Highness had gone, followed by the Sergeant and soldiers, and Bathurst was alone with his beautiful white rose.

"And 'tis to you I owe my life," he whispered for the twentieth time, as kneeling at her feet he buried his head in the folds of her gown.

"I have done so little," she murmured, "one poor prayer ... when you had done so much."

"And now," he said, looking straight into the exquisite depths of her blue eyes, "now you have robbed me of one great happiness, which may never come to me again."

"Robbed you? ... of happiness?..."

"The happiness of dying for you."

But she looked down at him, smiling now through a mist of happy tears.

"Nay, sir," she whispered, "and when the Duke has no longer need of you, will you not live ... for me?"

He folded her in his arms, and held her closely, very closely to his strong, brave heart.

"Always at your feet," he murmured passionately, "and as your humble slave, my dream."

And as his lips sought hers once more, she whispered under her breath,—

"My husband!"

"My dream!—My wife!"

―――

Outside the crowd of villagers were shouting lustily,—
"Three cheers for the Duke of Cumberland!"

Milton Keynes UK
Ingram Content Group UK Ltd.
UKHW022154250224
438379UK00006B/753